W9-CLG-627

One Prayer Away

One Prayer Away

Kendra
Norman-Bellamy

MOODY PUBLISHERS
CHICAGO

© 2006 by
KENDRA NORMAN-BELLAMY

All rights reserved. No part of this book may be reproduced in any form without permission in writing from the publisher, except in the case of brief quotations embodied in critical articles or reviews.

Cover Design: Carlton Bruett Design
Cover Image: Getty Images
Interior Design: Ragont Design
Editors: Suzette Dinwiddie and Cheryl Dunlop

ISBN-13: 978-0-7394-7564-5

Printed in the United States of America

"I thank my God upon every remembrance of you."
(Philippians 1:3)

Jimmy L. Holmes,
for being an eternal inspiration.
Tonja Holmes,
for always celebrating every accomplishment I made.
Clinton & Willie Mae Bellamy,
for loving me like a daughter.
Valeria Bellamy,
for being my friend long before you were my sister-in-law.

Each of you is proof that while death takes away life,
it does not take away love.
I will love each of you always.

~ One ~

It had been a long morning at the office, and the incomplete files he'd left on his desk promised to make it an even longer afternoon. Mitchell Andrews was happy for the much-needed break that brought him and his business partner, Christopher Jackson, to their favorite eatery.

The air in Bob's Steak & Chop House was thick with the combined smells of soups, steaks, and potatoes. As he unconsciously closed his eyes and inhaled deeply, Mitchell was almost certain that he caught a whiff of the fried calamari that the couple at the table nearest them shared as an appetizer. Or maybe it was all just a figment of his imagination conjured by the rumble in his stomach. He'd missed breakfast this morning, something his grandmother would have scolded him for if she were still alive. Hearing footsteps approaching and assuming it was their waitress finally delivering their ordered meals, Mitchell opened his eyes.

"Virtue!" Gasping, Mitchell stood suddenly from his chair, causing it to hit the uncarpeted floor with such force that the resounding thud made him the center of attention.

She was a slightly older but more beautiful copy of the woman he had fallen in love with years before. It was a decade ago that Mitchell had first seen eyes like hers, hair like hers, and teeth like hers. On that mid-August day of their initial meeting, she had unknowingly teased him with her eyelashes, and she owned a smile that qualified her orthodontist for a medal of excellence. It was a direct contrast to the look of horror she now directed toward the man whose outburst had startled her. Apparently having come in to enjoy a quiet afternoon of dining alone, she took several steps backward and pulled her purse close to her body as if fearful that in a restaurant full of dining patrons, Mitchell would dare to rob her.

"Mitch, man, what's wrong with you?" Chris stood and grabbed Mitchell's arm before turning to the woman who was still paralyzed with fear. "I'm sorry, ma'am." It was all Chris could say in his friend's defense. "I'm sorry."

Whatever plans the woman had for lunch were immediately changed. With Mitchell unable to take his eyes away in spite of Chris's tugging, she backed away and rushed to exit the front door. The bizarre mayhem had ended, but the eyes from neighboring tables repeatedly glanced in the men's direction long after Mitchell managed to lower himself back into the chair that Chris had brought to an upright position.

"Man, what was that?" Chris whispered, trying to mask his embarrassment behind sips of water. "You got the whole restaurant thinking you're on crack or something."

Taking a quick look around, Mitchell realized that his partner was only mildly overstating the facts. Every table that he saw seemed to have at least one occupant who looked in his direction as though he needed an exorcist. Closing his eyes, Mitchell took slow, deep breaths like he was taught to do during his tenure at the Betty Ford Center in California. His days of alcoholism had ended nearly three years ago, but his heart hadn't raced at this pace since his first week there when he had found himself in actual tears, begging and literally fighting for a taste of vodka.

"Let's go," Mitchell said, his voice steady but pleading. The stares that were coming from all directions were burning into his skin.

"We haven't even gotten our meals yet, man. Didn't you just say a few minutes ago that you were starving? What's wrong with you?" Chris had gotten no answer to that question the first time he had asked.

It would be a three-mile trek back to the office, and Dallas's unusually low November temperatures would make it seem twice as long, but he'd take his chances. Standing, Mitchell grabbed his wool coat from the empty chair beside him and stood to slip his arms in the sleeves.

"What are you doing?" Utter confusion could be seen on Chris's face as he spoke. "Where are you going?"

"Back to the office." Mitchell held out his hand to stop Chris from rising from his seat. "The walk will be good for me. I need to clear my head. See you later."

Two

*F*riday morning Mitchell stood at the window of his office, staring out at nothing in particular. Not able to go back to sleep after awaking before the sun had even come up, he'd gotten up and ultimately arrived at work two hours earlier than normal. The snapshot in his mind of seeing Virtue three weeks ago hadn't yet faded and showed no indication that it would any time soon. Mitchell's daytime hours had been spent wrestling with renewed guilt, and his nighttime dreams were haunted by the memories that had been responsible for riddling him with the unforgettable shame of it all. Forgiveness . . . that's what Chris had assured Mitchell that God had granted him three years ago when he responded to the altar call at his new church home. But Chris didn't know about Virtue, and all of a sudden, ever since Mitchell had seen her fear and panic, he didn't feel that the sins that involved her had been included in the forgiveness package. He felt as though the monster that had taken up residence in him all those years ago had returned with the intention to own him in a whole new way.

Back then, in the days that birthed the madness, Detroit, Michigan, had been Mitchell's home. With the blessings of his lifetime guardians, he'd relocated there permanently after acquiring his associate degree in business administration from Lewis College of Business, where he had majored in accounting. On the weekends, he had begun spending much of his time nearly two hundred miles away in Kollen Hall at Hope College in Holland, Michigan, wooing one of the school's few black female dance majors.

Grandma Kate, the only mother Mitchell had ever known, had wanted him to pursue higher education at a school closer to their Dallas home, but she had eventually conceded. After their youngest daughter died in childbirth, Isaac and Kate Andrews had taken custody of their then-infant grandson and raised Mitchell as their own. Her oldest son, Kent, lived in Detroit. He'd promised to keep an eye on Mitchell during college and make sure that he had everything he needed.

It was in late November after Thanksgiving when Isaac Andrews made the trip to Detroit at his grandson's request to help Mitchell and Virtue move from what had been a bachelor pad into a new two-bedroom apartment that would more easily accommodate his new bride and the family they were already making plans for. It had been a wonderful four-day bonding period that Mitchell would never forget. It was the week that the Detroit Lions played the visiting Dallas Cowboys, and Grandpa Isaac earned bragging rights when Dallas easily walked away with the win. Mitchell and his uncle Kent thought they'd never hear the last of his elation.

As Grandpa Isaac's time in Detroit neared its end, the unexpected happened. Back in Dallas, while carrying a load of laundry from one room to another, Grandma Kate fell and broke her hip. When Mitchell and his grandfather got the call from Parkland Hospital about her accident, they immediately began searching for earlier flights. Kate had told her husband to keep his current flight schedule, which would bring him back home the following day. She told him that she would be fine until he got there, but Mitchell urged his grandfather to leave earlier anyway. Grandma Kate had always put the well-being of others before her own. She'd never wanted to feel like a burden, and Mitchell knew that she was encouraging her husband to stay only because she didn't want to live with the thought that Isaac's visit with his grandson had been shortened because of her fall.

Isaac had taken his grandson's advice, but the flight he booked never made it to its destination. Mitchell still remembered his disbelief when he'd heard the Delta flight number announced on the evening news. He called the airline in hopes that an error had been made, and then for two solid hours he cried, wondering how he was going to break the news to his grandmother. It was a task that he never had the chance to carry out. Before he could call the hospital, the hospital called him. Kate's son, Kent, had watched the news too, and he called Dallas before Mitchell could. The devastating news that her husband of fifty-two years was dead was more than Kate's heart could take. Hospital officials said she went into cardiac arrest ten minutes after ending her call from Kent, and attempts to revive her had been unsuccessful. Five days later, Mitchell was attending a double funeral with a photo standing in for Grandpa Isaac's charred remains. Virtue had tried to be a source of strength for him, but Mitchell proved to be inconsolable.

Life after his grandparents' death had been brutal, causing Mitchell to go through a series of changes that ultimately destroyed his entire existence as he'd known it. First, when he needed them the most, the remaining Andrews family members alienated him, blaming Mitchell for their loved ones' untimely demise. Isaac and Kate both had been in their early seventies, but they had been in good physical and mental condition. Kent said they would have easily lived another ten years had Mitchell not gone against his mother's wishes and put his father on the plane. Kent took no blame for making the call that triggered his mother's heart failure. He said she would have had to find out sooner or later, and however she learned of her husband's fate, it would have killed her. Her death and the death of Isaac Andrews was nobody's fault but Mitchell's.

In the year that followed, family situations worsened. Mitchell's grandparents had willed their home to him, sparking more hatred from their offspring. The four biological children had equally shared the $250,000 life insurance payout, but that wasn't enough for them. They wanted the home too, but Mitchell fought them to the bitter end. The house was all he had left of his grandparents. He wasn't going to allow them to strip him of it. The year-long legal battle ended with the courts honoring the wording in the will. The rejection by his family gradually took its toll on Mitchell, leading to depression.

Two years after his grandparents died, his bout of depression worsened. In the end, it led to the loss of his job at a prestigious financial firm. The bottle became his best friend, and what began as a periodic means of taking the edge off of life became a daily habit that Mitchell couldn't shake on his own. For three years, it ruled his total existence and drove him to lash out at everyone, including those who loved him and tried to help him.

Finally, after driving away everybody, including the woman he loved, and up to his knees in debt from his lack of viable income, Mitchell had sought help from Alcoholics Anonymous. The meetings proved that he couldn't shake the habit, even with the help of professionals. He re-enrolled in the program so often that he grew tired of hearing himself admit that he had a problem. The Betty Ford Center in California was his desperate last recourse. It was there, through God's divine grace, that Mitchell killed the habit before it killed him. But during that month he'd lived at the center, he lost almost everything he had because of the numerous months he'd avoided paying his bills to finance his habit. In the year that followed, his attempts to find gainful employment failed, and he had no choice but to move back to Dallas into the home that his grandparents had left him six years earlier. It was the best thing he could have done for himself.

The last three years had been a dramatic time of healing and rebirth. Three months after Mitchell settled in Dallas, he landed a new job with an accounting firm, now named Jackson, Jackson & Andrews, CPA. He had seen the advertisement in the newspaper and had gone to the firm, then called Jackson & Son, CPA. That's where his life began to change on more than just a physical level.

After leaving the initial interview that had been scheduled for a Thursday morning, Mitchell felt confident that he would be called back for a follow-up. He and Christopher Jackson seemed to connect immediately upon introductions. Even though his attempts at finding employment in Detroit had produced nothing, Mitchell took on a new positive attitude as he sat in Chris's spacious office, answering questions about his professional background. Numbers were Mitchell's specialty, and he was born to be an accountant. In his prime, he had been the best at what he did, and there wasn't a question that Chris asked that broke Mitchell's skilled eye contact or made him fumble over his knowledgeable words. Mitchell's confidence had not been misplaced. By the end of the business day on Thursday, he'd gotten the call that he was to be among a select group of three who would be interviewed for a final time before the decision was made on who would get the offered position.

But by the time the Saturday interview was over, Mitchell was just as sure that he *wouldn't* be the one hired as he was sure that he would be one of those called back after the initial conference. During the final interview, questions that he was less confident about were asked, and Mitchell squirmed in his seat, searching for a roundabout way to answer them. He had prepared an answer for the question of why he'd left his former job, but Chris had already done his homework, and Mitchell hadn't prepared for that. His less-than-honest answer that he'd left his job in Detroit to make the move to Dallas was quickly challenged.

"Is that so? Well, your employer tells me that you were fired due to substance abuse several months before the date that you gave me for your relocation. He says that you're an alcoholic. Would you like to elaborate on that?"

No! That was the answer that Mitchell screamed in his head, but he knew he had to say something. He couldn't let this job opportunity slip away without a fight. He'd come too far to allow everything to fall apart now. Mitchell was trapped, and there was nothing left to do other than tell the truth. It was painful and shameful, but he did it anyway. Mitchell was shocked when Chris didn't immediately dismiss him, and he was even more surprised when Chris revealed his own personal story of pain. Having recently lost his father to a massive stroke, Chris could relate to Mitchell's sense of loss. Chris's father had also been his best friend, and he too had gone through a period of depression after his father's death. The elder Mr. Jackson's demise was the reason Chris needed help keeping the business afloat.

"How'd you get through it, man?" Mitchell asked him after Chris shared the story of Willie James Jackson Jr.

"Sometimes I'm tempted to ask myself the same question," Chris responded. He let out a small chuckle, but his face showed no amusement. "Dad's been gone now for eighteen months," he continued. "At first I told myself that I wasn't going to replace him. It seemed almost disrespectful to his memory. But the workload is way too heavy for one person to try to handle, and the way I see it, if I lose the business that my father struggled to make successful, that would be an even bigger disrespect.

"How'd I get through it?" he reverted back to the question that Mitchell had asked earlier. "I had to stop trying to do it by myself. I had shut everybody out of my life, basically. I was being selfish and not even considering the fact that my mother and my baby sister needed me to help them get through it too. I wasn't the only one who Dad's death affected, but it felt like it.

"I'll never forget the Sunday morning my mother and Ursula came to my house and just about physically pulled me out of my pool of sorrow. I was wallowing hard, man," Chris continued with another laugh. "I didn't know how pitiful I'd become until I took a real good look in the mirror that day. I was a mess on the inside, and it was beginning to show real hard on the outside.

"Ursula kept saying, 'Are you missing Daddy so much that you want to die and go and be with him? 'Cause that's what you're doing, Christopher James Jackson. You're killing yourself. Then what are me and Mama gonna do? You've got to be a man here. If Daddy didn't teach you but *one* thing, it was how to be a man. He's turning over in his grave right now if he can see the poor example of a man that I'm looking at right now!'" He mimicked her voice as he recalled her words.

"That was kind of harsh," Mitchell observed.

"It was a harsh reality," Chris admitted, "but I think she saved my life. It was tough love, but she was right. I learned a lesson from her that day. I'm eleven years her senior. Ursula was barely more than a teenager, but she gave me a reality check that day. I was the only man left in the immediate family. We had a brother between the two of us who had died two years earlier fighting the war in Iraq, so our family was just getting through the healing process from that tragedy. Since I'm the oldest, my father had always told me that if anything happened to him, it was my responsibility to step up and be the man of the house, so to speak.

"I didn't live in the same town with Mama and Ursula anymore. Immediately after Dad died, they moved to Los Angeles to be closer to my mom's family, but they were still my responsibility. Daddy owned apartments that he leased and actually willed to me with my mom's approval. In the months after his death, several tenants dishonored their contracts and moved out because I wasn't honoring my obligations to the buildings. I had really failed Daddy at that point."

"But that kind of hurt and loss takes time to heal," Mitchell defended with his own situation in mind. "It doesn't go away overnight."

"True." Chris nodded in agreement. "But Dad had been dead for about nine months at that time."

"Nine months?" Mitchell grimaced as an oath escaped his lips. "Nine months ain't nothing. I grieved way longer than that after my grandparents' death. Sometimes I still do."

Chris nodded as if he understood, and Mitchell was unprepared for Chris's next words and the conversation that followed. "But from what you've told me, you didn't —and still don't—have any family support. More importantly, and I'm taking a guess here, but I also assume that you didn't have spiritual support."

"What do you mean?"

"I mean, you didn't have a church or a pastor that you could turn to for strength and guidance on how to handle what you were feeling on the inside."

"I didn't need that. I had dealt with death before," Mitchell rationalized. "My mother died while giving birth to me, and I never even knew my father, so he's as good as dead as far as I'm concerned."

"But your grandparents were the first people that you loved and lost tragically," Chris pointed out. "In reality, you never knew either of your parents, so you didn't get to love them as your parents. The people that you loved as your parents were your first tragic losses, and the way your family crucified you added to the fuel that drove you over the edge."

"I suppose."

"Having my pastor to pray with me and my church family as well as my natural family to support me really helped out," Chris continued. "They were there all along, but I just had to open myself to accept the hands that were reaching for my rescue. Once I stopped trying to do it by myself, it was just a matter of days before my life was back on a positive track."

"Well, I guess God picks and chooses those who He'll help like that," Mitchell mumbled. "He didn't seem to be anywhere around when I was in the dumps."

"Did you ever look for Him?" Chris asked.

"*Look* for Him?"

"Through prayer, I mean. Did you ever ask Him for help? Did you seek His guidance?"

"I can't say that I did," Mitchell confessed. "Not that He would have helped me out anyway. I can't remember the last time I did anything for Him. You know what I mean?"

"Yeah, man." Chris nodded. "Believe it or not, I know exactly what you mean. But you can't look at God as you look at mortal man. With us, it's all about you scratching my back and me scratching yours. With God, it's not a matter of what you've done for Him lately. He'll still help you if you ask Him to.

"I'd gone to church my whole life. My dad was the head deacon there, and from the time we were babies, he kept us in church. Still, with all that religion and sound teaching in my background, I'd never been faced with nothing this hard, man. Even my little brother's death wasn't this hard. We'd prepared ourselves for his death, to a certain degree. I mean, when you go to war, there's a chance that you won't return. We'd hoped that he would and we'd prayed that he would, but we prepared ourselves for the worst. Jonah's death was hard, but at least he died for something he believed in. *This* . . . my father's death . . . was the toughest thing I'd ever experienced. I had to put all those years of spiritual teachings to work. In the Bible, Philippians chapter three, verses thirteen and fourteen became my favorite Scripture. It helped me to move on."

"So you don't miss your dad anymore?" Mitchell asked.

"Every day of my life." Chris pointed at his father's picture on the wall. Aside from an oil painting of a fisherman at sea, it was the only wall decoration in his sizeable office. "I still love that man. But now, a year and a half later, I don't get depressed when I think about his death. I know Dad is in a much better place. The joke in all of this is that he used to tell me all the time, as a kid, that I couldn't fool him with any of my childhood shenanigans. He said nothing I did was new. Whatever I could think of doing, he had already done before, and there was no place that I could go that he hadn't been first. I laugh about that now because even when I get to heaven, he would have been there before me."

"Chris." His secretary interrupted their chat when she slightly opened the office door. "Your next appointment is here."

"Thanks, Barbara," Chris said. "Give me five minutes, and then send him in."

Mitchell looked down at the watch on his wrist. "I suppose we got a little off track and didn't cover all of the interview questions."

"I guess." Chris smiled. "But we covered enough for me to work with. I have two other appointments this afternoon," he continued as he stood and extended his hand toward Mitchell. "I'll be in touch."

"Thank you." On his way to the exit, Mitchell passed the applicant who had arrived on time, thus interrupting the talk that had made him feel more like a patient than a prospect. The man wore a pin-striped black suit and sported a leather portfolio that hung from his shoulder. Glancing at his own face in a mirror on the foyer wall, Mitchell realized that the only thing hanging from his shoulders was the emotional baggage he'd been carrying around for more years than he cared to count.

He remembered not having much hope for the position when he left Chris's office. He was sure that the lie he'd told to cover his undisciplined recent past didn't do much to increase his chances. But Mitchell was wrong. By Saturday night, Chris had made his decision, and miraculously, he'd rejected the well-dressed gentleman who Mitchell was sure would get the position and had somehow decided that the still-broken man with the sordid past was the best one for the job.

Two weeks after Mitchell began working with Chris, he accepted an invitation to join him for worship services at the local church he attended. That Sunday, the preacher spoke on David and how he, though thought of as the least in his father's household, was chosen to be king. In some strange way, Mitchell felt as though he could relate to David. When he went home that day, he read the entire Scripture on David and realized that, like David, he too had been chosen over those who looked the part. Somehow, through Chris, God had chosen him. It would be another month before Mitchell would make the walk from his place on the fifth-row pew to the altar. He could still remember Chris waiting for him with open arms as he made his way back to his seat after he surrendered his life to Christ.

That day—the day he invited Christ into his life—all of the guilt and shame of Mitchell's past existence were erased. He'd been able to move forward with renewed spirit and a determination to make the next segment of his life better than the previous. Mitchell's hard work had truly paid off with great rewards. Living a life free of alcoholism and having a steady, well-paying job for the past three years had afforded him the clear head and the resources to get everything back that he'd loved and lost during his years of living in the cloud of a drunken stupor. Everything, that is, except Virtue.

⊷ *Three* ⊶

*G*ood morning," Chris called through Mitchell's open office door, snatching Mitchell's faraway thoughts of his first Christian experience back to the present.

It had been a long night, but even though Mitchell had only gotten a few hours of sleep, he felt rested and refreshed. For hours last night, he'd sat up and watched the flames lick hungrily at the wood in front of him. He didn't use his fireplace often, but when he did it seemed to render a certain level of calm to his innermost being. He'd fallen asleep on the sofa in the warmth that the flames shared with his living room, but he was permanently stirred only three hours later.

A year ago, he'd had the home that his grandparents shared completely remodeled to give it modernized comfort without taking away the welcoming feel that their presence had given it. The fireplace in the living room was one of the memorable aspects of the house that he wanted to keep simple. Other than adding a custom-made wooden mantel, it remained unchanged.

"Good morning," Mitchell replied as he began moving from the spot where he'd stood for so long that his legs had begun to grow numb.

"Is it cold enough out there for you?"

Mitchell laughed and then said, "The weatherman said that it would be unusually cold for these parts for the next several days, and he wasn't kidding. It's freezing out there."

"And it's going to get even colder as the week progresses," Chris said. "I heard that we may even get snow in some areas."

"It feels cold enough to snow right now," Mitchell remarked while finally taking a seat behind his desk. He was grateful for the opportunity to break away from his earlier dismal thoughts and get to more pleasant tasks.

With Chris gone to his own office, Mitchell got back to the files that awaited his attention. Barbara was running late today, so he had stepped into the hall long enough to prepare his own hot cup of water before returning to his assigned work space. Winter or summer, hot apple cider was his favorite drink. Perhaps it was the tart sweetness that attracted his taste buds. He'd often wondered if his body had found the flavor to be a feasible substitute for the drink it once craved. Whatever the case, Mitchell loved it and kept packets of the mixes in his drawer to add to the water that the coffeemaker provided.

Coffee had never been his drink of choice. Barbara and Chris raved over the varied, flavored crèmes that they used to give their caffeine kick a wide range of tastes. For Mitchell, it mattered not what international creamer was added; it was still coffee and still distasteful. Once in a while, he would drink hot chocolate, usually on nights when he felt particularly lonely. The kind with marshmallows really comforted him. It was the kind *she* always drank.

"I know you told me a couple of weeks ago that you didn't want to discuss this," Chris said, walking in and interrupting a fond memory. "But you and I have talked about almost everything imaginable since the time you started working here. Why is it that you can't talk to me about what happened at Bob's Steak & Chop House?"

Mitchell looked at him without responding. He thought he'd put a permanent end to this topic that same afternoon when Chris rejoined him at the office.

"Come on," Chris urged. "How bad can it be? You told me about your mom, your grandparents, your boozing, your fear of spiders, your bed-wetting . . ."

"Hey!" Mitchell said, taking a quick look around his office as though he thought someone would hear. "Lower your voice, man. That was traumatic stuff for a thirteen-year-old boy to deal with."

Chris's face scrunched up into a frown. "*Thirteen*? You didn't tell me you were thirteen. I thought maybe you were seven or eight. A thirteen-year-old is like a grown man leaking all over himself at night, man."

"Will you close the door on your way out?" Mitchell said, retrieving a folder from his briefcase. But Chris made no immediate attempt to obey.

"My point is that whatever it is that happened between you and this Vicky girl can't be any more embarrassing than that."

"I don't want to talk about it, Chris."

Taking a sip from his coffee mug, Chris made a grunting sound. "Well, whoever she was and whatever part she played in your life, she must have been quite the looker. The girl you scared off in your little mistaken identity blunder sure was."

Dropping his eyes to his desk, Mitchell smiled. Chris was right; Virtue was as striking as ever. He remembered her as a woman who'd always taken pride in her appearance, and that hadn't changed. Virtue stood only 5'5" in height, but her long, shapely legs and her habit of wearing three-inch heels gave her the illusion of a much taller woman. Her shoulder-length hair was still full of body and moved with every turn of her head. Years of dancing had kept her curves smooth and her body taut. Even in his dumbstruck state, Mitchell had been able to notice all of that before she had fled the restaurant.

Mitchell's lengthy silence sent Chris the message that he wanted to be left alone, but in truth, Mitchell's thoughts had momentarily snared him. He was brought back to himself when he saw Chris walking toward the door. For the first time, Mitchell found himself wanting to talk about a subject that had been taboo for years.

"Her name is Virtue, and there was no mistake made on my part except to run her away seven years ago."

His words stopped Chris in his tracks, and he turned to look at Mitchell as though he wasn't sure his ears had heard what they'd heard. The chime of the front door alerted them of Barbara's arrival, and Chris closed the door to Mitchell's office and then sat in the chair directly across from his desk. He didn't speak, but his eyes were full of questions. In a matter of seconds, Mitchell answered the most dominant one.

"Virtue is . . . Virtue *was* my wife."

Losing complete interest in the coffee he'd just been enjoying, Chris placed the still-full cup on his partner's desk and then pushed it to the side. "Your *what*?"

"My wife. The woman who walked in the restaurant used to be my wife. That was the first time I'd seen her since I struck her for the second time during one of my drunken rages."

Chris was still having trouble processing Mitchell's first few words. "You have a wife?"

"Had," Mitchell corrected.

"Have . . . had . . . whatever." Chris shrugged. "How, in three years, have I not known that you were once married?"

"You never asked." Mitchell knew that the answer wasn't a valid one, but he also knew that Chris wouldn't press him to give a more detailed one. Instead, Chris changed the question and proposed a new one.

"How long had it been since you'd seen her?"

"We'd just gotten married less than a year before my grandparents died, so I quickly became a different man than the man she married. Virtue hung in with me for almost three years, which was probably more than most women would have. But when the drinking started and then got out of control to the point where I was taking my frustrations out on her, she left. That terrified look that she had on her face at Bob's was the same look of horror that she had the first time I hit her. I thought I'd lost her then because she stormed out of the house, leaving me there to wallow in self-pity all by myself. But when I woke up the next morning, she was right there beside me in the bed. She came back."

"And you hit her again?" Chris was clearly fascinated by this story that he'd never heard before.

Mitchell nodded, surprised at how easy it was for him to share the most shameful part of his life with his friend. He'd held it inside himself for so long that he'd not noticed that it was not only a secret, but a burden. Telling Chris about it felt liberating.

"It must have been pretty bad the second time around for her to leave permanently," Chris said after Mitchell quietly drifted back in time.

"Two weeks later I hit her twice as hard as the first time," Mitchell explained. He shook his head in regret as he recalled the day it happened. "She hadn't done anything wrong. Every day she was going to work and trying to pay the bills that I couldn't because of my expensive addiction. She had just graduated from Hope College that summer and was settling in a routine of teaching ballet for first through fifth grade students at a local elementary school. Virtue had barely walked in the door that day before I nailed her with all of my complaints and accusations."

"Such as?"

"It didn't matter, man. Anything I could think of, I was saying it. I complained of not being able to find clean underwear because she hadn't done the laundry. I accused her of seeing another man because she'd gotten home an hour later than normal that day. I complained about being hungry because she hadn't cooked dinner."

"Did you really think she was seeing another man?"

"I was intoxicated, Chris. Drunk people are some of the world's most stupid people. I was smashed and I was an idiot. It wasn't about dinner or the laundry, and it sure wasn't about another man. I knew Virtue better than that. If she really wanted to be with another man, she would have just abandoned me like everybody else in my life had. I was just angry at myself for what happened to my grandparents and for losing my job and my family and for becoming a colossal failure. Virtue reminded me of the good things in life and all I could see and wanted to see were the bad. The first time I hit her, it was just a slap across the face. Not that that wasn't bad enough," Mitchell quickly added. "But it was nothing in comparison to the last time I hit her. I used my fist, and the blow was so hard that she flipped over the sofa and hit her head on the coffee table. As drunk as I was, I could see the instant swelling that followed. She didn't even bother to pack."

"That was the last time you saw her?"

"Yeah. Seven years ago." Mitchell pulled his keys from his top drawer and held them up so Chris could see them. Dangling between two of the keys was a gold wedding band with small diamonds embedded on the top. "This is all that I have to really remind me of what I had with her. When the movers came a couple of weeks later, they took every garment and every photo that had her in it, including the wedding album. Virtue had to be with them on the day they came. I wasn't home when they came and got her stuff, but I don't know how they would have known what to take had she not been there. When I got in that afternoon, it looked like I'd never shared that apartment with anybody. All of her things . . . everything was gone. It was like she'd vanished without a trace."

Chris stood and took a few steps across the floor before turning back to Mitchell. "Who filed for divorce?"

"She did, a few months later. I probably never would have filed, because I didn't want to be divorced. In spite of the way I mistreated her, I loved Virtue. I still . . ." Mitchell's voice drifted, and when it returned, the previous thought was left incomplete. "I guess in the back of my mind, I'd held on to the hope that she'd eventually return to me like she did after the first attack. But I had no such luck. I didn't even contest the divorce. I'd put her through enough, and she deserved to be happy. I was still struggling to find sobriety, so I knew I wasn't what she needed or wanted."

"And you'd never seen her again until the other day?"

"It wasn't for lack of trying, though," Mitchell said with a laugh. "After I got my life together, I would look for her periodically, not knowing if I really wanted to find her or not. I guess what I was most afraid of was seeing that terrified look in her eyes. Like the one she displayed three weeks ago."

"When was the last time you looked for her?"

"Remember last year when I spent my vacation in Detroit? That was the last time I looked. Her parents had moved, so they were no longer in the place where I'd known them to live. For years I'd been afraid of going to them, knowing that they'd known what I did to their only child. Her father never really liked me to begin with, so I was actually kind of frightened about how he would react to seeing the man who hit his daughter. But I manned up and said it was time that I faced the music. Whatever he said or did to me, I deserved that plus some more. But when I got there, I found out that they'd moved away."

Chris had made his way back to the chair he'd abandoned during Mitchell's explanation. The coffee in his cup was lukewarm, and he frowned after taking a swallow. He replaced the cup on the desktop and leaned back in his chair, shaking his head in disbelief of what he'd just heard.

"Man, you need to write a book," he said. "In our premarital counseling session with Rev. Inman last week, Lisa and I were asked to talk about the most tragic marital stories we'd ever heard, not including her own experiences, of course. When it was my turn, I just sat there looking like my last name was Huxtable. My parents have been married for almost fifty years, and Ursula and her husband have a good marriage. If I had heard your story a week ago, I could have made Lisa's tale of her coworker's bitter divorce and custody battle sound like an episode of *Sesame Street*."

A sudden overwhelming sadness engulfed Mitchell, and all at once he fought the threat of tears. For years he'd prayed for a chance to rectify the unforgivable sin he'd committed when he dared to lay his hands on his wife. He had foolishly taken for granted that he'd wake up the next morning with her in the bed beside him as in the previous case. Virtue's failure to return devastated him, and he spent almost every sober moment of the days following the fight looking for her. After two days passed and she hadn't returned home, Mitchell had gone to her job at the school where she taught dance and was surprised that she'd quit the job she loved with a simple phone call to her boss. Mitchell began to feel panic setting in. He was almost certain that she had found refuge with her parents, but each time he called, he got no answer. None of Mitchell's messages were returned, and without a vehicle he couldn't make the hour-long drive to their house. At least, that was the excuse he'd used at the time. Today was the first day that he'd been able to admit that fear was the real reason he didn't find a way to make the visit.

Since gaining a close relationship with Christ, Mitchell

had obtained a level of peace, believing that his prayers had been heard and that God had given him an immeasurable amount of patience to wait for Virtue to reenter his life. All those years of praying for a chance, and when he finally saw her, Mitchell was too dumbfounded to form any words other than her name. There was so much more that needed to be said. He'd never apologized. He'd never had another opportunity to tell her how much he loved her. Perhaps most of all, Mitchell needed to show her how much he'd changed. He wanted her to witness the differences in his life. Instead, all he'd been able to do was see a woman who was nearly frightened to death just by the very sight of him.

Mitchell unconsciously closed his eyes and tried to block out the image of the look in her eyes just before she'd dashed from the restaurant as though her life depended on how quickly she could escape. His meditation was broken when he heard Chris mutter five words.

"You think she's remarried now?"

It was a probability that Mitchell had given no thought to. Or perhaps it was one that he felt would not be so if he just didn't give it consideration. Virtue was an intelligent, gifted woman who was beautiful both inside and out. It only stood to reason that a man much smarter than Mitchell had seen what a jewel she was and had leapt at the opportunity to treat her like the queen she deserved to be treated as.

"I'm sorry," Chris said, realizing that he'd struck a chord with his last statement.

"It's okay," Mitchell said, suddenly wanting more than anything to end the conversation. "I'm sure she has. Like I said, she deserves to be happy."

Both men sat in silence for several moments. Mitchell's mind was bombarded with thoughts, just as it had been every day for the past three weeks. Although he'd never forgotten Virtue or the love he had shared with her,

Mitchell thought that he'd successfully moved on and accepted that that part of his life was over. As remorseful as he was for everything that had happened between them, he thought that he'd accepted the responsibility, gotten forgiveness, and would move on with his future, never having to revisit that part of his past.

Seeing Virtue had changed everything. It opened a flood of questions in his mind. *What is she doing in Dallas? How has her life been affected by what I did to her? Has Virtue ever found it in her heart to forgive me? And, if so, why did she run? What is she doing in Dallas?*

The question of her presence in Dallas was the one that repeated itself the most. Mitchell couldn't help but give way to the possibility that Virtue had somehow, maybe by divine order, made her way to the same city that he now called home. It would be ironic and quite coincidental given the fact that, as far as he knew she had no family ties here. Chris's question of whether she'd remarried weighed heavily in the back of Mitchell's mind. If he were a gambling man, Mitchell would bet money that she had. Even so, he still wanted to seize the opportunity, if one actually existed, to apologize. She may never find it in her heart to forgive him, and that was understandable as far as Mitchell was concerned; but he'd prayed for it, and if God was opening the door to allow it to happen, he needed to seize the moment.

But how?

Just as the thought formed in Mitchell's mind, Chris's voice overshadowed it.

"You still love her, don't you?"

Mitchell looked up and found Chris looking directly at him, asking a question that his eyes indicated he already knew the answer to. The obvious truth would be simple to say, but Mitchell wasn't sure whether he wanted to verbally admit his lingering love for his ex-wife. The answer might have been simple, but it was a painful truth. And if

Virtue's heart indeed belonged to another man now, it would be a *pointless* truth.

"When a man is as big of a drunk as I was, Chris, very little else means anything to him, even love." Avoiding a direct answer to the question seemed like a safer route to take. "I was barely clearheaded long enough to even think about love. Virtue slept in the bed most nights and I passed out on the sofa, opting instead to sleep with Pearl."

Chris looked at him in a mixture of surprise and disgust. It was clearly not the response he'd been expecting. "Pearl? You mean you actually carried on an affair, with your wife in the next room?"

"What can I say?" Mitchell shrugged. "Pearl was smooth, elegant, supple, full-bodied, and just a little bit spicy. She made me relax, and I loved going to sleep with her in my arms."

"I don't mean no disrespect, man, but no wonder Virtue left your sorry behind. And listen to you. Even now, you make it sound like this relationship with Pearl was deeper than your relationship with your wife. It sounds like it was serious, man."

Mitchell looked at the profound expression on his friend's face and burst into laughter, unable to continue the façade. After the emotional overrun of thoughts that had nearly broken him just moments ago, the laughter was a welcome change. Mitchell's outburst seemed to cause Chris's concerns to diminish but his confusion to double. Once Mitchell stopped laughing, he explained himself.

"Pearl is the brand of vodka I used to drink, Chris. Believe me, there was no real love there. We just used each other. I used vodka to drown my sorrows, and vodka used me to infiltrate my life and tear it to smithereens. Pearl cost me twenty-four dollars a bottle and, eventually, everything else too."

Chris broke into a hearty laugh at the realization of it all, but his next words were halted by the sound of his telephone ringing in his office down the hall. Barbara answered, but it was only a matter of seconds before she called for him.

"We'll finish this conversation later," Chris said just before walking from the room and once again leaving his partner to his thoughts.

Mitchell knew that he wasn't off the hook. He knew his best friend well. Chris was perceptive enough to know when Mitchell wasn't ready to talk about an issue, and he was always kind and wise enough to back away when needed. But Chris was also determined. Mitchell knew that when he came back, the question of whether or not there was still love in his heart for Virtue would be high on the list of conversation pieces. This time, Mitchell had avoided answering. Next time, he knew he wouldn't be so fortunate.

Four

*I*t had taken eight months for Virtue to seek the help she needed following a series of misfortunes that began with her separation and ultimate divorce from the man she had once called her soul mate and ended with the burial of her beloved mother. Seven years seemed like a lifetime ago, and in a sense it was, but seeing Mitchell Andrews during her visit to Dallas had all but erased the healing that her year-long therapy had helped her to gain. Now here she sat again on Dr. Beverly Oliver's couch, doing what she did best —crying.

"Listen, Virtue," Beverly said as she took slow, quiet steps toward her patient, turned friend, turned patient again. "I know life threw you a curveball with this one, but you don't have to let it be a setback for you. God has been too good to you for you to allow this one sighting to destroy all the strides that you made. For the past three weeks, you've been walking backward. You can't fall apart because of this. I won't let you."

With a quick, involuntary jerk of her body, caused by

the gasp she took in an attempt to control her tears Virtue struggled to force a smile in the direction of her therapist. Beverly was a godsend. It was really the only word that adequately described her. Virtue was, for the most part, a loner, and she credited her life's experiences for making her that way. She'd been in Houston for more than five years now, and there was still no one her own age that she would define as a friend. She worshiped with a thousand other church members every Sunday and rehearsed with a dozen praise dancers three times a week, but once their time in their respective settings was over, there was little or no communication until the routine began again.

Following her breakup from Mitchell, she'd made several moves in search of a better life. For a little while, she remained in Detroit, but she took advantage of a job opportunity that relocated her to Flint, Michigan. When an even better opportunity presented itself in Houston, Virtue accepted, not once expecting to run into Mitchell Andrews. He loved Detroit, and she couldn't imagine what had brought him back to his childhood home of Dallas.

Virtue had just made her move from Flint to Houston when she met the then-forty-nine-year-old woman who was to become her mentor and friend. Beverly had been standing at the exit doors, serving as an usher, at the Temple of Jerusalem Church on the first Sunday in June three and a half years ago. Virtue often recalled the day with bittersweet fondness. It was a day that marked the beginning of a long journey to hope and healing. On that day, just like today, Beverly walked up to her and placed a fresh Kleenex in her hand to absorb the flow of tears that ran so heavily down Virtue's cheeks that they pooled at her chin and overflowed into large drops that landed on her skirt.

The cushions on the couch where Virtue sat sank under the pressure as Beverly joined her. The woman, well-respected in her field, had the striking beauty of a retired model, but a trunk that was more reminiscent of a retired

Model T. Her hips were full and wide, but every pound of her was full of love and kindness. To Virtue, Beverly had become a mother, a friend, and a therapist, all in one. Not having friends her age left no feeling of void in Virtue's life. Following that Sunday morning service, Virtue's unlikely heroine invited her to her home for dinner, and Virtue never left. Not permanently anyway. She found out that Beverly was a practicing psychiatrist who used her expertise in a center for abused women.

Whoever said that the first step was the hardest decision was right. Although outwardly Virtue had convinced herself that she could make it through her traumatic experiences on her own, inwardly she knew she needed help. Her life was slowly crumbling, and she had gotten to the point where she felt plagued with thoughts of ending it all. In Virtue's mind, there was little left to live for. She was hurting in a way that was slowly killing her, both mentally and physically. Virtue's walking into the Temple of Jerusalem Church had long ago been defined by both women as an act of God. With the mental battle that had been going on inside Virtue, had she not seen the church on the corner lot that morning and somehow gathered enough wits about her to wander in, she was sure that she would have taken her life that very day.

As a reminder of the miracle God had performed, Virtue had kept the bottle of pills that she'd purchased from the drugstore that Sunday morning. She'd endured enough pain in her lifetime. She didn't need to die in the same manner in which she'd lived. Her plans had been to go home, write a letter for whoever would have the misfortune of finding her body, and end her life's sufferings. But God had different plans.

Virtue made it clear early in her first conversation with Beverly that she would not live in the housing that the center offered. After she was convinced that Virtue's ex-husband was not a dangerous man who might be stalking her, Beverly stopped pressing but insisted that Virtue move in with her so that she would not be alone. It had taken a fair amount of coaxing on Beverly's part, but Virtue agreed to the arrangement, realizing that it would also spare her many of the expenses that her two-bedroom apartment required. The arrangement worked perfectly, and in the end Virtue was grateful for the professional and personal attention she got from the licensed expert. Both Beverly and the Temple of Jerusalem became beacons of hope and salvation for Virtue.

"You do know that nothing happens by accident, right?" Beverly said, using her hand to force Virtue to look directly at her. "God is in control of everything, and just like He directed your path and led you to church back in yonder years, He also led you to that restaurant."

Virtue often saw eye-to-eye with Beverly's conclusions, but this time the vigorous shaking of her head showed her utter disagreement. "No," Virtue refuted. "That was the devil's doing. God wouldn't do this to me, Beverly. Not after all that I went through with that man. Not after all the pain and hurt. God wouldn't do that."

Beverly sat back in her spot on the sofa. Although Beverly didn't readily dispute the declaration, Virtue could tell that her friend still held to her own findings. But Virtue knew better. There was no way that God would have directed her to Bob's Steak & Chop House if He had known. . . .

Catching herself, Virtue reevaluated her line of thinking. *Okay . . . God knows all things, so of course He knew that Mitchell would be there, but my running into him was not orchestrated by God. I had been saying that I had a taste for Chinese food. Had I followed my own mind, I would have gone to a different restaurant anyway. I was out of God's will.*

"Virtue, our thoughts are not God's thoughts and our ways are not His ways," Beverly said in a manner that made Virtue feel that Beverly had read her thoughts. "By our understanding, it would seem foolish—brutal even—

for God to put you in the path of the man who hurt you so deeply. But sometimes God takes the foolish and uses it to show us things that we may not see otherwise. It's like Elder Bradley preached a couple of months ago. Sometimes God has to remind us that . . ."

Virtue had heard enough. "You know what God uses to remind me of Mitchell?" she challenged. "This!"

Using her fingers, Virtue created a part that separated her thick strands of hair. "Do you see this scar?" she demanded. "This is from the gash that I received as a result of his violence. If I had fallen differently, the impact could have killed me, Beverly. It's easy for somebody like you, who have never experienced any kind of domestic abuse, to quote Scriptures and cite appropriate sermons that make me out to be the villain. But I wonder if you could see it so simply if you were the one who lived through what I did. It's pretty hard to forgive and forget when you have permanent scars to remind you of it every single day of your life. And if my unwillingness to wipe the slate clean and run up and shake Mitchell Andrews's hand makes me a bad Christian, then oh, well!"

By the time her rant ended, Virtue's tears had once again begun pouring. Taking on more the role of a mother than a therapist, Beverly reached over and pulled Virtue against her, so that her head rested on Beverly's chest. Nothing was said for several minutes. Even after Virtue's tears had slowed, her head remained in its comfortable place, and she stared at the warm colors in the fibers of the carpeted floor.

"Do you love him?"

Beverly's words froze Virtue. Everything seemed to momentarily stop. Her tears, her breathing, her heartbeat —all of it was lost in time. Her immediate instinct was to jump to her feet in a fit of rage and scream at Beverly for even suggesting such a thing. Mitchell Andrews had struck her, and in doing so, he had torn their entire lives apart.

Because of it, she'd been left with nowhere to call home. Because of it, she'd had no strong shoulder to lean on in the trying times that followed. Love him? *She hated him.*

"Virtue?" Beverly spoke in a calm, soothing tone. "Do you love him?"

The urge to throw an Emmy-winning tantrum remained, but Virtue couldn't get her body to cooperate with her mind. No one had asked her that question since her mother had asked it the first time she'd taken Mitchell to meet her parents. Virtue still remembered the conversation like it was yesterday.

"He seems like a nice young man, Virtue," Peggy had said that day as she and her daughter worked together to put the dishes in the dishwasher following dinner. "He's handsome too."

Virtue blushed. She was glad that her mother seemed to approve. "Yeah, he is kind of cute, isn't he?" she'd replied. "He's really nice, Mom. At first I thought he was just another man trying to play the game, but he's different. I can tell. He's so . . . sweet and considerate. I guess, in a way, he's a lot like Daddy."

Peggy's eyes momentarily clouded over, but a wide grin quickly spread across her face and erased the fleeting former reaction. "Well, I don't think I've ever seen you so taken by a man, Virtue. This sounds serious."

As Virtue recalled, she'd never responded to her mother's implication. Instead she blushed deeper and placed the last plate into the dishwasher. As soon as she closed the door and stood to her full height, Peggy reached forward and removed several stray locks of hair from her daughter's face and tucked them behind her ear.

"Do you love him?" Peggy had asked.

Just the sound of the question had had an emotional effect on Virtue. She found herself almost speechless, but when she nodded her positive response and managed a soft, "Yes, I love him," there was no look of surprise from her mother. It was obvious that Peggy had already known the answer before she'd asked the question.

"Now tell me."

Both women had turned to see Mitchell standing in the opening that separated the kitchen from the living room where he had been sitting and chatting with Virtue's father. Embarrassed by what she knew Mitchell had witnessed, Virtue used her hands to cover her face. A few quiet moments passed before she felt Mitchell's hands tugging at the makeshift veil she'd provided. When she'd reluctantly lowered her hands, she found that the three-person gathering had been reduced to two. At some point during Virtue's reaction, Peggy had walked away and left Virtue to face her admittance alone.

"Tell me," Mitchell whispered.

Suddenly uncomfortable with the man she'd been nothing but at ease with for the past month, Virtue dropped her eyes and shifted her feet. Her mouth became parched, and the roof of it begged for moisture that her dry tongue couldn't provide.

"Tell you what?" she asked, knowing full well that Mitchell wasn't naive enough to think she was clueless about what he meant.

"Tell me," he had repeated. This time he cupped her face in his hands and forced her to return his gaze.

Virtue didn't know why her eyes filled with water, but they did, and she couldn't stop the spill that followed. Mitchell didn't flinch in his position. His eyes remained locked on hers, and his face was so close to Virtue's that she could almost taste his lips.

"Tell me, Virtue." His eyes were pleading. *"Tell me,"* he urged for the fifth time.

Her voice broke and it was barely above a whisper, but Virtue knew that Mitchell understood the three words that he'd been begging to hear. They had barely escaped her lips when he covered hers with his. The temporary drought that her mouth had endured was quickly brought to an end. Admitting her love for Mitchell and having him mirror her feelings had brought about a whole new chapter in Virtue's life. When she met his grandparents three months later, Virtue knew that this was the family she wanted to be a part of. She loved everything about Mitchell. Only a fictitious character like Cinderella or Snow White could relate to what she felt. She'd met her Prince Charming, only hers came in black; and instead of a white horse, he rode a dark grey Chrysler New Yorker. It had been a love story that was never supposed to end. But it did.

Virtue's mental trip back in time came to an end too. Her time was up. She'd waited too long to breathe. She'd waited too long to shed another tear. She'd waited too long to restart her beating heart, and she'd waited too long to answer. Her silence, as far as Beverly was concerned, gave consent. Even knowing the conclusion her therapist had drawn, Virtue couldn't find the strength to dispute it.

"Sweetheart, don't you see?" Beverly said, using her hands to push Virtue back into an upright position. "The reason you are so broken and angry isn't because you saw your ex-husband. It's not because you saw the person who you see as responsible for tearing your life apart. It's not even because you saw the man who delivered the blow that gave you that permanent scar. It's because you came face-to-face with all of that and you still have love for him."

Five

*F*ive years ago, when any of Virtue's sessions with Beverly came to an end, she would leave the battered women's center feeling like she'd made another stride, overcome another obstacle, defeated another demon. But following today's meeting she felt the onset of depression. Virtue had heard every word that Beverly had said, and she certainly could see how she'd arrived at all of her conclusions; but Virtue knew herself, and regardless of her inability to answer at the time, she knew that she had no love in her heart for the man who had stomped on it and broken it into a thousand unidentifiable pieces.

"No, I don't love him," she said aloud. She could kick herself for not being able to verbalize it sooner.

Having completed her shampoo and shower, Virtue stepped from the stall and dried herself. Years of exercising and dancing combined with her selective eating resulted in the well-toned body that was reflected in the mirror. Virtue had never fought the battles of the bulge that Beverly had told her about, but, in turn, Beverly had never had Virtue's physical and emotional battles. In her mind, Virtue reasoned that she'd make the swap any day.

With her hair and her body wrapped in matching thick, rose-colored towels, she stepped from her bathroom and sat on the edge of her bed. Virtue loved her two-bedroom townhouse. She'd purchased it once she finished her year-long therapy and settled into her current job as the leader of the praise dance team at Temple of Jerusalem. There, she trained dancers and taught routines that were performed every Sunday morning during praise and worship services. The emotional, Spirit-filled moves of her students added much depth to the services, and the church paid her well for what her expertise brought to the growing congregation. It was the most fulfilling job that she'd ever had.

Virtue reached in the bottom drawer of her nightstand and pulled out the jewelry box that she kept buried beneath her college yearbook and other collectible papers that she rarely ever reviewed. She hadn't looked inside the box in more than a year. It was such a beautiful ring. From the angle where she sat, the overhead light reflected off the half-carat solitaire and the chips of diamonds that were set in the matching band. It had been a symbol of eternal love and devotion that she'd gladly accepted more than nine years ago. If she and Mitchell had remained married, they would be celebrating their tenth anniversary this Christmas.

Virtue remembered the first day she had met Mitchell. It was just after Valentine's Day, and she had made the two-and-a-half-hour drive from Holland to Detroit to spend the weekend at home to help her mom as she recuperated from an injury to her arm. While out shopping together the day before she was to drive back to the campus, Virtue and her mother made a stop by Motown Market on West Grand Boulevard to pick up a few items for her to take back and stock in the refrigerator in her dorm room. Mitchell's and her meeting almost seemed like destiny.

Virtue and her mom had already completed their shopping and were loading the items in the car when Virtue decided she wanted to pick up a few more cans of the mandarin oranges that were on sale. That quick run brought her together with the man she'd marry just ten months later.

She'd been in her second year at her four-year liberal arts college, and Mitchell was only a few weeks away from graduation at the two-year, historically Black college that he attended. Mitchell's grandparents died just months after she'd married him, but she had been accepted with open arms into the Andrews family. Her heart went out to him, but nothing she did seemed to be able to console his grief. In the months that had followed, Mitchell's sadness and the hurt from the abandonment of his surviving relatives turned into bitterness and anger. He became short-tempered, unapproachable, and untrustworthy.

Months had passed before Virtue came to realize that he had a drinking problem. He stopped going to work regularly, and the monies that they had been saving to take their delayed honeymoon began mysteriously disappearing from their joint savings account. The first time she'd approached Mitchell about her concerns was the first time he hit her. Virtue remembered being stunned into a speechless oblivion. Her first consideration was to run to her parents' house, but she knew that with her father's temperament, going to them would only exacerbate the situation. Instead, she filled her car with gas and spent the next several hours circling the city. When she was too tired and sleepy to drive any longer, she returned home and was elated that her husband had literally drunk himself to sleep. Virtue justified his lashing out and even blamed herself for provoking it, citing her knowledge that he was already feeling bad enough with his family situation. She also convinced herself that Mitchell's drinking was just a temporary habit brought on by grief.

Instead of getting better, Mitchell's drinking had

worsened; and before long, it had cost him his gainful employment. The tighter their finances got, the more irritable Mitchell became. On the day that his car was repossessed, he trashed the bathroom while Virtue was at work. When she got home, she saw opened bottles of medication strewn across the floor, and she panicked. Mitchell lay motionless on the living room sofa. Her first fear was that he'd overdosed. Waking him turned out to be a mistake that would eternally change both their lives.

As it turned out, he hadn't overdosed or even taken any medicine at all. He was just intoxicated, as had become his way of life. Mitchell awakened angry that Virtue had dared to disturb his drunken afternoon slumber. He began yelling about her being a poor excuse for a wife. There was no dinner on the table, he'd said; the house was a mess, and he'd had to fish underwear from the dirty-clothes hamper because there were no clean ones in his drawers.

She should have just continued to ignore him. Instead, Virtue opened her mouth to defend herself and earned herself a wallop across the face that sent her tumbling. Getting up from the spill was a struggle. Her vision was momentarily blurred, her head spun, and when she touched the sore spot, blood appeared on her hands. It was a life that she had said she'd never live, and if she stayed another day, Virtue knew she'd be sentencing herself to years of this kind of mistreatment. Love made her want to stay, but as Mitchell continued ranting and sputtering foul words at her, it was fear that had led her through the front door with only her purse and the clothes on her back.

A tear rolled down her cheek as she sat on the side of the bed staring at the ring she'd removed from her finger on the day she filed for divorce from her abuser. Maybe she should have seen the possibility, but Virtue had been totally blindsided. No one could have ever told her that her marriage would have turned out the way it had. When she'd met Mitchell in the canned goods aisle at Motown

Market, it'd felt like love at first sight. He was smart, kind, handsome, and destined for success. Mitchell Andrews was everything she wanted in a mate. Early in their relationship, Virtue told her mother that a love like she'd found with Mitchell only came once in a lifetime. How could she have been so wrong? Had her upbringing been so sheltered that it left her ill prepared for the real world? Sometimes Virtue didn't know who it was she was angriest at: Mitchell, for his pretentious behavior that led had her to believe that he was such a wonderful individual, or herself, for being a woman who could be so easily deceived.

Virtue whisked away another tear. Mitchell had been her first everything. He had been her first real boyfriend. Sure, there had been crushes and interests before him, but none of them personified true love. By every definition, Mitchell was *the one*. Virtue had had no real spiritual foundation when they began dating, but with the day of their marriage set in the not-so-distant future, Mitchell agreed to wait. It wasn't easy for either one of them. Waiting tested their commitments and their wills to the nth degree, but they succeeded. Knowing that he wasn't accustomed to waiting made his willingness to do so mean even more to Virtue. Mitchell hadn't just waited for her; he had waited *with* her.

Virtue put the ring away and stretched across the bed. For a moment, she stared at the light fixture that was attached to the ceiling of her dancer-themed bedroom. The border that lined her bedroom walls displayed the repeated image of a dancer holding a long ribbon in her hand as she twirled in her performance garb. The pink and green border not only showed the love Virtue had for her vocation, but the pride she had in her chosen sorority as well. She squeezed her eyelids together and tried to flush out the thoughts of her failed marriage and the circumstances surrounding it. As much as she tried, she found little success. Virtue hadn't thought this deeply about Mitchell in years.

If she could rewrite the recent past, she'd certainly delete the moment that she had made the last-minute decision to turn into the lot of the restaurant in Dallas.

Why didn't you just go for Chinese? she asked herself while turning over and tightening the towel around her body.

Now that the relationship was over and the marriage was dissolved, Virtue was sure that her former husband had filed her name right along with all of the other women he'd conquered before and after her. The thought of it was sickening. Virtue rarely got to bed before eleven o'clock at night, but since she couldn't rid herself of the thoughts of her past life, she welcomed the heavy eyelids that threatened to mark this evening's bedtime at nine thirty. She reasoned that she'd sleep the night away. Tomorrow was Saturday, and she'd be sure to keep her weekend busy. It was time to shake herself of the three weeks of anguish that seeing Mitchell had brought on. There was no way she could go through this for another week. A month of Sundays would not pass and find her still fighting this seven-year-old battle. She just wouldn't allow it.

six

*C*onfessing the details of the thirty-two-month marriage he'd been keeping secret from even those closest to him had granted Mitchell a sense of relief, but it also fueled his desire to find his former wife and beg her forgiveness for all the hurt and pain that he'd caused her. It was way too late to save their marriage, but for his own peace of mind Mitchell needed to hear her say that she'd forgiven him. Or maybe he just needed to feel a sense of detachment from the dastardly act that he was sure she identified him by. Maybe he needed her to forgive him before he could fully forgive himself. Whichever was the case, Mitchell was determined to own up to his stupidity and beg her pardon. From the way Virtue had cringed in fear at the sight of him and dashed away in apparent panic, it was clear that the turmoil he'd created was still fresh in her memory. The years (even the drunken ones) hadn't been enough to erase it from his mind either.

Arriving late, Mitchell parked his new Toyota Tundra in the lot of Living Word Cathedral. He had overslept after failing to set his alarm before he dozed off the night before. The usher who stepped aside so Mitchell could enter the sanctuary looked at him with scolding in her eyes. Mitchell almost laughed. It wasn't as if she wasn't accustomed to his late arrival. The reward for his tardiness was always the same. Like most Sundays, Mitchell would have to settle for an empty space near the back of the church; and if he wanted to get a good view of his pastor, he'd have to look up at the large-screen monitors that hung from the ceiling.

The sermon had just begun as Mitchell entered the sanctuary. Living Word Cathedral was the meeting place of choice for roughly three thousand worshipers each Sunday morning; and Lionel Inman, in Mitchell's opinion, could stand up to any top-rated television preacher in the world. Still in his midforties, Rev. Inman possessed biblical wisdom that far exceeded his years. There were certainly more seasoned preachers in Dallas, but a more knowledgeable one would be difficult to find.

Growing up with his grandparents, Mitchell could count on one hand the number of times he'd gone to church, and every single one of them was for a funeral. Isaac and Kate Andrews had been two of the most kindhearted and giving people Mitchell had ever known, but spiritual they were not. Grandpa Isaac would have given the shirt off his back to another man in need, but if anyone ever had the misfortune of crossing him the wrong way, he could curse like a drunken sailor. When he ran out of bona fide swear words to use, he created bogus ones. They may not have been found in *Webster's Dictionary*, but if they were directed at anyone in particular, that person knew he'd just been cussed out.

Grandma Kate had been different. Mitchell couldn't think of a time when he'd ever heard her use any foul language. She referred to such as unladylike. But apparently she didn't feel the same way about lying. Kate would tell an untruth without thinking twice about it. She'd say she spent all day looking for something when she'd actually spent the day in front of the television set, or she would tell a friend who called that she had company, when, in reality, she just didn't want to talk to the person. Mitchell had been sharing the couch with her once as she watched one of her favorite soap operas when his grandfather called. One of the first things Grandpa Isaac would ask when he phoned home was, "What's going on at the house?" This particular day, his grandmother told him she was starting dinner and had just put the pots on the stove. Mitchell hadn't even looked away from the television screen. Grandma Kate had told "little lies" like that all the time, so to hear her spit out one on a moment's notice was no surprise.

Grandpa Isaac had referred to church as "organized religion." Preachers, in his eyes, were all crooks in suits, and the people who gathered to listen to them each week were pathetic and gullible. He said he believed in God but could serve Him right in the comfort of his home, and if anyone ever accused him of not being a Christian, he'd cuss that person out too. The few times that Mitchell had gone to church, he'd done so with his grandmother, but they were all to pay respects to the dead. If Kate knew somebody who was third cousin to the deceased, she'd be there, dressed in black and weeping into a handkerchief as though it were a personal loss. Most times her crying was dignified and quiet, but if it was one of those funerals where the mourners got carried away, Grandma Kate would not be upstaged. She could howl, grab caskets, and pass out with the best of them, and every once in a while, she did.

When Mitchell and Virtue got married, Virtue's childhood pastor conducted the ceremony in the Detroit church where her parents still attended. It was the first time in Mitchell's life that he could remember stepping foot in a church wherein everybody was alive and well.

When he'd first walked through the doors of Living Word Cathedral three years ago, Mitchell felt a bit out of place. He knew worshiping was something people did regularly, but it wasn't the norm for him. He was twenty-eight years old at the time but felt like a child who'd just entered his kindergarten classroom for the very first time. Aside from Chris's, every face in the building was strange; and when the preacher spoke, every word seemed to be directed at him. Mitchell had wanted to grab a blanket, stick his thumb in his mouth, and retreat into the nearest corner; but Chris insisted that he not only sit through the service, but meet Rev. Inman personally afterward.

In an instant, Mitchell felt comfortable when he shook the smiling preacher's hand. After attending that first time, he knew he'd be returning the following Sunday and the Sunday after that. Ultimately, he joined the ministry and had missed very few services since. As he now looked at the words in the Bible that he held in his hand, Mitchell smiled in reflection. He wondered what his grandfather would think if he could see him sitting in a church and absorbing the words that Rev. Inman spoke.

"Where are you running off to?"

The familiar voice stopped Mitchell as he neared the parking lot to head for his truck after the benediction had been given. He turned around to look into the face of one of the prettiest women he'd met since moving back to his hometown. At times, Mitchell still had lingering doubts about Lisa Edwards and her loyalty to his best friend; but she made Chris happy, and in the end, that was all that mattered. Breaking into a grin that he hoped didn't carry shadows of his doubt, Mitchell reached out and accepted the offered embrace from the woman who would become Mrs. Jackson just before Valentine's Day.

"Hey," he responded. "Where's Chris?"

The bulk of Mitchell's doubt was rooted in the way Lisa interacted with him, especially when Chris wasn't around. Mitchell had tried to define her playful winks and frequent touches as harmless flirting or as a part of her friendly personality. But sometimes he found it hard to convince himself that all of it was done in innocence. Her bold reactions seemed tailor-made just for him and only seemed to happen when Chris was nowhere in sight. To say that Lisa made him uncomfortable was an overstatement, but Mitchell did become uneasy at times, especially when they were not in the presence of others, as they were right now.

"He's in that crowd somewhere," she responded, nodding her head toward the open doors of the church. "Where are you headed? You're not gonna hang with us this afternoon? Chris and I are going to grab something to eat."

The position of third wheel was getting old, and Mitchell was ready to resign. He'd been the odd man out ever since Chris and Lisa began dating a year and a half ago. Once they married, he knew he couldn't continue to spend his weekends with them, so it was best to begin the weaning process while the choice was still his. He'd made preparations to eat at home today.

"I marinated some seafood last night," he told her while simultaneously shaking his head. "I think I'm gonna just dine in today."

Lisa took a quick look around as though making sure her response couldn't be overheard. Apparently not satisfied with their degree of privacy, she grabbed Mitchell by the arm and led him closer to the parked cars. Mitchell braced himself for what he thought would be one of her advances.

"Is it because of *her*?" Lisa stressed the pronoun as though hearing her name might rub Mitchell the wrong way. "Do you not want to go out because you think you'll see her again?"

Mitchell gave a short laugh. It was no surprise to him

that Chris had shared the confidential information with his fiancée. "Lisa, if I thought I'd have the chance to see Virtue again by going out with you guys, I'd go in a heartbeat. Maybe I'd get the chance to save face for what happened the last time." Mitchell noticed Lisa's grimace, but continued. "I'm just not really in the mood for eating out today. Besides, I have some things that I need to take care of."

Lisa narrowed her eyes and peered up at him, obviously unconvinced that he was being completely honest with her. "What things?"

At thirty-three, Lisa was a year older than Chris, but she could pass for a woman in her midtwenties. Like Virtue, she stood at five feet eight inches with the help of three-inch heels, and her fair-skinned, cosmetic-free face was decorated with freckles just around her nose. She had brown eyes and wore her reddish, natural hair in locks that were about ten inches in length and dangled just above her shoulders. She was quite the attractive one, but she could also be meddlesome.

When he made no attempt to answer her question, Lisa delivered a painless punch to his arm and continued. "And why didn't you tell me you used to be married? I could have been a good ear for you. You know I was married before too. We could have shared stories about our ex's. I know I could have told you a few that would probably make the hairs stand up on your head." She took a quick look around and then leaned in closer and whispered, "And I could also tell you a few that would make you blush."

Taking a step backward, Mitchell shifted his position and pulled his arm away from the uncomfortable touch that Lisa hadn't ended since she jabbed him. "My failed marriage isn't exactly something I'm proud of, Lisa. I was at fault for losing Virtue, and that's not something I want to sit around and discuss on a regular basis."

"Oh, please," she said with a carefree wave of her hand.

"Everybody fails at something in their lifetime. It's no different. That's how we grow as Christians, Mitchell. We can't wallow in our failures. We'll never move on if we don't get over our pasts, and what better way to get over it than by talking about it?"

"I suppose." Mitchell shrugged. "I have to admit that I did feel a bit better after talking to Chris."

"Talking to Christopher is good. But sometimes you need to talk to someone who can relate. You know, someone who's been where you've been and knows where it is that you're trying to go." Lisa's hand was back on Mitchell's arm. "Sometimes it helps when the person you're talking to has faced the same fears and endured the same loneliness that you have."

Her words sounded genuine, but there was a level of suggestiveness in Lisa's tone that Mitchell couldn't ignore. It wasn't a first for her. She did it all the time, and just like in times before, Mitchell chose not to say anything that might encourage her to continue. His unresponsiveness was intended to make her change the subject, but when he did not readily reply, Lisa reached deeper.

"The 'L word' has a way of making a man clam up," she said. "Most women think that love is the hardest thing for a man to talk about, but I've found that *loneliness* is the emotion that they are most afraid of. See how you totally shut down at the mention of it? Christians get lonely too, Mitchell, and there's nothing wrong with it. It's a human emotion, but it's not one that you have to shy away from talking about. That's what I mean when I say that you need to talk to someone who's been where you are. I've been there, Mitchell. Sometimes I still deal with it, and I could certainly use somebody like you to help me. So anytime you feel . . . lonely, you can always come to me. I'm here for you. You know, whenever you need to talk . . . or whatever."

It was the sound of the "or whatever" that troubled him the most. More than anything, Mitchell wanted Chris to show up. An overwhelming sense of relief engulfed him when he looked out into the distance and saw his friend walk out onto the porch of the church.

Steady streams of people, satisfied with their chance to talk to Rev. Inman, were filing from the double-glass doors that led to the outside. Children had begun running through the grass, unfazed by the dropping outside temperature. The lengthy service seemed to have given them a new appreciation for the outdoors. While some members lingered and chatted, others made quick beelines for their cars to avoid the cold.

One couple in particular caught Mitchell's eye as they walked hand in hand toward the street. They only lived a block away and generally walked to Sunday morning services. Even in the nippy weather, they seemed to be in no hurry to get home. Their love and the company of each other was enough to supply the warmth they needed.

Hearing her call his name, Mitchell turned back to Lisa.

"Are you mad at me now?" she asked. "I didn't mean to upset you. I know men can be egotistical and don't particularly like to be reminded of their weaknesses. I'm sorry if I offended you. I was just trying to help."

"I'm not mad at you, Lisa. I'm just not in the mood to talk about Virtue right now."

"Who's talking about Virtue? I'm not in the mood to talk about her either. I can relate to that too. I don't want to talk about my ex either. Felander's not worth my breath, let alone my time. And look at that! We've got another thing in common. Both our ex's have crazy names. I thought Felander had a jacked-up name, but what drunk woman would name her daughter something like Virtue?"

The line had been crossed, but before Mitchell could respond, Chris trotted across the lawn and came to a breathless rest at the back of the car where the two of them stood. It was difficult, but Mitchell forced a smile through the heat of his anger and accepted the brotherly pound that Chris offered.

"What's up, man?" Chris said, panting. "For a minute, I thought that you had missed church today. You were even later than usual."

"I overslept," Mitchell explained. "I made it in time to hear the message, though."

"Well, the future Mrs. and I are going to get a bite to eat," Chris said as he slipped his arm around his fiancée and pulled her closer to him. "You can hop in the car with us and we'll bring you back to get your truck afterwards."

"Yeah, Mitch. We'd love to have you join us."

I'll bet you would, Mitchell thought and then immediately punished himself inwardly for thinking the worst of Lisa's urging. He knew lots of women who had the tendency to be overly friendly. That didn't mean that they were offering themselves for a deeper relationship with every guy they flirted with. Chris had the intelligence of a Yale graduate. He would know if his girl was capable of being unfaithful.

"Come on, Mitch," Lisa urged, touching his arm again. This time her touch didn't have the same feel as the ones she'd given prior to Chris's arrival. This time, it didn't challenge Mitchell's comfort level.

"No thanks, guys. I'll pass today but maybe later."

Chris looked at him in disbelief. "You're not eating? You sick or something?"

Laughing at his friend's expression, Mitchell shook his head. "I didn't say I wasn't going to eat; I just meant that I'd pass on eating out."

Although he didn't do it often, Mitchell was a superb cook who had learned almost everything he knew about meal preparation from his grandmother. The spicy oven-fried tilapia that he had planned for today was one of Grandma Kate's favorites. He'd cooked it for Virtue on their first date. It was one of her favorites too. At least, it used to be.

"You sure, man?" Chris asked. "We don't have to go to Bob's today. We can go somewhere else if you like."

Mitchell smiled but shook his head, declining once more. He was tempted to try one last time to convince both of them that his refusal of their invitation had nothing to do with seeing Virtue, but it wasn't worth the trouble. It was clear to Mitchell that his friends would never really understand the place he was in. The sighting of his wife didn't make him want to hide from her. Instead, it had renewed his quest to find her and clear his conscience.

"Maybe next week," Mitchell said. "I have some research to do anyway, so I need to be near my laptop. I'll catch you guys later."

With a wave of his hand, he made an escape and walked through the maze of vehicles pulling from the lot, finally reaching his own. Once inside, he breathed a sigh of relief. Revealing his marriage may have unburdened him to a certain extent, but talking about the failure of it was still painfully difficult. Mitchell joined the fight to escape the parking lot and headed toward home. During the drive, he saw Christmas lights that were left on to twinkle even during the daytime hours. The city of Dallas had sprung into the holiday season as soon as Thanksgiving had passed, but there was no festive lighting beckoning for Mitchell as he turned into his driveway. The December holiday was no longer a favorite of his.

As soon as he changed into more comfortable clothes, he fired up his computer and then went into the kitchen to start dinner. He preheated the oven while he took the fish from the refrigerator where it had been marinating in the spicy mixture for the past fourteen hours. Laying four fillets in the foil-lined pan, he placed them in the oven and set the timer for half an hour. That would give him enough time to make headway on the project ahead of him.

Saying a quick prayer before typing the name "Virtue Lynne Andrews" in the search criteria of his laptop, Mitchell watched while the hour-glass-shaped icon made its calculations. Regardless of what Lisa said, he thought Virtue's name was both beautiful and appropriate.

Seven

When she'd graduated from Hope College, Virtue had had big dreams of performing before thousands of people who would admire and adore her as she entertained them with the grace and beauty of creative dance. In a sense, she was living her dream, but not in the manner that her limited foresight had planned. Instead of swaying on a stage somewhere in Harlem or on Broadway, Virtue found herself doing so to the sounds of worship music at Temple of Jerusalem Church. God had taken a talent that some dubbed secular and made it useful for His glory.

It had taken some time, but Virtue had finally come to the understanding that God knew all along what she needed most, and it didn't involve bright lights and curtain calls. Leading the praise team at her church was a result of her salvation from an existence that had begun to feel hollow and meaningless. Escaping from her abusive marriage may have been the right thing to do, but it was in no way the easy way out. Leaving Mitchell was most likely the hardest thing Virtue had ever done in her life, and it had had a long-lasting effect on her. Hardly a day had passed in the seven years since she had walked away that she didn't think of him in some way. Virtue always found herself wondering where Mitchell was, what he was doing, *how* he was doing. Some time ago, she'd even resigned herself to the fact that he'd most likely drunk himself to death or perhaps been killed as he drove his car in an impaired state of mind. The fact that she even cared one way or the other would often make her angry with herself.

Sunday mornings had at one time been like another phase of therapy that helped to get her beyond the worries of everyday life. Being in church, hearing the Word of God, and dancing had all been much-needed aspects of her graduation from what Beverly often called "a broken yesterday to a bright tomorrow." It had taken time, and not a single step of her deliverance was easy, but Virtue had passed all of her tests with flying colors. Now, as the music blared through the speaker system and the harmonic sounds of the Voices of Jerusalem began to sing along, giving her and the dance troupe their cue, Virtue felt as though she needed this breakthrough as much as she needed the one she'd gotten the very first time she'd taken the floor.

Holding a long colorful strand of cloth in her hand, she led the line of a half-dozen chosen ones who burst through the back doors of the church and worshiped God using the powerful dramatization of dance. As the leader of the dance ministry, Virtue rarely was among the ones who performed. Instead she worked behind the scenes, teaching the steps to the teenagers and younger adults who put them into action on Sunday mornings. So today the membership was delighted to see Virtue take the lead. Although at thirty-one she was older than all of the other troupe members, Virtue was by far the most graceful, most powerful, and most emotional. Because of her formal training, her technique was often flawless, and her ability to bring a song to life frequently brought worshipful tears to the eyes of the onlookers. For her, it was more than a gift; it was a passion and a divine calling. Today was one of those days when there were tearstained cheeks throughout the sanctuary. Kirk Franklin's one-time hit "The Reason Why We Sing" had never been so moving.

Having finished their routine and made their exit, Virtue and the others scampered back to the dressing room. She gave them a few quick reminders as they prepared the outfits for their next performance. While they readied for the next song that signaled their reentrance, Virtue slipped into her own dressing room and into her own clothes. The performance they'd just completed would be her only active involvement for the day. Over the last three years since she'd taken over the position that had been left vacant by a scandal that resulted in the demotion of her predecessor, Virtue had done wonders with the dance troupe. The roster had grown both physically and spiritually under her leadership, and the routines were more anointed and charismatic. Elder Bradley often called Virtue "God's angel of praise." The congregation, for the most part, agreed.

"Excuse me, Virtue. I haven't heard anything since I turned in my application to join the dance ministry two Sundays ago. Did you get the paperwork? I know y'all ain't trying to discriminate."

Renee Bell was one of the very few who disagreed with Elder Bradley's view and Virtue knew why. Renee's sister Dondra had been the former leader of the praise dancers, and when "secret sins" that no one seemed to want to talk about were revealed, Elder Bradley wasted no time relieving both her and her coconspirator from their leadership duties. For a full twelve months, the church functioned without a dance troupe. Elder Bradley often said that they'd do without one before he allowed such atrocities to go on in God's house. Upon her dismissal, Dondra (along with the husband of one of the church's most dedicated ushers) chose to leave the ministry altogether and take their affair elsewhere. It was a scandal that rocked Temple of Jerusalem, but the church and those who were injured the most survived.

Maybe *that* was why Beverly had connected so well with Virtue. Although it wasn't a subject that they discussed frequently, Virtue could imagine the level of betrayal that Beverly had endured when she found out that her husband, who also happened to be on the ministerial board, was not only *capable* of being unfaithful, but was a *practicing* adulterer. Virtue imagined that it must have felt much like the betrayal she suffered through when she was forced to accept the fact that her husband was an abuser—both of alcohol and of her.

"Yes, Renee, I received your paperwork. And no, we're not discriminating; we're just not taking in any new members right now."

Virtue was glad that she didn't have to struggle with the decision of whether or not to be honest. Her explanation was true. The two slots that had been open for the troupe had been filled just before she got Renee's application. Virtue remembered breathing a sigh of relief and sending soft praises to heaven when she retrieved Renee's submission from her in-box. She wouldn't have chosen her anyway. Virtue wasn't naive enough to believe that Renee would come without drama. She was still extremely bitter about her sister's firing, and Virtue knew that Renee wouldn't be a positive addition to the ministry. The members of the dance troupe complemented one another well. Adding Renee to the mix could be just the ingredient that would make them lose their spiritual synchronization. Choosing her would be like rolling out the welcome mat for trouble.

"You lying," Renee accused as she reached between the pages of her Bible and pulled out a folded sheet of paper. "It says right here in the church bulletin that there are openings for the dance team. Lying ain't no better sin than any other. You need to be taken down from your position."

Renee tried very little to hide her animosity toward everyone who she felt had wronged her sister, therefore disrespecting her entire family. Virtue found it amazing that Renee seemed not to be able to see that Dondra had brought the harsh actions upon herself. Virtue turned her eyes briefly to the ceiling before looking back in Renee's direction and taking the paper that the woman held eye-level to Virtue's face.

"This bulletin is dated three Sundays ago, Renee. Had you turned in your application at that time, it would have been considered along with the other eight that we received. We filled the available slots last week, and the new dancers are going through the standard training period before they will be released to perform. So no lies are being told here. As with the other six applicants that were not chosen, we will keep your paperwork on file should another need for growth arise."

Snatching the bulletin from Virtue's hand and then taking a quick look at the date, Renee huffed in suppressed anger before crumpling it into a mangled mass. Satisfied that she had caused the paper enough pain, Renee then took it and shoved it into the pocket of Virtue's jacket.

"You can do the same with my application," Renee said. "You can ball it up and stick it in your pocket . . . or *wherever* else it'll fit. I don't care to be your second choice. For the record, I don't believe for a minute that the positions have already been filled. But if they have, it's your loss, not mine."

With that, Renee tossed Virtue a condescending look and then turned to walk away. As she brushed past Beverly, who was headed in their direction, a coy grin crossed Renee's face, and she made a U-turn that brought her right back to the place she'd just left. The expression on her face told them, even before her words did, that she'd dare not let an opportunity pass when she could say something that could ruffle the feathers of both the women she despised most.

Snapping her fingers as though she'd inadvertently left out some pertinent piece of information, Renee looked directly at Beverly and said, "Oh, by the way, my sister is pregnant. She's giving Lester the baby that you apparently never could. I guess he finally found a *real* woman. They're getting married too. Would either of you like a formal invitation?"

"Renee!" Virtue was livid. She wanted to say more . . . far more than she even should have, in fact. Fierce, offensive words that she hadn't sputtered in years were slowly forming in a sea of fury that was rising from Virtue's belly. Beverly's touch to her arm stopped what probably would have been a reaction that Virtue would have regretted later.

Beverly's eyes locked into Renee's and remained there. "No, thank you," she said with a smile that appeared just as genuine as Renee's ill-timed revelation. "But please give her my condolences, will you? I'm sure she'll find out more sooner than later that my barrenness isn't *really* what caused Lester to stray."

Beverly's cool composure clearly wasn't the reaction that Renee had hoped to see. And her sharp prediction wasn't what she'd hoped to hear either. Renee's smirk disappeared and was replaced by narrowed eyes that seemed to give a hint of warning just before she walked away. To Virtue it almost felt like a silent threat. While she didn't fear Renee, Virtue often wondered why the resentful sibling continued to make Temple of Jerusalem her home. It was obvious that she wasn't happy there. During services, she sat stone-faced and, for the most part, was unresponsive throughout, no matter how spirited the atmosphere was. Sometimes Virtue wondered if Renee was just there to see if the church would eventually die from the venomous spirit that she brought along with her every time she walked through the doors.

"I'm so sorry, Beverly," Virtue said as she hugged her friend. "You so didn't deserve that."

Beverly returned her embrace but chuckled. "Honey, I'm too smart and too old to be taken down by adolescent tactics. Lester ain't been mine since the first time he thought in his heart to lay with that child. I can't be concerned with what they do."

"I know, but still . . ."

"Virtue, Lester is fifty-seven years old, and that girl he's running around with is young enough to be his daughter. I've forgotten more than she's ever learnt, but one thing she's definitely gonna learn is that a man who will cheat on his first wife will cheat on his second one too. I know Lester wanted babies. We both did, but I was already pretty much past my childbearing years when he took up with Dondra. If it was about babies, he would have left a long time ago. Without God, Lester's not going to be able to be any more faithful to her than he was to me."

"But you all were married for what—*thirty* years? It's not like he didn't know how to be faithful. Dondra probably seduced him and turned him into something that he wasn't."

"Maybe so," Beverly said, nodding, "but *he* made the choice to leave me permanently to be with her. She didn't make him do that. If Lester had told me it was all a terrible one-time mistake and had been willing to get counseling and work through it with me, I would have given him another chance. But he didn't. He carried on that affair for months, all while standing behind the pulpit preaching—like he didn't even believe there really was a God. Even the Bible calls people like that a fool, Virtue. Lester is an old fool, but he's not my fool to worry about anymore. God will be Lester's judge. He did me wrong, yes. But if I want to get my crown, I have to forgive him even though he never asked for it. Truth be told, them getting married is what they need to do. If they're going to be carrying on like they're married, the least they can do is make it legal."

Once again, Beverly had exemplified what it meant to rise above it all, leaving her young admirer in awe. "Maybe I'll be like you one day when I grow up," Virtue remarked.

Beverly laughed as the two of them embraced again before heading for the exit doors. "You just stick with me, honey," she said. "Before it's over, both of us are gonna learn a new lesson or two. Wait and see."

~ Eight ~

*O*n Monday morning, the amount of work that needed to be done was evident from the stack of folders on Mitchell's desk. As the last few weeks of the year ticked away, the corporations that contracted the services of Jackson, Jackson & Andrews were rushed to get end-of-the-year accounting issues complete. But as important as it was that Mitchell not fall behind, he was failing miserably in his quest to focus on the business files in front of him. Instead, his eyes continued to stray to the information that he'd printed from his computer last night.

It was almost frightening how easy it had been to find information on his ex-wife, but in this case he was thankful. Typing both Virtue's maiden and married names in the search criteria had brought up a number of references, beginning with the roster of her graduation class from Hope College in Michigan. A number of ideas had traveled through Mitchell's mind of the route Virtue might have taken with her degree, but none came close to the one that he found.

"Here's your hot water, Mr. Andrews."

Mitchell looked up from his papers and managed to flash an appreciative smile in Barbara's direction as she set the steaming cup on a coaster. He dumped the powdered mixture from the pack into his cup and stirred slowly, still deep in thought. Mitchell's search had left him baffled. He'd gotten the information he needed, but now he had no idea what to do with it.

"You want to talk about it?"

Chris's voice startled him. Shaking his head, Mitchell said, "No, not really."

"It's about your ex-wife, isn't it?" Before he could respond, Chris continued. "Man, this whole Virtue thing is eating at you from the inside out. That's the same folder you were working on when I came by an hour and a half ago."

Mitchell closed the folder with more force than was necessary, and slid it away from his work space. As he rubbed his hands over his freshly cut hair, he heard the door close. Without immediately looking up, he knew that Chris hadn't left him alone. When Mitchell raised his head, his partner was sitting in the chair across from his desk.

"I'm listening," Chris said.

Mitchell hesitated, but the silence that followed was brief. "I thought finding Virtue would bring me peace of mind, but instead, it's working me over even more than seven years of not knowing where she was at all did. I'm just frustrating myself with this battle of should I approach her or shouldn't I. Sometimes I feel like no matter what I do, I'm going to regret it. I can't help but feel that this is a lose-lose situation."

"Why?" Chris asked with interest. "What did you find out about her? Has she remarried?"

That was one of the aspects of finding her that had brought Mitchell a sense of relief. "I don't think so. Surprisingly enough, she still has my name, so I doubt very seriously that she's remarried. But her marital status has nothing to do with my dilemma."

"What, then?"

It was hard for Mitchell to put his racing thoughts into words. He'd seen Virtue dance on a stage several times, and he knew where her heart's desire lay. Virtue wasn't just a good dancer; she was an *incredible* dancer who had major potential. Mitchell had trouble believing that by choice, she didn't do something great with her talent. Over the years when he thought of her, he pictured Virtue having ties with the Alvin Ailey American Dance Theater in New York. She'd always loved their productions, and she idolized Judith Jamison. Tormenting guilt had mounted on Mitchell ever since he'd traced her steps to the Temple of Jerusalem, a church in Houston that didn't even have a television ministry to show her performances to the world. For Mitchell, it was agonizing to have to wonder if he'd played some role in her lowered ambitions, and he voiced his concerns to Chris.

"Dancing on a stage was what Virtue loved to do," Mitchell concluded. "I'd hate to think that she didn't pursue that because of me. I said some mean things to her when I was under the influence. I remember telling her that she didn't have what it took to make it as a dancer. Making her feel like a failure was my way of building my own diminished self-esteem. What if what I did and said made her lose all of her drive to succeed at what she loved to do most? What if she settled?"

Chris's next words gave Mitchell a wake-up call that he couldn't believe he'd even needed. "Settled? What do you mean, settled? Mitch, are you saying that being called upon by some agent or employer to dance for entertainment on a New York stage is a greater achievement than being called by God to worship through the ministry of dance?"

Mitchell felt more ashamed than he dared to reveal. Chris's analogy wasn't what he'd meant, but it was exactly what his words had suggested. Mitchell wanted to try to explain himself in greater detail, but he didn't think it would do any good. No one could truly understand his line of thinking. Not even Chris, who Mitchell saw as the man who could understand him more than anyone.

Since he'd seen Virtue, Mitchell had come to believe that unless a man had walked in his shoes, lived his life, lost his battles, and committed his sins, he couldn't truly understand his pain. The pain that Mitchell carried was the type that never truly went away. It left in seasons, but it always returned to remind him of the man that he'd once been, the man that forces of evil still wrestled to make him return to. Each time the pain of Mitchell's past revisited him, the hurt was deeper; and every time it faded, it left more questions for him to battle through.

Rubbing his palms over his eyes as though they had suddenly been splashed with acid, Mitchell tried to wipe away the memories of yesteryear. He hated that he couldn't totally rid himself of the flashes in his head that re-appeared every time he allowed himself to dwell on the past. The clips of the nights he'd drink until he literally passed out; the days he didn't have enough drive to get out of his pajamas; the weeks and months that his existence defined *wretched*; the morning he struck Virtue for the first time; the day the love in her eyes turned to fear; the evening he struck her for the second time and lost her forever . . . all of these haunting memories were the ones that God, for some reason, hadn't erased when He freed Mitchell of the habit that had been the cause of them all.

"Mitch!" Chris reached out and used force to pry his friend's hand from his face. He'd been calling Mitchell's name for the past several moments, but Mitchell had been too deep in his tormenting thoughts to hear him. "Mitch, that's enough," Chris said while forcing Mitchell to look at him. "You've done about all you can do with this for now. You're gonna make yourself ill if you keep this pattern of yours going much longer. You're not getting enough rest, and eventually that's going to start affecting every aspect of your life, including your job. We'll talk about this some more later, but right now you need to get your mind off of your indecision where Virtue is concerned and on to matters that are easier to work through. We're approaching the end of the year, man, and you know we have a lot to get done before the clock strikes midnight on the thirty-first. I know finding your ex and apologizing to her is important to you, Mitch, but you need to step back from it for a few days, maybe even a few weeks. If you get sick over this, you're going to be no good to anyone, including Virtue."

"I know," Mitchell replied, wiping his forehead and shaking his head to clear it. "I've been trying to concentrate on the stupid portfolios. I'll get them done."

"Dang skippy, partner," Chris said. "You can call these folders any kind of name you please, but remember that completing them is what keeps our doors open and what pays our bills. This company was founded by the blood, sweat, and tears of Willie James Jackson Jr., and he prided himself in professionalism and prompt service. I continued his legacy for nearly two years all by myself, and when I brought you in I did so with the assurance that you'd keep this business's reputation a priority. And the only way you can do that is by completing these *stupid* portfolios.

"Now, I want you to find Virtue and clear your conscience just as much as you do, Mitch, but not at the expense of it affecting your performance here. I made my daddy a promise." Chris stopped long enough to count the incomplete folders on Mitchell's desk. "You've got twelve assignments to complete and less than three weeks to get them done. Can I still rely on you?"

Mitchell clenched his jaw and swallowed. He knew Chris was right. This was nobody's problem but his, and he couldn't force those around him to be affected by it. That was what he'd done all those years ago with Virtue. He'd made her suffer because he was in so much pain, and that was the reason he was in this predicament. In slow motion, Mitchell nodded his answer and then watched his friend stand to leave. Just before he walked through the open door, Chris turned to face him.

"I'm on your side, Mitch. I don't want you to think that just because I have a great relationship with Lisa that I don't feel you on this. But I wouldn't truly be your friend if I didn't tell you the truth about what I felt. And what I feel right now is that you are agonizing too much over this. You need to stop trying to figure this out on your own and maybe start praying about your next step. On your own, you might make the wrong choice. I might even slip up and advise you in the wrong direction. But the one person who we both know won't ever steer you wrong is God."

Mitchell stared at his closed door long after Chris made his exit. He had heard every word that his partner had said, but some stood out more than others.

"I hope you're right," Mitchell whispered as he redirected his thoughts and picked up another folder from his stack. "I hope you're right."

~ Nine ~

*T*en years ago, when Beverly accepted the position of a therapist and counselor at the Houston Center for Women, she'd thought that she was just taking on a job that would fulfill her desire to help women who had been made to suffer the abuse of domestic violence. But since the destruction of her own marriage, she'd begun to see her appointment at the center as more.

Aside from the comfortable office that she occupied every day to serve those in need of mental and emotional therapy, the HCW also included a one-hundred-bed shelter where survivors of domestic violence, women and children, could live until they felt safe enough to start new, independent lives for themselves. Even with her conventional education, Beverly had, in her mind, thought of abuse as something of a more physical nature. Most of the women she saw on a daily basis had been sexually abused or, like Virtue, physically harmed at the hands of the men they once shared their lives with. But now Beverly saw abuse as much, much more.

Having had her whole world come to a crashing halt without her even seeing the brakes that would bring it there, Beverly now understood a different level of violence. For her, it seemed even deeper than emotional abuse because that was something that she was trained to know how to deal with. What Lester had done to her was so much crueler as far as Beverly was concerned. She masked her hurt well; but every now and then, like today, the heat of the invisible mask smothered her, and she had to remove it to show her true emotions. Wiping a lone tear from her cheek, Beverly took a sip from her cup of water that was left over from the lunch she'd finished nearly three hours earlier. It was room temperature, just the way she liked it.

In truth, days like this one, when she felt the full brunt of Lester's cruelty, were few and far between. But every year, at least once a year, she cried. When she thought of the evil intent behind Renee's words yesterday, a part of Beverly wished that she'd have allowed Virtue to give the girl the tongue lashing that she deserved. Beverly's education had taught her that lashing out wasn't the way to deal with these sorts of things. But appropriate or not, knowing that Renee had been hurt in some small way for the callous things she said would have certainly satisfied Beverly's human side—the side of her that grew up in the rough neighborhoods of Miami, where people like Renee were often dealt with harshly.

Prayer had indeed been the lifeline that saved Beverly from what could easily have been a total meltdown after her husband of thirty-one years left. Another tear dropped from her eyes and landed on the calendar that covered much of her desk. Today would have been their thirty-fourth anniversary, the third one that had come and gone since Lester abandoned her for a girl almost half his age. It was only on their anniversary date that Beverly cried, but unlike the early days of her ordeal, she no longer saw her tears as weakness, but as a symbol of strength. In spite of the hurt and shame of it all, she had risen victoriously and had proven to herself as well as anyone else who doubted her ability to live independently, that she could.

Beverly often admitted to patients in her sessions that being alone was one of her greatest fears. She'd gone from depending on her parents to depending on her husband. Before Lester's desertion, Beverly had never lived alone and had never had to solely sustain herself. For the first few weeks, she'd fretted about the little things: how she would be able to pay her mortgage; how she'd function, no longer having a man to depend upon for the feeling of safety during the night hours; who would keep the car serviced and the lawn manicured? Many responsibilities that she'd never had to worry about were thrown at her all at once.

In that moment of her life, Beverly found herself understanding why many of the battered women she saw made the dangerous choice to go back to their abusers. Fear controlled them and made them believe that they *needed* these men in their lives in order to survive. Most times, it was the men who had convinced them that they were nothing without them. And in the end, no matter what Beverly told them in their conferences with her, the women chose to go back. Fear was such a controlling factor, and when Beverly finally came to the understanding that what she was feeling was fear, she was able to face it, make her prayers specific, and trust God for the strength she needed.

She hadn't seen Lester in almost three years, and the river of love that she used to have for him had turned into a cesspool a long time ago. Still, sometimes she reflected on the hurt that his downright disrespect of her had caused. When Beverly wept now, she felt as though she was not only crying for herself, but for Virtue and all eighty-eight of the women and children who currently occupied the beds at HCW. Degreed education had made Beverly qualified to tell the women at the shelter how to go on, but divine experience had made her worthy of *showing* them.

Using a soft handkerchief, she dabbed at each eye, careful not to smudge the foundation that she'd so carefully applied that morning. Her crying cycle had ended, and Beverly found reprieve in knowing that it would be at least another year before she'd have to do it again. It would be another hour before her last client for the day would arrive, so she settled back in her chair and took advantage of the free time that she had by sorting through the mail that had been placed in her box earlier in the afternoon. None of it was urgent; it was mostly sales flyers and other advertisements. Beverly opened an envelope from Black Expressions Book Club and began flipping through the pages of their most recent catalog, searching for a book that might catch her eye. When her office closed over the approaching Christmas holiday, she'd need something to read while she sat snuggled in her favorite blanket near her fireplace.

With both her parents deceased, and since she and Lester never had any children or grandchildren, Christmas had never been a big day of celebration in Beverly's house. She usually cooked a hearty meal and she and Lester had eaten together just before going to the church to help deliver meals to the area shelters that needed them the most. When Lester first left, Beverly thought that Christmas would become a holiday that she'd be forced to spend alone, but God had brought Virtue into her life and changed all of that.

Sometimes it seemed beyond coincidence that the young, broken woman was sent to her for mending. So much about Virtue reminded Beverly of herself. It was more than the fact that they'd both endured broken marriages. Like Beverly, Virtue had gotten married during the Christmas season. Both of them had endured tragedy in their lives that forced them to face the truth about family members and close friends. Secretly, Beverly had always wanted to be a dancer, but she'd never had the courage to try. The hips that her mother had given her were not made for dancing.

When she really thought about it, Beverly sometimes cringed at the remembrance of how, not too far in the distant past, she'd watched Dondra lead the praise dancers during worship services and been astonished. Like Virtue, Dondra's technique was masterful. But unlike Virtue, her praise was *not* genuine.

Beverly's eyes continued to search through the Black Expressions catalog, but her thoughts remained on her friend. Virtue often said that Beverly had saved her life, but sometimes Beverly thought that it was the other way around. Although she had released her anger over the situation of Lester and Dondra, Beverly hadn't quite let go of the pain. Seeing Virtue's hurt somehow made Beverly forget her own. On a daily basis she would see several ladies who still carried emotional and physical scars that their abusers had initiated, but seeing Virtue's affected Beverly differently. In an instant, Virtue became the daughter that she'd never had. She not only wanted to educate her she wanted to protect and nurture her.

Oddly though, as dear as she had come to see Virtue, Beverly could never find it within herself to be angry toward the man who had inflicted pain on her and caused the scar on her head that Virtue often spoke of. There was something about him—this man she'd never met—that made Beverly pity him and pray for him. Somehow, though Beverly never voiced it, she couldn't quite categorize Mitchell with the other abusers that she heard about during sessions with the women who shared the details of their lives with her. Almost all of the men she'd been told about constantly used their victims as punching bags or for sexual gratification. Their stories didn't match the ones she'd heard from Virtue.

Then again, perhaps Beverly's lenience toward Mitchell was because she could still see the emotional attachment that Virtue had for him. She didn't want to love him, but Beverly knew that she did. And Virtue's wasn't the addictive, misguided love that Beverly often saw in the women she counseled. Those women were lost without their abusers, and Beverly had seen them crawl back to unchanged men more times than she cared to acknowledge.

Virtue's love was different. She had freed herself from Mitchell, gotten her total life together, and had had more than one opportunity to move on in other relationships. Yet she remained single, refusing to acknowledge her love for her ex-husband, but also refusing to allow her suppressed feelings to force her to make the wrong choice. As confusing as it might be to those who had not studied the nature of the abuser and the abused, to Beverly it was clear and commendable.

A knock on the door snapped her from her place of deep thought. Beverly looked at the watch on her wrist. Her appointment was more than half an hour early. Taking a moment to clear the scattered mail from her desk, Beverly stood as she normally did before giving permission for entrance.

"Come in." The door opened, and she was surprised at whom she saw. "Well, hello," Beverly said as she walked around her desk to greet Virtue. "I wasn't expecting you today. Is everything all right?"

As she stepped closer, Beverly noted the redness of Virtue's eyes, and she instantly knew that something was wrong. She didn't reply, and Beverly felt Virtue melt in her arms as they embraced as though the hug was what she needed more than anything. Understanding the silent plea for support, Beverly tightened her grip and didn't press for an answer. Instead she allowed Virtue's quiet tears to fall undisturbed on the silk fabric of her suit jacket.

"He knows where I am."

The words were muffled because her face was pressed against Beverly's shoulder, but she understood every word that Virtue had said. Pulling away so that she could have eye-to-eye contact with her, Beverly searched Virtue's face, not really knowing what it was she was looking for.

"*Who* knows where you are?" she asked as if she didn't know the answer.

"Mitchell."

"How do you know?"

"He left a message on the machine in my office at church."

"Saying what?" Beverly probed.

"That he desperately needed to speak with me face-to-face." Virtue freed herself from Beverly's hold, sank onto a nearby chair, and pulled sheets of tissue from a box that sat on the table beside her. "He didn't say much else. Just that it was important. He kept saying that he understood if I didn't trust him, and he said that I could bring as many people with me as I wanted to if I feel I need protection."

Beverly smoothed her hands over her head to make sure that none of the hairs in her neatly styled bun had been misplaced during her embrace with Virtue. Taking several steps backward, she turned and walked the distance to her office window and stared out. A million thoughts were racing through her head all at the same time. In a normal session, according to what she'd been told about the abuser, she would advise her client not to meet with him. Beverly had read too many case studies in which the abuser would beg the victim to come back to him, only to abuse her again. Sometimes the abuse worsened. Sometimes it turned deadly.

Why she did not feel the same apprehension about Mitchell, Beverly couldn't explain. The last thing she wanted to do was to send Virtue into the lion's den, but there was something calming about knowing Mitchell wanted to see Virtue that made Beverly believe that it was a safe decision.

She almost voiced her opinion but rethought her position. It would be unethical, in the position that she was in, for her to make that decision for Virtue. Had her friend approached her away from the office, perhaps Beverly would have felt more comfortable with offering personal advice. But in her office at HCW she had to think like a counselor, not a friend.

"What are you going to do?" she asked Virtue without turning to face her.

"Well, I'm not going to meet with him, if that's what you're worried about," Virtue blurted. "I don't know what he wants, but if he can't say it to an answering machine, he won't say it at all."

It wasn't the answer that Beverly had hoped for, and she was glad that her window-watching hid her look of disappointment. She understood Virtue's lingering bitterness, but Beverly still struggled with the unexplainable trust she had for the man who had caused Virtue so much pain.

"Why?" Being the professional that she was, Beverly was able to ask the one-word question without it sounding judgmental or accusing.

"Because whatever he has to say, I don't want to hear," Virtue answered. "Who does Mitchell think he is anyway? I haven't heard from him in years; now all of a sudden he has something that he needs to tell me? *Whatever*!" she huffed.

Virtue's words were laced with hostility, but Beverly also captured a hint of something else. As heated as Virtue's tone was, her voice carried a slight but noticeable quiver, indicating that somewhere there were more tears that wanted to be set free. Virtue succeeded in holding them back, but when Beverly turned from the window and faced her, she was sure that she saw more pain than anger in Virtue's expression.

"Are you afraid to meet with him?" Beverly asked.

Virtue was quick to shake her head. "Absolutely not," she insisted. "If he thinks I'm the same woman who allowed him to slap her around back then, he couldn't be more wrong. I can't even believe he shaped his mouth to say that I could bring people with me if I wanted to, like I need a bodyguard. For all he knows, *he* might be the one who would need protection."

Beverly chuckled as she walked back toward her desk and sat in the chair behind it. Virtue had misinterpreted her question. When Beverly asked if she was afraid to meet with him, she wasn't asking whether Virtue feared that Mitchell would hit her again. Beverly's question was far more complex. What she really wanted to know was if Virtue's real concern was that being in close quarters with Mitchell again and talking to him in person would unleash the affection that not seeing him had allowed her to discount. Those feelings had played no part in signing the papers that ended their three-year marriage. Those were the emotions that Virtue succeeded in hiding from everyone except Beverly.

On one hand, Beverly wanted to explain herself further, but it was no use. She knew Virtue would deny it. Sometimes she wondered if Virtue was even aware of her true feelings. She'd refuted them for so long that she seemed to have convinced herself into believing that nothing remained of the love that she and Mitchell had once shared. Beverly chose her next words carefully.

"Sometimes putting true closure on a situation is the only way to truly get beyond it, Virtue," Beverly said, making sure that her tone sounded like that of a therapist.

"What do you mean?"

Her tactic had worked. Virtue didn't become defensive or jump to conclusions like she often did when they spoke to each other about this subject away from the office. Beverly continued.

"There was never any real closure put on your relationship with your ex-husband, and there really should be. The last time he hit you, you left, and the two of you never saw one another or spoke to one another again. No doubt, there are some things that you really needed to say to him. You needed to let him know how much he hurt you and how disappointed you were in him for forcing you to end what was supposed to be a lifetime commitment."

Looking directly across her desk at Virtue, Beverly knew that she'd struck a chord and was on the right track.

"Not only that," she continued, "but I'm sure there were some things that Mitchell needed to say as well. As far-fetched as it may seem, he might need you to hear him say that he regrets the hurt and pain that he caused. You may not want to hear it, but in order for him to move on, he may need to say it to you. Who knows? Perhaps he's grown up over the past seven years. He may have tried to pick up the pieces and even remarried."

Beverly noted the drop in Virtue's face when she voiced the possibility of Mitchell being in another committed relationship, but she moved on without addressing it.

"The bottom line is: God has commanded us to forgive. I'm not saying that you are supposed to be able to forget everything that happened; I'm only suggesting that Mitchell may be looking for the chance to clear his conscience. For the sake of his present life, he may need that."

"I don't owe him anything, Beverly," Virtue said, her voice unstable once more.

"I know." Beverly nodded. "But Jesus didn't owe us anything either. Yet He paid it all. Think about that."

~ Ten ~

Mitchell was surprised on Wednesday morning when he arrived at Jackson, Jackson & Andrews ahead of his always-prompt partner. Seven more minutes and Chris would be what Mitchell was generally known to be—late. With Chris constantly preaching sermons on annoying little things like how being on time could be the difference between the failure and success of a business, his late arrival would give Mitchell something to needle him about today. He was sure Chris would blame today's dragging on the sniffles that he battled through yesterday. December's change of weather had taken a toll on many of the citizens of Dallas. Mitchell felt lucky that he'd not so much as sneezed yet this season.

"The water is already hot," Barbara said as he spoke to her on his way to his office. "I'll bring you a cup in just a minute."

Noting the wad of tissue on Barbara's desk, Mitchell felt that, just to be on the safe side, he'd excuse her from her morning duties. "No bother, Barbara. I'll get it myself. Thanks."

With both her and Chris fighting runny noses and other cold-related symptoms, Mitchell was left to wonder whether his apple cider packed some secret weapon that their coffee didn't. As he turned the corner and walked through his office's open door, Mitchell noticed that he was whistling a tune. What the tune was, he wasn't exactly sure, but it was a good sign. He couldn't remember the last time he had whistled while he prepared for work.

Today, Mitchell felt more relaxed than he had in weeks. That was mostly due to the fact that he'd had the most restful night he'd had in weeks. He still hadn't spoken directly with Virtue, but having reached out to her and offered an olive branch of sorts had lightened what he now knew was a burdensome load that had been riding his shoulders for the better part of seven years.

Yesterday he'd sat at his desk and watched his phone, wondering if Virtue would call him as he'd asked and contemplating what he'd say if she did. Twice during the work hours and once after he'd gotten home, Mitchell had picked up the telephone and began dialing the number to her office at the Houston church. It wasn't until after he'd eaten dinner and was taking his shower that reality finally set in. Virtue had probably gotten his message Monday afternoon. The reason she hadn't returned his call after more than twenty-four hours was because she didn't want to. Once Mitchell accepted the truth that she never would, he was able to release much of his anxiety. The disappointment that she'd chosen not to talk to or meet with him continued to linger, but Mitchell recounted the facts and understood her decision. During his prayer time last night, he'd found a level of peace in knowing that he'd tried. After all, trying was all he could do.

"Any word from Chris this morning?" Mitchell asked after putting his belongings in his office and stepping back out into the hallway to fill his cup with water.

"I spoke with him a little earlier," Barbara called back. "He said he'd be in."

"Four minutes," Mitchell whispered with a grin as he looked at the clock on his office wall just before emptying a packet of drink mix in the steaming cup and settling in the chair behind his desk.

Working with Chris sometimes brought out the kid in him. Christopher James Jackson was by all definitions a serious businessman. When it came to the company that his father had founded, Chris didn't cut corners or do anything with mediocrity. Every completed file had to reek of excellence, and every customer had to feel as if he or she was the most valued one on the roster. Yet, despite his need for perfection, Chris knew how to relax and enjoy life. He was the brother that Mitchell never had. Oftentimes, Mitchell saw Chris as the poster child for the faithful friend that Solomon spoke of in Proverbs 18:24.

"Man!" he whispered in disappointment at the sound of the front door buzzer. "Two more minutes and I would have had you."

Getting up from behind his mass of paperwork that he'd just begun working on, Mitchell prepared to walk out and greet his partner, but the ringing of his telephone stopped him in his tracks. He reasoned that he'd just catch Chris when he made his stop in the hall outside his door. Chris never started his morning without coffee. Picking up the telephone, Mitchell said, "Good morning. Mitchell Andrews speaking."

The voice on the other end of the line had a hint of familiarity, but it was far more raspy than normal.

"Hey, Mitch."

"Chris?" Mitchell asked after a brief hesitation. "Is that you?"

"Yeah. Hold on a sec."

Looking again through his open door into the hallway, Mitchell was now confused. He was sure that it was Chris who had entered the front door of the office just moments earlier, but apparently he had guessed wrong. Mitchell held the phone and waited while listening to Chris release a fit of heavy coughs. His cold had worsened.

"I'm not gonna be able to come in today, man," he growled after he'd caught his breath. "I'm gonna do what I can at my computer here at home, but I don't want to bring this into the office."

"And I appreciate that, Wolfman Jack," Mitchell teased, hoping to conjure up a laugh from his friend. "If you get lonely over there, you might want to send for Barbara. She's not sounding too good either."

"Yeah, I spoke to her earlier. She said she wasn't feeling her best, but she wanted to tough it out. I told her to go on home when you got there, but she told me if I could come in to work sounding like I did, then she could definitely do it." Chris paused to cough again, but this time it didn't sound as painful as the first. He begged Mitchell's pardon and continued. "Since I'm not coming in now and I feel partly responsible for Barbara's cold, I sent a replacement for her today so she could go on home and get some rest."

Mitchell frowned. "A replacement?"

"Good morning, Mr. Andrews," a voice sang from behind him.

Mitchell turned to face the door, and his heart seemed to plummet. Standing in his doorway, dressed in a pair of chocolate-colored corduroy pants and a cream cropped sweater, was Lisa. Mitchell licked his lips in an attempt to ease the sudden dryness. Chris's hoarse voice did little to break the tension.

"Yeah. I called Lisa. She's on vacation from work this week, and she's accustomed to receptionist work. I figured that you'd be way more comfortable having her there with you for a couple of days than having to deal with some stranger from a temp agency."

You thought wrong. For a minute Mitchell wondered if

the comeback had bounced from his brain and had escaped through his lips. He looked back toward the door, and Lisa was still standing there, smiling. It was apparent that his thoughts had remained his own. Just a moment ago, he'd been all for Barbara going home and getting the rest she needed, but that was when Mitchell thought that he'd be manning the office alone. It would be a challenge, but in Mitchell's mind it wouldn't be nearly the challenge that he was in for now.

"I'm going to go and lie down now," Chris said. "I just got a headache that came out of nowhere."

Me too, Mitchell thought.

"Lisa should be there in a little bit. I'll call later and check on you after I get some rest. Okay?"

Mitchell bit his lip. A part of him wanted to yell at Chris for sending a replacement without asking whether or not he wanted one. But Mitchell knew that his friend was looking out for the business. He couldn't rightfully blame Chris for putting him in this uncomfortable position. Chris didn't know that his girlfriend's friendliness sometimes felt like forwardness, and Mitchell only had himself to blame for not making it known. Even with his back turned to the door, Mitchell could still sense Lisa's presence behind him. He could feel her eyes burning into the back of his neck, singeing the hairs on his flesh.

"Mitch? Are you still there?" Chris's croaky voice pulled him back into reality.

"Yeah," Mitchell said.

"You're okay with Lisa filling in, aren't you? I know you have a lot to do and you're used to working with Barbara, who rarely ever needs to interrupt you for anything. But it shouldn't be much different with Lisa. With her skills, she shouldn't need to bother you too much. She knows her way around an office pretty well. I'll keep the phone nearby so I can hear it ring. Call me if any fires need to be put out."

"Don't worry," Mitchell said, not sure whether he was trying to convince Chris or himself. "I've got everything under control here. You just take care of yourself."

Ending the phone call and turning to face the door once again, Mitchell found Lisa still standing there as though she were waiting for her orders for the day. She broke into a pearly white grin that magnified the slant in her almond-shaped eyes. Running her fingers through her natural locks, Lisa took two steps inside of Mitchell's office and looked around as if it were her first time there.

"If it weren't for the stacks of papers on your desk, I'd say that no one even worked in here. You keep a clean office, Mitchell. That's odd for most men that I know. It's a rare but attractive trait to have."

Although it sounded more like a come-on than a compliment, Mitchell thanked her and then took brisk steps to bring himself back behind his desk. The sooner he set a tone of business, the better. Just as he sat in his chair, Barbara stepped in the doorway behind Lisa and turned down her lips as she readjusted the strap of her pocketbook that hung over her right shoulder.

"Chris is kicking me out," she announced to Mitchell's amusement.

He needed the laugh that her dry tone, combined with her facial expression, brought out of him. "I know," Mitchell said. "Chris just wants to be sure that you're okay, Barbara. A little bit of rest is probably just what the doctor ordered."

"Umph," Barbara grunted. "Well, okay then. Do you want me to stick around and show Lisa a few things before I go? I don't mind."

Mitchell saw a chance to erase some of his alone time with Lisa and was just about to take Barbara up on her offer, but Lisa's response was quicker.

"Oh no, Ms. Barbara," she assured her, all while giving Barbara a slight nudge to rush her exit. "I do office work five days a week, and we have way more traffic coming through my office than you all have here. Don't worry about me; I can handle this. You just go home and take care of that cold before it gets any worse."

When both women disappeared from his office en route to the front of the business, Mitchell closed his eyes and released a heavy sigh that was propelled by exasperation. His vexation was becoming evident again, and Mitchell searched for a way to get it under control. He knew that Lisa would be returning soon, and he didn't want the tension that her appearance had made to be obvious.

"It's just one day," he spoke to himself, hoping that it wasn't just wishful thinking.

Unlike Chris, Barbara just had a severe case of the sniffles. Mitchell hoped that her condition wouldn't worsen overnight like Chris's had. He reasoned within himself that he could somehow pull himself together and ignore his suspicions about Lisa for one day. Having to put on a façade of comfort for any longer, though, might be more of a challenge than he could handle.

As normal, Mitchell turned his radio on and tuned in to one of his favorite local stations. Good music helped him to work better. It had been that way for as long as he could remember. Grandma Kate had an old piano that his grandfather had bought her, and she played daily during the childhood years that Mitchell spent in their home. There was something about the melody the piano offered that seemed to sharpen his mind. The best time for studying or doing his homework was when his grandmother's fingers danced across the ivory keys.

By the time he was ten, his love for the music had turned into an interest in the instrument itself. Mitchell could remember the day he'd played his first piece by ear. It shocked both his grandparents. He had watched his grandmother play many times, but Mitchell had never had any formal lessons. It was an inborn gift that none of them realized he had. By the time he was thirteen, his technique was like that of a man who'd had classical training.

"My, my, my," Mitchell recalled Kate saying one day as she sat on the sofa and tapped her feet to the rhythm of the tune he played. "It looks like we've got ourselves a regular ole Little Richard on our hands."

Pulling the newspaper away from his face and repositioning his after-dinner stogy in the side of his mouth, Mitchell's grandfather had muttered an oath and then grunted the words, "I shole hope not."

When he'd met Virtue in the store that day and soon thereafter found out that she was a dance major, it felt as if their being together was inevitable. He'd never accompanied her as she danced, but he had a portable keyboard that he'd play sometimes, just to show off for her. Virtue liked that. They enjoyed many of the same things and shared similar long-term aspirations for their lives. They had been the perfect match . . . until he started drinking.

Memories of hitting Virtue threatened to form in his head, but Mitchell pushed them away and replaced them with more pleasant thoughts. Their wedding was the second most exciting moment of his life. It had to take a backseat to the wedding night. Mitchell closed his eyes for a moment and lost himself in the memories.

He recalled the soft music and the scent of vanilla that filled the room from the candles that provided the only light they needed. He remembered the feel of Virtue's skin. It felt like fresh rose petals beneath the touch of his hands. She wore a long, satin, peach-colored gown that night—Mitchell remembered it like it was yesterday. He recalled the sultry way it covered her body and the flowing way it fell from her at the command of his fingers. Everything about that night and many of the nights that followed was etched in Mitchell's mind like the permanent carvings on an Egyptian wall. He had yearned for his role as Virtue's husband many times over the past years, but it had been quite some time since he'd missed her like he did today. Every kiss, every curve, every touch . . .

"Mitchell, are you all right?"

Mitchell opened his eyes and found that the hand that gently touched his cheek wasn't attached to the woman in his daydreams. Quickly pulling his face away, Mitchell glanced up at Lisa, who stood at his desk with a look of concern on her face.

"Are you all right?" she repeated.

"I'm fine," Mitchell said without hesitation. His embarrassment from her catching him drifting to another place and time was overshadowed by his curiosity as to why she was standing over him in the first place. "Do you need something?" he asked.

"No. I was just stopping in to see if *you* needed something when I noticed that you appeared to be falling asleep at your desk."

Mitchell readjusted his chair and grabbed a folder from the stack on his desk. "I'm fine, Lisa," he reassured her. "You can just stay up front and take care of the incoming calls. I have a lot of work to do, so if you can take messages for me, I'd appreciate it. Other than that, I think I can handle it. Thanks."

Lisa chuckled as she began taking a few steps away. It wasn't a laugh of humor, but the one that Mitchell defined as the titter that preceded the flirt. She almost always did it right before one of her playful touches or just before some dubious remark that Mitchell found unnerving. And this time was no different. Just before reaching the doorway, Lisa turned and flashed him one of the smiles that flaunted just how beautiful she really was.

"Christopher told me to come in and help you out in *whatever* way you needed," she said. "So you'd better take advantage of my *skills* while you have me all to yourself."

It wasn't *what* she said as much as it was *the way* that she said it. There seemed to be special emphasis placed on "whatever" and "skills." Anybody else could have said those same words and Mitchell wouldn't be reading between the lines for their true meaning. But with Lisa he did. Watching her turn and walk away with a slow, exaggerated sway of her hips, Mitchell took a sip from his lukewarm drink and opened the file he'd retrieved earlier.

"It's just one day," he said, whispering the reminder to himself and hoping that the hands of the clock on the wall in front of him would read his thoughts and cooperate.

~ Eleven ~

If a cluttered desk is the sign of a cluttered mind, then what does an empty desk mean? Virtue sat in front of her computer screen but stared mindlessly at the colorful sign she'd purchased nearly two years ago. Now it decorated the corner of her desk at Temple of Jerusalem, but when it first caught her eye it had rested on a shelf in a quaint little gift shop in New Orleans.

When her year-long therapy at the Houston Center for Women had finally come to an end, Virtue felt like a new woman from the inside out. Her mind's next mission had been to wipe the slate clean and start a new life without the burden that her past had forced her to carry around like a malignant tumor. The extended mental and spiritual therapy had given Virtue a new lease on life, and she'd decided to celebrate, back then, with a cruise to the Bahamas.

Sitting on the balcony of her cabin aboard the *Royal Caribbean* was like an added measure of rehabilitation. The waters that rippled in soft waves below the ship sparkled under the sun in the daytime hours and glistened beneath the moonlit skies at night. For as far back into her childhood as she could recall, Virtue had always wanted to go on a cruise. She loved the water. Whether it came in the form of a walk on the beach, a dip in the pool, or just a relaxing bubble bath, water, like music, had always been a source of escape. So, shortly before they married, when Mitchell asked her how she wanted to spend her honeymoon, the answer rolled off of Virtue's tongue naturally. The Bahamian cruise was the dream vacation that they'd been saving for, but Mitchell's lack of employment and his expensive drinking habit had drained the account where the money had been stored for safe-keeping. It didn't stop her, though. Virtue took the initiative to fulfill her own dream. But she was forced to do it without Mitchell.

"May I come in?"

Virtue's trance was broken, and she brought her attention to the doorway of her office where Minister Efunsgun Fynn stood, knocking lightly with one hand and holding a large manila envelope in the other.

"Sure, Fynn," Virtue responded. She had known the preacher for several months before she even knew what his first name was. He'd taught her how to pronounce it (*Efoon-shay-goon*), but for Virtue, it was easier not to. Like everyone else, she chose to call him by his surname. He didn't seem to mind.

Taking long, slow steps into her office, Fynn made himself comfortable, choosing to sit in a chair that was facing Virtue on the opposite side of her desk. Of African descent, Fynn had strong native features that announced his origin even before his accent could give it away. The product of an African father and an African-American mother, the youth pastor of Temple of Jerusalem had spent all of his thirty-eight years in the United States, but his native accent was still very distinct.

"You look to be a bit . . . shall I say, distracted," he observed with caution. "Is everything well with you?"

Fynn was one of the few people at the church who would feel comfortable enough to address Virtue about any matter that might seem delicate. Even though her presence in Temple of Jerusalem was prominent, Virtue knew very few of the members on a personal level. Fynn was one of several men, since her divorce, who had asked her out and one of a very select few whose invitation Virtue had accepted.

He seemed to be a well-informed, dedicated Christian and had wasted very little time making his intentions known, but it didn't take long for Virtue to realize that there was no future for her and Fynn. At least, not in the kind of relationship that he desired. Some of the traditional family expectations that had been passed on to Fynn by his father, grandfather, and other staunch African men before him were too much for Virtue. Or perhaps they'd just given her an excuse to avoid the pressure of becoming more involved with Fynn than she desired. In the end, maybe she just wasn't ready to once again place her trust in the lifetime of bonding that courtship and marriage were supposed to bring.

When Virtue remained trapped in silent thoughts, Fynn spoke again. "Virtue, what's going on?" He leaned in closer, searching her face with concern in his dark eyes.

"Nothing," she replied, reasoning that it was at least partly true. "I'm working on choreographing a dance routine. Elder Bradley wants me to perform solo at the Christmas banquet this year."

"Well, it must be intense," Fynn said with a chuckle. "You appeared to be lost in it when I first approached your doorway."

His words prompted Virtue to wonder just how long Fynn had been standing at her door before he made his presence known, but she didn't ask. Instead, she chose words that she hoped would abbreviate his visit. "I'm working against time. Elder Bradley just told me about this a couple of days ago, and I only have a couple of weeks to get it all together."

"Well, I'm sure he's not worried," Fynn said, displaying a wide grin, showing teeth that almost seemed to glow next to his smooth midnight skin. He made no attempts to give her the privacy that she hoped for. "You're brilliant, Virtue. You can dance in your sleep. I'm sure you won't have a problem putting this together."

Virtue laughed. "Thanks. I'm glad one of us is confident."

"My love, I have enough confidence for both of us."

My love. The words sobered Virtue. She stared at her computer screen for a moment and then began pecking at the keys, pretending to be adding on to the composition in front of her. Without even looking at him, Virtue could feel Fynn's eyes boring into her, and she knew that her outward show had accomplished little other than to amuse him. His soft laughter proved her right.

"Did I ever tell you the meaning of my name?" he asked.

Virtue squirmed in her chair, but finally looked at him from across the desk. She didn't know where he was headed with his question, but she was sure that it was a place that would just add to her discomfort. "Yes. You're named after your father."

"Not *after* my father," Fynn enlightened. "At least not in the same manner in which American men name their sons. Efunsgun means son of Obatala. Obatala is the name that my grandfather gave to my father. I say that to say this: Just like my father, I am a very smart man, Virtue. Therefore, it is not easy to fool me with words or actions. I know I made you uneasy when I addressed you as 'my love.' But I call you such because I see you as such. You have been running for a long time with no man to guide you. I too have spent enough years alone with no woman to walk behind me. I believe that God wants us to be one—to complete each other. But you must believe that too in order for us to walk in a perfect line."

Your sweet words could melt the dew right off of the morning glory, Virtue said to herself in mock allure.

"So what brings you here today?" she said, sending an indirect message that this was a subject that she had no interest in discussing. "You don't usually come in on Wednesdays."

Fynn chuckled again, making it quite clear that he wasn't blind to her tactic. He played along, though. "I just needed to come in and pick up a few papers," he said while tapping the envelope that lay on his lap. "The youth ministry is playing a part in the Christmas gala as well, so I guess both of us will be busy over the next few days, huh?"

"Looks like." Virtue forced a quick smile and then began typing again.

As if to underscore his earlier statement, Fynn remained seated, and although Virtue wasn't looking at him, she could sense his wide-mouthed grin. He was expecting her to stop working, submit to his silent insistence, and bring the conversation back to his earlier point, but she had no desire to. The extended stillness that remained in her office was painful, but she was determined to beat him at his own test of wits.

"God said that it is not good for man to be alone," Fynn finally spoke. Virtue had succeeded in not bowing to the pressure, but unfortunately for her, that hadn't discouraged him. "As far back as the days of Adam, God made it known that He designed the woman for the man. I am a man nearing his fortieth year, with no former wives or dependants, an education that exceeds many, and most importantly, a love for the same God that you serve. I have no baggage. Is that not enough for you? How long will you fight this and force me to be alone, Virtue?"

Withdrawing her fingers from the keyboard in front of her, Virtue settled back in her seat and forced her eyes to meet the intimidating eyes of Efunsgun Fynn. On one hand, his words infuriated her, but knowing that he meant well in spite of them was the ingredient that kept her response calm.

"Fynn, please don't let me *force* you to be alone. You are a nice man, and if you are indeed all the things that you just outlined, I'm sure that there are women in and outside of this church's congregation who would be more than willing to walk beside, or should I say, *behind* you."

His eyes told her that he'd not failed to grasp the sarcasm of her chosen words, but before he could interrupt with a reply, Virtue held up her hand to stop him. Leaning forward with her elbows resting on the desk in front of her, Virtue continued.

"All I'm saying is the same thing that I've been telling you for the past year. I like you, Fynn; I really do. And I respect you in your capacity as a leader here at Temple of Jerusalem. However, I would be misleading you if I told you that I was interested in a possible lifetime commitment to you, because I'm not. Unlike you, I have a past that includes a former spouse, and although I have no children, I do have baggage. The baggage that I carry doesn't allow me to open my heart just yet."

"God does not wish for you to hold on to that kind of hindrance, Virtue. You are cheating yourself out of a full life by insisting on holding to your past."

"You think I'm doing this by choice?" Virtue asked, pushing the keyboard of her computer to the side as she spoke. "You think I *want* to have these apprehensions my whole life?" Her eyes burned, and a lone tear made a single moist path down the front of her cheek.

Reaching across the papers on her desk, Fynn placed his hand on top of hers. The laughter that had been in his eyes earlier was all gone and had been replaced by a genuine look of concern.

"I'm not accusing you, Virtue," he said in a low tone, as if there could possibly be someone listening just outside the open door. "But perhaps you should ask that question of yourself and not of me. Search your soul. Could it be possible that you are intentionally holding on to your past? Is there something or *someone* there that you don't want to fully release?"

Virtue was all set to lash out at him for his insinuation, but Fynn began speaking again before she could form her words.

"He *hurt* you, Virtue," he said in a tone that almost seemed belittling. Somehow his delivery made Virtue feel like a child in a classroom wherein the teacher had to talk slowly in order for his students to have any hope of grasping an understanding. "Any man who dares to do that isn't a man at all, and he does not deserve any part of you, especially not your heart. I'm offering you the life that every woman of God deserves to have. One that every other woman would envy and long for. One with a husband to make her complete and to fertilize her with the babies that God designed her to birth. One whose home is . . ."

Pulling her hand from beneath his, Virtue held it up, stopping Fynn in midsentence and then taking a moment to regroup so that her words didn't sound as angry as she felt. "First of all, Mitchell doesn't have my heart. He beat that out of me seven years ago. Do you see this?" She parted her hairs to display the scar that they covered. "How can I love somebody who did *this* to me? So you're wrong, Fynn. You don't have to remind me of what he did to me, because I have this to do that for me every single day. You're wrong on so many different levels. I don't need you or any other man to *complete* me."

"Virtue . . ."

"No, Fynn, you've had your say. Let me have mine." When he settled back in his chair, Virtue continued. "I'm quite capable of living my life to the fullest as a single woman, fulfilling my purpose by teaching creative dance as a means of worship. God equipped me for a lot more

101

than having babies, and I have far more options than one that requires your *fertilizer*. A marriage is comprised of more than a man, a woman, and babies, Fynn. It requires *love*."

"I do love you, Virtue."

Virtue was taken aback. She'd never heard him say the words before. She knew that Fynn was attracted to her, and she'd even heard him voice his desires for her to be his bride. But Virtue had never heard him declare his love for her. She hadn't planned on fighting that line of defense, but since he'd put her in such an uncomfortable place, she prepared herself to do just that. Now, more than ever, Fynn needed her to be honest. She wanted to be completely up front with him, but she didn't want to hurt him in the process. Virtue hesitated and took care to be sure that her next words didn't sound harsh.

"But . . . but I don't love *you*, Fynn. You have to know that. I never meant to lead you to believe . . ."

"I am very well aware of that, Virtue," he said in a manner that reflected his lack of astonishment.

At first, Virtue felt an overwhelming sense of relief. She would have been both regretful and embarrassed had he told her that she'd done something to make him feel that she'd viewed him as anything other than a friend. But her reprieve was soon overshadowed by confusion. If Fynn knew that she didn't love him, why would he be so adamant about them being together? His next words answered her question, but did little to lessen her frustration with the matter.

"When our people were captured and taken from Africa, we were not only stripped of our home, but also our traditions, and forced to take on the customs of European America. In our heritage, marriage was never about love; it wasn't a necessary factor. Still today, in my homeland of Niger, many girls are told who to marry before they ever reach their teen years. The parents know who is best for them. They choose a boy whose family has common beliefs or a man who they are sure will give her the life she deserves. Love often comes later. She *learns* to love him. You will *learn* to love me."

Virtue looked at him in disbelief, stunned that he would even suggest such a thing. Whether they'd been forced out of Africa or not, they were no longer there, and Americans didn't practice African customs. To Virtue's ears, his words not only sounded primitive, but downright insane. Fynn read her thoughts through her silent reaction and tried again.

"Look at us as Christians, Virtue," he said. "We weren't born saved. We weren't born loving God. We were born in sin and shaped in iniquity. Someone had to *teach* us the way of the Lord, and in turn, we *learned* to love Him. I'm not saying that those who wait for love before they marry are wrong. I'm only asking you to broaden the narrowness of what this foreign society has brainwashed us to believe is the *only* way. Look how many marriages fall apart after the wife and husband were supposed to be so eternally in love. Look how *yours* fell apart. Loving a man beforehand is no guarantee that the love will last forever. Half of all marriages end in divorce. These are marriages where love is most often declared beforehand. So marrying me and *learning* to love me is no bigger risk. Think about that, my love."

Virtue didn't know whether to laugh from hysteria or scream in annoyance. She did neither. Instead, she sat in silence and watched Fynn rise from his seat and stand at a full height of just over six feet. She didn't move or speak, even when he reached forth and gently touched her chin with his hand before turning to leave. All she could do was watch while her voice sat dormant somewhere in the pit of her stomach.

Just before he left, Fynn turned to face her and flashed the bright, tooth-filled smile that had become his identifying characteristic at Temple of Jerusalem.

"*Think* about it," he repeated.

Twelve

Chris turned over in his bed, once again awakened by the combination of his own coughing, the chills that the continuous sweating brought on, and a recurring bad headache that he blamed on the fever that just wouldn't break. He'd draped himself with extra covers earlier because he was cold, but now he was so hot that it felt as though he'd set his thermostat on high. Tossing the heavy linen aside and forcing his aching body from the mattress, Chris rubbed his hand across his forehead and wiped away beads of perspiration.

The dream he'd been having was trapped in a fog in his mind. Chris tried to recall it clearly but couldn't. He knew it had something to do with his wedding, though. Lisa was in the dream and so was he. But just as they were proclaimed man and wife, something would happen to mess up an otherwise flawless wedding day.

"No time for getting cold feet, Christopher," he told himself with a laugh. His sister had warned him that he'd start getting wedding jitters as the date came closer. Ursula said that it happened to all men. Chris had disputed her, but now he was beginning to believe it was true.

"I sure hope I didn't give this to you, Barbara," he said, changing his thoughts as he struggled to stand and maintain his balance.

At the advice of Rev. Inman, who had stopped by earlier in the morning to pray for him, Chris had gone to the doctor, chauffeured by his pastor. Just as Chris suspected but hoped wasn't accurate, he had the flu. The doctor called it an "acute respiratory infection," but he'd had the flu enough times to know what it felt like.

After leaving the doctor's office, Rev. Inman had been kind enough to take Chris to the drugstore to get his prescription filled. Taking the large, hard-to-swallow pills was supposed to make him feel better, but quite honestly, Chris felt worse now than he had before he'd crawled into bed for his afternoon nap. The label called for him to take the medicine with food, but juice was the best he could do. He had no appetite for solid foods, and the uneasy feeling in his stomach at the time told him that solid food probably wasn't the best idea.

The current rumbling in his stomach, though, was a clear cry for a meal, but Chris didn't have the energy to make his way to the kitchen. It took all the strength he had just to walk to the hallway to adjust his thermostat. Rev. Inman had placed an extra glass of orange juice by his bed earlier. That would have to suffice until his fiancée came by later to check on him.

"Thank God for Lisa."

Chris mumbled the words while he leaned against the wall of the hallway for added support. The short walk had sapped him of nearly all of his strength, and he needed a moment to rest before making the short return trip. He couldn't recall the last time he'd been so ill. If he'd passed what he had on to Barbara, it would be next week before she could return to work.

Barbara was more than a dedicated employee. As the secretary that Willie James Jackson Jr. had hired when he first started the business twenty-eight years ago, she was a fixture at Jackson, Jackson & Andrews. Barbara hated missing work. As a sixty-year-old widow who lived alone, the job was proof of her independence and her worth. Chris knew that he'd have to insist that she take another day away from the office, but he had no problems doing so. He'd promised his father two things: that he'd take care of his mother and sister and that he'd treat Barbara well for all of her years of service.

When Chris had called Lisa early this morning to tell her of his condition and ask her to sacrifice one of her vacation days to fill in for Barbara, he had expected her to be hesitant. He'd even prepared himself for the small possibility of her saying no. He would have been disappointed, but he wouldn't have blamed her for declining. It wasn't often that she took days in succession away from her job. Chris was glad that she didn't refuse his plea. It spoke volumes to him that she'd be so willing to help him in his time of need.

She's so good for me, he thought as he slowly started back toward his bedroom. Catching a glimpse of the glowing numbers on the clock that sat on his nightstand, Chris noticed that he'd slept most of the afternoon away. It was later than he'd initially thought. Lisa would be here any moment. Just the thought of it seemed to ease the queasiness in his stomach. Help was on the way, and it was coming in the form of his future bride.

When Chris had last called the office to check on everything, Lisa told him that she'd fill in until Friday, if necessary. He'd told her that one day should be sufficient; but now, not knowing if he'd passed the fullness of his viral infection on to Barbara, Chris wasn't sure that he wouldn't have to call Lisa back. For certain, *he* wouldn't be back in the office before Friday, and he could only imagine that the same would go for Barbara. Even if she didn't get as sick as he was, he'd insist that she take at least one more day to fully recuperate.

While he took small swallows of the orange juice, Chris's desire for food seemed to heighten. He hadn't had an appetite all day, but suddenly hunger was getting the best of him. The sips turned into gulps, quenching his dry throat but burning it in the places that had become raw from consistent fits of coughing. It didn't take long for Chris to realize that drinking the citrus drink on a nearly empty stomach wasn't the best decision. Tight knots formed in his stomach, or at least that was what it felt like. One moment it felt as though he would vomit, and the next there was only an excruciating pain that he could only imagine to be comparable to the pains of a woman giving birth or the passing of a kidney stone—whichever was worse. He was in a kneeling position beside the bed when his house alarm beeped, signifying that someone had entered.

Chris hoped that it was Lisa, but at this point, he'd settle for a burglar. As long as the intruder would spare his life, Chris wouldn't care if he robbed him of all of his possessions. All he'd ask is that the thief would leave the bed and help him get back in it. The rest of his belongings were of no current value to him.

"Christopher? Sweetie, are you all right? What are you doing on the floor?"

A moan was the only response that Chris could muster as Lisa rushed to his side. He wanted to tell her not to get too close, but he found that he didn't have to. She'd already taken the precautions of wearing a mask and gloves. Her position in the administrative department of a local children's clinic had trained her well for situations such as this.

"Why didn't you call me?" Lisa asked through grunts as she helped him from the floor to the bed. "You're burning up, Chris," she added, after placing the back of her hand against his forehead. "Did you take your meds?"

"Yeah, babe," he managed to say as he lay back on the pillow and exhaled through the pain.

"Is it time to take it again?"

Chris watched as Lisa picked up the bottle from the table beside him and read the label. He knew exactly what her next question would be, and while he was saying it in his thoughts, she was voicing it out loud.

"Sweetie, did you take this on an empty stomach?"

With the juice that he drank earlier, his stomach hadn't been completely empty when he took his morning dosage, but Chris had no time to respond.

"That's why you're on the floor," Lisa concluded. "It's time to take it again, but not before I get some food in you. I'm going to microwave some of that canned chicken noodle soup that you have in the kitchen and let you eat that before taking any more medicine. Don't you go anywhere. I'll be right back."

Don't go anywhere? If Chris had had enough strength, he would have laughed at the thought. Moving from his bed was something that he couldn't do even if he wanted to. It was all he could do just to reposition himself on the mattress so that he would be more comfortable. Beads of sweat surfaced on Chris's skin as another wave of coughing made its round. The chills that he'd felt earlier in the day had returned, prompting him to once again cover himself with the blanket he'd tossed aside earlier. In addition, his lack of sleep was beginning to catch up with him.

"I noticed that you have tomato soup in the cabinet too," Lisa said as she stepped in the open doorway of his bedroom, disturbing the onset of sleep. "You want me to mix some of that in with your chicken noodle?"

Chris looked toward her and offered a weak smile. "Come here," he whispered.

"What?"

"Come here," he repeated.

Lisa took a few steps in the direction of his bed and

then stopped long enough to cover her nose and mouth with her mask. The combination of the mask and gloves made her look like an OR nurse who was preparing to help a doctor perform some important surgical procedure. Even with most of her face covered, with the exception of her eyes, Chris thought Lisa was beautiful. Her eyes, pecan brown, were perhaps her strongest feature.

"Come here," Chris said for the third time while reaching one arm upward.

Understanding what he wanted, Lisa set the two soup cans on the table beside his bed and bent down to deliver the kiss that Chris beckoned for. The fabric of the mask prevented their lips from touching, but Chris was almost sure that he could taste hers just the same.

"Thanks for coming, babe," he said after releasing her.

"Where else would I be?" Lisa asked. She kept her face close to his and stroked his cheek with her gloved hand. "You're sick, Christopher. Those vows say in sickness or in health, don't they? I guess I might as well get an idea now of what you're like when you're not feeling well. There are gonna be days like this, you know. You'd do it for me, wouldn't you?"

When she was this close to him, Lisa made Chris's heart beat at twice its normal rate. He was already weak from the effects of the flu and lack of nourishment, but Chris felt the little strength he had left dissolve beneath the gentle touch of Lisa's hand. He closed his eyes and relished the thought that only a few weeks remained before he would be with her in every way.

"I'd do anything for you," Chris whispered.

He opened his eyes as he felt her pulling away. She stood for a moment, and even though the mask continued to hide much of her face from Chris, he could tell from her eyes that she was smiling. He watched as she reached beside the bed and retrieved the cans that she'd placed there earlier.

"Give me a few minutes," she said as she began backing away. "I'm going to make you all better."

Analyzing that this was as good a time as any to ask the favor, Chris spoke. "Babe?"

"Yes?"

"About tomorrow," he mumbled. "I think I might need you to fill in for Barbara again. I'm sorry. If I could make it in, I wouldn't worry about it. Together, Mitch and I could hold down the place without much of a problem. But with only him there . . ."

"It's okay, Chris," she assured him. "I'll do it."

"You sure? I hate asking you to do this. I know this isn't how you planned to spend your vacation. I can contact the temp agency and have them send someone over if necessary."

Lisa pulled the mask from her face, allowing Chris to capture the fullness of her smile. Seeing it helped to lessen Chris's doubts about her genuine willingness to return to Jackson, Jackson & Andrews. "I said I'll do it," she reiterated. "There's no need to call the temp agency. Mitch and I work well together."

Chris grinned. "I told him not to work you too hard. He didn't, did he?"

"He didn't work me hard enough," Lisa said with a laugh. "Maybe you're the reason why he never had anything for me to do all day except answer the telephone. I knew there was more that I could be doing."

"A lot more," Chris agreed. "When I call him this evening, I'll tell him to let you help with those files that are stacked on the floors of both our offices. We were working on a purge project before those end-of-the-year orders started rushing in. You can start in my office, and if you get finished early, you can start on the ones in his."

"Good," Lisa said in a satisfied tone. "I'm glad you're getting the extra rest. Maybe if you sleep in late tomorrow you'll be well enough to make it to our last session with Rev. Inman. What do you think?"

"Let's hope so," Chris said as he watched her disappear through the doorway.

He fully relaxed his back against the mattress when he heard the clatter of pots in the kitchen. Lisa had worked at the clinic for nearly six years, and she loved working with the medical staff there. For the past several weeks, Chris had been trying to find a way to approach her about coming to work for him once they were married. He couldn't imagine a better-case scenario than one that would have them spending both their days and their nights together. At first he thought that getting her to change employers would be a difficult sell. But with the way she'd been so open to the idea of working at the accounting firm during her vacation, Chris found new confidence that his future bride would consider his suggestion that she play an active role in the business that his father had left for him to carry on.

Turning over in the bed, Chris picked up his cell phone. He always kept it on the pillow beside him when he was in bed. Mitchell would be happy to know that he wouldn't have to carry out business alone tomorrow. And it would encourage him even more to know that Lisa was willing to fill in again and that she would be helping to get the file project complete.

Getting Mitchell's voice mail wasn't standard for this time of the afternoon. Generally, he kept his cell with him, and most days Mitchell went straight home from the office. The only exceptions were the days when work had been more stressful than normal. On those rare occasions, Mitchell would detour from his regular route home and stop on Preston Road to put his membership to LA Fitness Center to use. He said a good one-hour run on the tread-mill did wonders for clearing his head and relieving the stress of the workday.

"Hey, Mitch," Chris said after being prompted to leave his message. "Where are you, man? A brother could be over here dying. The least you could do is come by and check on me. Good thing I got Lisa, 'cause you ain't a bit of good. She's here now, working in Chris's Kitchen, preparing the soup of the day."

Chris tried to laugh at his own joke, but instead he had to battle with a spell of coughing. When he gathered himself, he continued. "Sorry. Just wanted to call to let you know that Lisa will be at the office helping you again tomorrow. I'm going to call Barbara and tell her to take another day. If she's feeling anything like I am, she'll be happy to hear it. I told Lisa about the file purging that we never finished, so let her work on those if the phones are quiet. I'm gonna try to get well enough to come in on Friday. Peace."

He had barely returned to his position lying on his back when Lisa walked into the room with a steaming bowl of soup in one hand and a large cup of orange juice in the other. She balanced them with care while she used her foot to pull Chris's tray closer to the bed. Sitting on the edge of his bed, Lisa took several moments to carefully mix the combination of soups with a spoon. She then pulled her mask away from her face and blew on the portion that she'd scooped up. Chris admired her every move and couldn't help but smile as he dragged his still-tired-and-sore body into a seated position. He didn't like being sick, but he loved the way Lisa took care of him.

"You're a jewel," he whispered as she brought the spoon toward his mouth.

"And don't you ever forget it," she whispered back.

~ *Thirteen* ~

*H*e said *what*?" Beverly's tone was demanding as she placed her coffee cup down and leaned across the dinner table as if she thought she'd misunderstood the end of Virtue's story.

It had been almost nightfall by the time Virtue completed the outline of her Christmas choreography. In her experiences as a dance instructor for the school she'd taught for back in Detroit as well as her position as the leader of the praise dance troupe, Virtue had found it to be more of a challenge to choreograph a solo piece than a routine for a group. But today, the difference in the techniques wasn't the reason that she'd struggled to get through. After Fynn left her to herself, it had been a battle for Virtue to get her thoughts together and concentrate on crafting the routine. Eventually, she'd had to step away from her computer and have a private talk with God before she could regain her focus. In time, she did manage to get her work done, but it hadn't been easy.

Before she left her office, Virtue had made the decision

that the disturbing conversation that she'd had with Fynn would remain only between the two of them. She thought that she'd been successful in hiding her mental anguish from her mentor, but by the time Beverly was clearing the dishes from the dinner table, Virtue knew better.

"I'm gonna get these dishes in the dishwasher and then bring us something to drink to go with dessert," Beverly had said more than half an hour ago. "Maybe after you get some of my apple pie in you, you'll be ready to talk."

On one hand, Virtue had been glad for the opportunity to get honest feedback from the older and wiser woman, but on the other, she dreaded reliving the moment. For more reasons than one, she found talking about her impromptu meeting with Fynn disturbing. Virtue sipped from her mug of hot chocolate while Beverly pounded the table in annoyance.

"Now, see? I always liked Minister Fynn, but he has truly bothered me with this one. Honey, that's the devil right there," she said. "And sometimes when people are letting the devil use them, you can't be sitting all nice. You got to put the devil in his place. He'll leave you alone then."

"Then why haven't you put Renee in her place yet?" Virtue challenged.

"Don't try and turn the tables or change the subject," Beverly said. "Renee will get hers in time, believe you me. But we're talking about Minister Fynn right now, and you'd better listen to me when I tell you that he needs to be put in his place."

Virtue was surprised by the magnitude of Beverly's disappointment. After all, she had been the one who encouraged Virtue to accept the preacher's invitation to accompany him on a first date back in early spring. In her sales pitch, Beverly had used words like "worthy mate," "respectable man of God," "great catch," "model Christian," and other convincing phrases. Now, after hearing a rerun of what had taken place in Virtue's office that afternoon, Beverly had completely switched gears.

"I was just so thrown by his suggestion that I marry him without being in love," Virtue thought out loud. "I wonder if those types of marriages really take place in Africa, and I wonder how many of them work." When she pulled her mug from her lips after taking a long sip, she found Beverly looking at her in disbelief.

"You're not thinking of taking him up on this insanity, are you?"

The frightening truth in Beverly's words was the biggest reason that Virtue was troubled by her discussion with Fynn. When he'd first suggested that she marry and learn to love him, Virtue had been appalled. She couldn't believe he'd been so bold as to say the words; but after he'd left her there, she began to feel perplexed, then found herself comparing the pros and cons . . .

"Virtue?" Beverly interrupted her thoughts.

"No," Virtue responded. Knowing that it was a lie, she came back with, "I don't know. I mean, I definitely don't love Fynn, but he made a pretty good argument. Love isn't enough to sustain a marriage. My failed marriage and the thousands of others before and since it are proof. And like he said, we aren't born loving God. That is something that we learn to do along the way."

"Stop it, Virtue!" Beverly snapped. "I can't believe what I'm hearing. First of all, I can't believe Minister Fynn would use God's Word to try and convince you that love is not a prerequisite to marriage. And secondly, I'm even more bewildered that you would give something so ridiculous a second thought. I know you know better than this, Virtue."

Virtue remained quiet. Embarrassment crept in, and like a child, she wanted to burst into tears or run to the nearest bedroom and lock herself inside. She wanted to deny giving Fynn's awkward proposal any serious consideration, but she couldn't, at least not in honesty. And Beverly had proved time and time again that she couldn't be easily deceived.

"Did I ever tell you what I did before becoming a counselor at HCW?"

Virtue shook her head in silence. Almost everything she'd known of Beverly's life had taken place in the ten years that Beverly had worked at the center.

"Well, let me tell you now," Beverly said. She took another sip from her coffee cup before placing it to the side. "I worked as a high school teacher in the social studies department. Doggone kids just about ran me crazy," she said, seeming to drift from the subject at hand. "I knew that I either had to find another profession or be willing to go to jail for hurting somebody's flip-mouthed child. I taught in the classroom for sixteen years. I knew I should have stopped at fifteen, because that last year almost got the best of me.

"For the last four years of the twenty years that I worked in the public school system, I was a guidance counselor. That was better, but not by much. What most of those raggedy children needed was a good whipping. I can't tell you how many times I had parents in my office crying and saying things like they had already spent ten thousand dollars or more to get professional help for their teenager's unruly behavior. *Ten thousand dollars?* Honey, if they'd have given me just ten dollars, seven days, and a two-by-four, I could have straightened that child right on up."

Beverly had been serious during her rant, but the tone of her words and her distorted facial expression drew laughter from Virtue. The humor was lost quickly when Beverly began talking again.

"Right about now, I need a two-by-four for you, Miss Thing," she said with a finger pointed in Virtue's direction. "Before you go gallivanting off and making stupid decisions that you'll regret for the rest of your life, you need to pick up a book and read it. I remember us studying Africa during my teaching years in Houston's public school system. We studied everything from their cultures and their religions to Africa's weather, crops, and the landscape. What Minister Fynn said to you is true. The parents do choose husbands for their daughters. Sometimes those daughters are as young as twelve, and they are forced to marry these sometimes-much-older men whether they want to or not.

"In Minister Fynn's family's homeland, they have close to a 60 percent rate of girls who are *forced* to marry between the ages of fifteen and nineteen. They are more like servants to their husbands than they are wives. Yes, our forefathers were forced from their native land and brought to America and turned into slaves. But now we are not under that same bondage. There are still plenty of prejudiced people around, but we have freedom here that doesn't exist in much of Africa. There, many of the women are treated as less than second-class citizens, and they remain in a different kind of bondage, forced to live lives they had no option of choosing.

"I listened to you talk about your conversation with Minister Fynn, and many of the words he said to you are a direct link to what he has been taught. He may not realize it, but he still has the mentality of his father and grandfather. Coming to America may have changed his family's physical addresses, but it didn't do much to change their mind-set. Just the mere fact that he would suggest that you marry him without loving him proves it. That should make you wonder what other traditions he holds on to. It's not uncommon in Niger for men to think women should not be educated or even think for themselves. Domestic violence is commonplace if a woman disagrees on any level with her husband, and I know how you feel about that subject. Fynn may have made it all sound attractive, but don't you underestimate love, girl. I may have been hurt by it, and you may have been hurt by it, but love identifies

119

God. The Bible says that God is love. That's just how power-ful it is."

Having finished her mini-sermon, Beverly sat back in her chair and resumed drinking her coffee. Virtue felt like a little girl who'd just taken a whipping from her mother. She sat with her eyes glued to the half-eaten apple pie in the saucer in front of her, saying nothing for fear of what she might say.

"Do you want to marry him, Virtue?"

Beverly's words brought Virtue's eyes from their down-ward stare. Shaking her head, she answered, "No. I don't want to marry anybody, Beverly. Fynn's words just had me thinking, that's all. He made it sound like our getting to-gether was God's will and somehow I was allowing my own hang-ups to serve as a hindrance to something that had been divinely orchestrated. I guess I was just confused for a minute. I should have just dismissed everything he said."

"Maybe not everything," Beverly said. When Virtue looked at her in bewilderment, Beverly continued. "You said that he suggested that you were intentionally holding on to your past for some reason. I happen to think he's right about that."

Virtue sat up straight in her chair. "What? What do you mean, you think he's right?"

"Mitchell has reached out to you at least twice since your accidental meeting in Dallas. Have you returned his calls?"

"No. And I'm not going to."

"Why?" Beverly challenged.

"How many times do we have to go over this?" Virtue said with a raised voice. "I've explained this to you before. I don't want to talk to him. He said everything I needed to hear when we parted ways in Michigan."

"Except maybe 'I'm sorry.'"

"I don't want to hear his apology, Beverly. It's way too

little, way too late. If I never see Mitchell Andrews's face again, it will be too soon for me."

"Really?"

Beverly had taken on the tone of a therapist, and Virtue didn't like it when she did that away from the office. It confused her and forced her to decipher what she should and should not say. She knew how to talk to Beverly as a friend, and she knew how to talk to her as a therapist. But Virtue was put in an uncomfortable place when she felt Beverly was setting her up to do both.

"I'm going to bed," she declared as she got up from the table. Virtue expected Beverly's voice to stop her, and it did.

"You're still holding on to him, Virtue," she said. "As long as you don't allow him to apologize, you can always hold on to him in some way, even if it is in a negative sense. You can always part your hairs and show your scar, blaming him for putting it there as long as you don't hear him voice his regrets and be forced to *truly* forgive him. Once you forgive him the way God instructs us to forgive those who do us wrong, you'll be obligated to release him and let him go."

The tears that had begun pooling in Virtue's eyes when she stood from her seat were now escaping, making mad dashes down her cheeks. "That's not true," she replied, all the while searching herself for what was true and what wasn't.

"Then prove me wrong," Beverly said, repeating the challenge she'd hinted toward earlier in the week. "How many years has it been, Virtue? You've taken many steps in the right direction since the day you left Mitchell. You found medicine to care for your physical wounds, you had prayer to help establish your spiritual life, and you sought counsel to help you cope with the mental anguish. But as good and as right as all of that is, you'll never find complete deliverance until you let go. It's time for you to face the truth, Virtue. Either you want to release him or you don't."

To Virtue, Beverly's words sounded accusing. Turning to face her, all Virtue could see was a blurred image of her friend. Her tears were so thick that they nearly blinded her. She didn't even bother to wipe them away.

"I released him when I filed those papers, Beverly," she defended.

"All those papers did was sever the legal bonds of your *marriage*. But love is a lot stronger than paper and ink."

Continuing the conversation was pointless. Virtue felt that nothing she said would be convincing enough for Beverly. How could she make her understand that she had no desire to revisit her painful past? Fynn may have been wrong about a lot of things, but he'd been right about at least one thing. She didn't owe Mitchell anything, and he didn't deserve anything from her. Without responding to Beverly's insistence, Virtue turned and took quick steps down the hallway that led to her bedroom. Once the door was securely closed behind her, she sank onto the floor, buried her face between her knees, and wept.

Fourteen

Rev. Lionel Inman was more than a pastor to his flock of faithful members; he was also a friend of the community and made himself accessible as much as possible in whatever capacity needed. His ministry wasn't limited to the pulpit of Living Word Cathedral. He also served as one of the chaplains at Baylor University Medical Center, a mentor in North Texas's Big Brother/Big Sister program, and visited the prison system often to introduce Christ to those who were incarcerated. Rev. Inman often testified that his life, void of an active father and short on the love and attention that a child needs, was the reason that as a young man he'd turned to a life of fast cars, loose women, and high crimes.

To many outsiders who hadn't been told his life's story, the relatively young preacher didn't seem qualified for the services that he carried out. There wasn't a noticeable grey strand of hair on his head, and without the Sunday suit and ministerial collar he looked no different than the average man next door. But there was a whole lot more to Lionel Inman than met the eye.

Just a few years ago, the forty-six-year-old preacher had been a leader of a much different kind. Born and raised in California, he'd made a dreadful but successful living selling drugs and women. A "pleasure engineer" is what he said he'd titled his decade-long profession. A ride in the back of a squad car was all the time it took for him to make an about-face. The arresting officer didn't claim to be a preacher, but he was definitely heaven-sent. Rev. Inman loved to share the story with the members of Living Word Cathedral, and they loved hearing how their pastor's typical arrest turned into anything but.

In a move that was by all accounts cause for suspicion, the arresting officer pulled the patrol car over to the side of the road two blocks away from the precinct. Rev. Inman said that he'd heard horror stories from many of his friends and even from some of "his women" who'd been picked up for soliciting undercover policemen. He thought he'd have a brutality story of his own when the white officer shut off his flashing lights, got out of the driver's seat, and climbed into the backseat with him. In a fair struggle, Rev. Inman said he would have had little trouble taking on the man who was at least four inches shorter and twenty-five pounds lighter than he. But with him still bound by handcuffs, the officer had an unfair advantage.

After closing the door, erasing any chance for his prisoner to escape, the officer reached under the front passenger seat. Rev. Inman said he'd tried not to show any signs of fear, but his insides cringed and he braced for the force of the nightstick. Instead, what the policeman pulled from beneath the seat was a weapon of another kind.

"I could get in trouble for this," the officer told him. "All it would take is for you to report my badge number to my superiors, and none of the years that I've served the LAPD and sacrificed my life for the safety of others would mean a thing. I'd be out of a job by morning."

Rev. Inman said the image of the gold badge with blue

writing became a permanent imprint in his mind. He'd already decided that he'd fix this racist white man who dared to try and intimidate him. The numbers 14188 seemed to sparkle from the streetlight that provided the only illumination in the area where the policeman had chosen to park his cruiser. *He'll be sorry he ever cuffed the hands of Lionel Inman,* he had reasoned. But it was the officer's next words that captured the future preacher's total attention.

"But even though I know you'll have the power to destroy my life as I know it, I've got to do this, because God told me to."

The man proceeded to write something on the first page of the leather-bound book. Rev. Inman said that he drew back when he saw the officer reach into his pocket afterward.

"Turn around."

"What?"

"Turn around," the officer said again. His voice was calm but authoritative at the same time.

Lionel continued to stare at him in defiance, and when the policeman finally understood the reason for his hesitation he burst into a hearty laugh that made his detainee even more confused.

"God wouldn't tell me to do that to you, sir," the officer said. He then held up his right hand and displayed a key. "You'll have to turn around if you want me to unlock you."

Rev. Inman said he turned as instructed, but the whole while he was trying to figure out the catch. Was this one of those things like he'd seen in *Murder in Mississippi*, the movie wherein Blair Underwood played James Chaney, the civil rights activist who was slain by Ku Klux Klan members after he refused to run in fear? Well, this wasn't 1964, and he wasn't about to go down without a fight. He turned back around quickly after feeling the metal pull away from his wrist.

"You're going to be somebody," the officer said, just as his former captive was about to draw back his fists. "God said you're going to be a vessel that He'll use to bring many lost souls to the cross. You're a preacher in the making. The people of Dallas, Texas, will never be the same once you walk on their soil."

With that, the man handed Lionel his first Bible. For the longest time, Rev. Inman said, the only thing he could do was to stare at the cover and wonder what on earth was wrong with the man who'd given it to him. He didn't move again until he heard the doors unlock.

"Go on now," the officer told him.

Lionel remembered spewing every swearword he could think of at the officer. They didn't even form a proper sentence, but they were an accurate result of his combination of fear, anger, and confusion. Shaking his head in defiance, Lionel added, "What you trying to pull, fool? I ain't crazy. *You* the one who's crazy. I ain't 'bout to go down like that. You're just trying to get me to get out of this car so you can shoot me in the back and say I was trying to escape."

The officer's reply was to remove his gun from his hip and empty the bullets on the floor of the squad car. After all of the bullets had fallen at his feet, the man dropped the gun on the floor with them and pointed toward the door behind Lionel.

"Go," he repeated.

Lionel hesitated, but finally obeyed. His first few moments of freedom, Rev. Inman had told his congregation, were more frightening than the entire episode, including the actual arrest and the time spent confined in the back of the car with the officer. He'd started out walking away from the car, but he'd broken into a sprint when he heard the car door open and close in the distance. That area of Los Angeles was home to Lionel. He ran through alleys and cut through backyards to be sure that the policeman couldn't trail him. He didn't stop running until he had reached the gated community where his illegal profession had allowed him to live in luxury. It wasn't until he was safe behind his latched door that Lionel realized he'd clutched the Bible in his hand the whole way.

To this day, he believed that the officer had been an angel that God had planted out on the street where Lionel had been read his rights. When he finally opened the Bible after four days of being too afraid to even leave his home, Rev. Inman read the inscription for the first time. The officer had written, *To: My Servant, Lionel; From: Your Savior, Jesus.* Lionel always carried fake identification whenever he was involved in illegal activities. The license that the officer had confiscated from him that night bore the name Elliot Woods. Never had he told him that his real name was Lionel. When the significance of it all settled in, his level of fear heightened. It would be another four days before Lionel would have enough courage to step outside his doors.

Two weeks later, he called the Los Angeles Police Department to ask about the man wearing 14188 on his badge and found out from them that the number didn't exist. In fear, he'd tried on several occasions to throw the Bible away; but each time he did, an indescribable force would have him retrieve it from the garbage can. Nothing about his life as he'd known it for ten years had been the same after that momentous night. He didn't feel comfortable in the pimp garb that had gotten him the respect of those within his circle. Within a matter of days he'd destroyed it all, and the women he'd used to achieve his noted status were released from the bondage they weren't even aware they were in.

Fruitless days and sleepless nights prompted the onset of what would become many hours of reading the pages in the Bible and kneeling tearfully on the floor beside his bed. John 3:16 became the Scripture he read every single day until he finally understood its meaning and asked God to give him the eternal life that was promised in His Word. By the end of the month, without a clue of what he was going to do once he got there, Lionel Inman had packed his belongings and was headed toward Texas.

Looking back, he still couldn't account for all that had taken place in his past to bring him to his present, but for every unexplainable detail, Rev. Inman had been thankful. Now, as he sat at his desk and sorted through the paperwork in front of him, he made good use of free time that had unexpectedly been presented to him.

Thursdays were by far Rev. Inman's busiest days at the church. It was the day that he scheduled most of his counseling sessions. He had already completed three of his five scheduled appointments, but the subjects of his fourth one were running late, rewarding him with a few minutes of availability that he was now using to prepare himself for Sunday morning's sermon. Though he was grateful for the additional study time, Rev. Inman had been looking forward to this meeting with Chris and Lisa. It was their last one, and one that he had hoped would give him the additional confidence he needed to perform their February ceremony without the reluctance that had been nudging at him for the past several weeks.

Rev. Inman's eyes stared at the pages of his notebook, but his thoughts were far from the words he had jotted on the paper. For quite some time he had been struggling with his lingering doubt about the upcoming vows that would be exchanged between two of his most loyal members. Rev. Inman had avoided bringing it up during sessions because he wouldn't have a clear answer if either of them asked why he felt that way. As a pastor and counselor, Rev. Inman knew that he had to be careful not to let his personal feelings mingle with the spiritual enlightenment that God gave him. Usually he was good at distinguishing one from the other. This time, however, he wasn't at all certain.

Christopher Jackson had been a member of Living Word Cathedral longer than Rev. Inman had been pastor. In the thirteen years that he'd served as leader of the congregation, the preacher had seen nothing to cause him to question Chris's character. Rev. Inman remembered the despair that Chris had endured after the death of his father. He had become distant, and depression had set in. But even in all of that, Chris's spiritual foundation remained strong. He was a hard worker and a leader in his community. Everyone respected the son that the elder Mr. Jackson left to carry on his legacy. Chris's strength and loyalty had been tested and tried. Even when his mother and sister uprooted from Dallas and relocated to California to start new lives, Chris stayed behind. His dedication to carrying on his father's business was nothing less than commendable.

It had been less than three years ago that Lisa walked through the doors of his church for the first time. Rev. Inman remembered her well because her presence demanded attention. When she walked in the door, heads turned. Many men in the church were impressed by her natural beauty, but it was Chris who had won her heart. The two of them made a handsome couple and seemed to get along well. Even during counseling, when they disagreed, there was never any disrespect. Rev. Inman liked that. One of the points he always made during the course of marriage counseling was the importance of regard between a husband and wife. So much about Chris and Lisa seemed to make them the perfect pair, but the pastor still wasn't convinced. A recent observation had caused his confidence in their bond to weaken.

For the first year of their courtship, Chris and Lisa only had eyes for each other, or so it seemed. But something had changed, and it hadn't escaped the watchful eyes of Rev. Inman. While there hadn't been a noticeable change in the way Lisa interacted with her fiancé, there *had* been a marked difference in the way she interacted with her fiancé's best friend. Rev. Inman noticed it for the first time four Sundays ago. While he'd been standing in his office, looking out of the window that faced the side parking lot of the church, he'd seen Lisa approach Mitchell Andrews from behind as he bent to load some belongings in the back of his Tundra. For a while, she'd said and did nothing except stand and watch in what looked a lot like lustful admiration.

Rev. Inman's telephone had rung that day and drawn him away from his watch. By the time he'd returned to the window, the three of them—Mitch, Lisa, and Chris—were standing together talking. Lisa's arm had a firm grip around Chris's waist, and all seemed well. Rev. Inman had convinced himself that he'd made more of the sighting than necessary, but since that time, he'd made several more observations of questionable behavior between Lisa and Mitch. He hated the probing question that had him hesitant to officiate at the pending wedding. Today he planned to get the answers he needed in order to clear his spirit.

Rev. Inman looked at his watch and noticed the lateness of the hour just as his telephone rang.

"Rev. Lionel Inman," he answered.

"Hey, Rev. Inman."

It was no surprise to him to hear Chris's voice on the other end of the line. As a matter of fact, Rev. Inman had almost said Chris's name when he answered. It was extremely rare for him to ever run late for any type of meeting, let alone his premarital counseling sessions. And from the sound of Chris's hoarse voice, Rev. Inman made the early speculation that he'd have to wait to get the answers to the questions that weighed on his mind.

∽ Fifteen ∽

Do I make you nervous?"

It was five minutes till closing, and as uncustomary as it was, Mitchell was already packing his briefcase in preparation to leave. This day had been even longer than yesterday, and top priority for him right now was to get his belongings packed and to head to the gym for another stress-relieving run. Last night, Mitchell had been en route to Chris's house to check on him when he'd listened to the message that had been left on his cell phone. He had achieved a personal best, thirty-minute, four-mile run and had left the fitness center feeling rejuvenated. But his high had quickly fizzled when he played the message left by his friend. Mitchell had been so agitated that he made an illegal U-turn in the road and headed home instead. Chris had to settle for a late-night phone call instead.

"Do you make me *what*?" Mitchell asked, knowing full well what Lisa had said the first time.

"You heard me." She took several steps that brought her closer to his desk and then repeated her question. "Do I make you nervous?"

"What kind of question is that?"

"One that requires an answer," she said with sarcasm.

Mitchell was temporarily rescued by the sound of the telephone ringing from the front desk. Lisa gave him a look that distinctly said, "I'll be back for an answer," and then rushed from his office to catch the call before it rolled into their voice mail. With her gone, Mitchell released a deep sigh. Maybe he should be glad that she had brought up the subject. It would give him a chance to address all of the concerns he'd kept to himself. But he hadn't been prepared for her to drop the issue on the table today. He still had a lot of work to do and needed to get home to his laptop—and to uninterrupted peace and quiet.

When he looked up from his briefcase again, Lisa was standing quietly in his doorway, leaning against the frame of it and almost seeming to strike a pose. Mitchell looked at her for a moment and then went back to work, putting another file inside the case before closing it. Avoiding her inquisitive eyes, he walked to the coatrack and pulled his leather jacket from it. He should have known better than to think she'd just take a hint and go away. Mitchell's back was turned to her, but the sound of her heels against the hardwood floors gave warning that she was once again approaching.

"Talk to me, Mitchell."

That was another thing that irked him. In his lifetime, no one had ever consistently referred to him as Mitchell except Virtue. He loved the way the relatively common name rolled off of his wife's tongue. He didn't know if it was intentional or not, but when Virtue had said his name, it almost sounded lyrical. Mitchell supposed that he'd subconsciously reserved being identified by his full first name for Virtue since hearing it from another was bothersome. Lisa didn't refer to him as such all of the time, but Mitchell took note that when she did, it was only in Chris's absence. For some reason, that made him leery too.

Slipping on his jacket and facing her, Mitchell said, "Talk to you about what?"

By now, she was standing directly in front of him. Mitchell tried to appear absorbed in his work, but in what looked like a calculated move, Lisa slid Mitchell's in-box over on his desk to make room for her rear. Sliding herself onto the oak desk, she sat and crossed her legs at the knees. By every definition, it was inappropriate, but Mitchell made a conscious attempt to bridle his tongue.

"What are you doing?" he asked.

"Waiting for you to answer my question." Lisa's matter-of-fact tone was unwavering. Placing her arms on her lap, she relayed her question for the third time. "Do I make you nervous?"

"Why would you make me nervous?" For Mitchell, avoiding a direct answer to the question seemed like the best route to take. He wanted to know where she was going with her suggestion before jumping to a conclusion that he might regret.

Lisa shrugged. "I don't know, but lately I get the feeling that I do, especially when we're alone. Don't get me wrong. I'm used to it. I seem to have that effect on most men."

Mitchell knew his car keys were in the pocket of his coat, but he patted the leather anyway and then walked past Lisa toward his briefcase, which was still on the desk behind where she sat. "I'm not most men, Lisa."

"I know," she said, switching positions so that she faced him once again. "With most men, I know why they're so intimidated. They're that way because they're interested and just aren't sure how to approach me, or even if they *should* approach me. But that couldn't be the case with you . . . could it?"

It was a hard judgment call to make. To Mitchell, her words felt a lot like a come-on, but on the other hand, she could be testing him to see just how loyal he was to his best friend. Maybe it wasn't even about Lisa wanting to establish something deeper with him. It could easily be that she was only trying to see if he'd make a move on her so that she could determine if the man her fiancé had chosen to serve as his best man was worthy. Mitchell wasn't sure what to think of Lisa's new line of reasoning, but whatever was her motive, he had heard just about enough.

"Lisa, we've both had a long and busy day. I'm sure you're as ready to get home as I am. Why don't we stop with the mind games and just go home? Barbara will be back in the morning, so you can take tomorrow and enjoy what's left of your vacation time. Chris will be sure that you get a check for your services."

"Get home for what, Mitchell?" she challenged, not budging from her spot on the corner of his desk. "At least I have a cat to greet me when I get to mine. You don't even have that. So why are you in such a hurry?"

Her insinuation that he didn't have much of a life would have angered him if it weren't so true.

"Why don't we go get a bite to eat?" Lisa offered.

Mitchell retrieved an overlooked folder from his desk and opened his briefcase to insert it in the inside pocket. "I can't; I have work to do," he replied, glad for a legitimate reason to turn down the offer. "That's why I'm taking these folders with me. Your duties here ended fifteen minutes ago. You could have been well on your way home by now. When I have this much work to do, my job doesn't end at the close of business."

"You're taking work home with you?"

There were too many questions being tossed out, but Mitchell was glad that at least they'd turned into questions that didn't unnerve him. "Most days I do, Lisa," he told her. "It's not uncommon."

"You're a dull somethin' 'nuther, ain't you?"

Mitchell broke into a hearty laugh. He couldn't recall hearing the term "somethin' 'nuther" since his grandmother had said it when he was a child. Grandma Kate was originally from a small town in South Georgia, and Grandpa Isaac had often referred to her chosen dialect as "country gibberish."

"Well, I've been called worse," he said as he closed his briefcase and scrambled the combination lock.

"You should smile more."

Her unexpected advice froze Mitchell in place for a moment. He finally became mobile again, but his movements were gradual. He didn't immediately voice his feelings, but he quickly learned that he didn't have to.

"See, there you go again," Lisa said. "Why do you clam up every time I pay you a compliment? Hasn't anyone ever told you that you have a nice smile?"

They had. During his childhood years in Dallas, Mitchell's grandmother had often referred to it as his mother's smile. Kate had had many good memories of her deceased daughter, and she referenced them as often as opportunities arose. Looking back, Mitchell felt that she did it so that those same memories—memories of a woman he'd never even met—would be etched in his mind too.

Lisa broke the lingering silence. "Come on, Mitchell. How many chances like this are you going to get? Once Chris and I are married, I won't be as free to spend this kind of time with you. I know there are things in that handsome head of yours that you want to talk about."

"Lisa . . ."

"Your ex-wife, maybe?" she probed. "I heard that you'd been trying to contact her. I don't know why, though. Some things are better left alone. I know how hard it is to just forget the past. Especially when stones were left unturned and questions were left unanswered. I told you I've been there. But it's their loss. You and I are good catches, Mitchell. If Felander and Virtue were too blind to see that, then they never deserved us anyway."

"Look," Mitchell said. "I don't know what sent you

and your ex-husband to divorce court, but it wasn't like that with Virtue and me. We broke up because . . ."

Mitchell stopped himself. He couldn't believe he was getting into this with Lisa. What happened between Virtue and him was not her concern. Neither was it his business what caused her divorce from Felander. Chris told Lisa everything else. It was hard for Mitchell to accept the possibility that she really didn't know his story already.

"Go on," she urged.

"I don't think so, Lisa. It's time to get out of here anyway."

Mitchell grasped the handle of his briefcase and pulled it from his desk. As if she had finally conceded, Lisa wiggled her way off of his desk and stood. But when he turned to head for the door, her hand stopped him. It was one of those touches that only happened when Chris wasn't around.

"If you turn down my dinner offer, you'll leave me with no choice," she said in a tone that was similar to that of the girls in the 1-900 commercials. "I'd have to go back to my initial question of why you feel uncomfortable when we're alone."

"Lisa . . ."

"Are you uncomfortable now, Mitchell?"

He wasn't facing her, but she stood directly beside him, and Mitchell could feel her breath as she spoke. The atmosphere had gone far past uncomfortable. With her so close to him now that parts of her body touched his, there was little doubt left now about what Lisa was trying to accomplish. Mitchell was too stunned by her blatant actions to speak or immediately move.

"What about now?"

Her latest step forward had placed her mouth within a fraction of an inch from his face. She was so close, in fact, that her body pressed against his and her lips grazed his neck, sending a strange ripple of chills down his right arm.

A woman hadn't stood this close to Mitchell in quite some time, and certainly not one as beautiful as Lisa. Mitchell's mind was telling him to step away, but his body didn't readily agree. The brush of Lisa's lips turned into one kiss to his neck and then another. All Mitchell could do was stand there while his spirit fought against his flesh in an all-out war of good versus evil.

"Do you want me, Mitchell?"

Lisa's voice was a seductive whisper, but the sudden words that broke the silent, mounting tension were enough to snap Mitchell from the gaping abyss that had begun to swallow him whole. At first his defiance sounded more like an inaudible mumble, but with renewed strength Mitchell took the step backward that his mind had ordered him to take moments earlier.

"Get out."

"What?" Lisa was visibly caught off guard by Mitchell's words.

"Get out," he repeated, louder this time.

"Mitchell . . ." Lisa took a step in an attempt to close the gap that Mitchell's retreat had put between them. She reached forward to touch his face, but his hand was quicker than hers.

"Ouch!" she groaned as he grabbed her wrist and snatched her arm away.

Releasing her, Mitchell took brisk steps toward his office door and stood in the open doorway, pointing in the direction that would lead her down the hall and to the front door. "I need you to leave," he said.

"Mitchell, why are you . . . ?"

"Go!" he yelled.

Lisa winced at the sudden change in his voice level and tone. She hesitated for a moment, but did as she was told. Mitchell stepped back as she reached his office door, taking special precautions so that she wouldn't have to touch him during her exit. He remained in his doorway and watched her as she snatched her belongings from Barbara's desk and flung the door open on her way out. Mitchell waited until he heard the automatic locks on the front door engage themselves before he moved from his place.

With his footsteps heavy from the weight of the burden of guilt and shame had placed in each of his shoes, Mitchell dragged himself to his desk and pulled out his chair. He needed to sit and find a way to get himself together before attempting to drive home. A new battle had begun inside of him now. His best friend's fiancée had just made an attempt to seduce him. It was a failed attempt, but not by far. A part of him felt just as responsible as Lisa had been. If he had ended the conversation earlier, none of what had happened in the last two minutes would have.

How was he going to tell Chris about this? His friend would be crushed. And if Mitchell told him the whole story, of how refusing her advances hadn't been the easiest choice to make, he would probably be angry as well. But he had to tell him. Someway, somehow, he had to tell Chris what had happened. This was something that he couldn't keep from him. Even at the risk of hurting Chris's feelings and breaking his heart, Mitchell knew he had to tell him.

The sudden ring of his telephone interrupted his thought process. After a brief hesitation, pondering whether or not he should allow the after-hours call to go to voice mail, Mitchell made the decision to answer. A part of him hoped that it was Chris. Admittedly, it would be the choice of a coward, but telling Chris over the phone would probably be easier than doing it in person. Very few clients knew his direct number. Business calls most often came in through the general line at the receptionist's desk, and Barbara forwarded them accordingly. The odds stacked up against the call being from anyone other than his business partner. The fifth ring would send the call rolling over to voice mail. It was ringing for the fourth time before Mitchell picked up.

"Mitchell Andrews."

"Hello, Mr. Andrews? I'm glad I caught you. You're just the man I need to speak to."

It was a female's voice, but it rang with no familiarity. She sounded relieved, prompting Mitchell to assume it was a desperate client. The closer the year came to its end, the more he got calls like this from people who needed the prompt service of a capable accountant. It was the reason his briefcase was already stuffed with homework.

"Yes, ma'am," he said. "What can I do for you?"

~∽ sixteen ∽~

Virtue sat in the corner booth nervously rubbing her hands together and wondering how she'd allowed herself to be suckered into such a thing. Even when she was a child, she had never succumbed to dares in order to prove herself. But someway, somehow, she had been scammed into doing it today.

"This is stupid," she said, suddenly standing.

"*Sit* down, Virtue!" Beverly whispered harshly. It was the second time in less than half an hour that she had had to take on the tone of a chastising mother in order to prevent Virtue from abandoning her at Piatto Ristorante, one of Houston's contemporary Italian restaurants. "You have come this far, and I'm not going to let you throw your progress away. He'll be here anytime now, and you're not going to have him come all this way only to find that you've bailed out."

"*I* didn't have him come anywhere, Beverly; *you* did. You never should have called him."

"Don't you even try to pin this on me," Beverly scolded. "It's not like I didn't clear it with you first."

"I wasn't thinking straight, and you know it," Virtue defended. "Now that I am, I've changed my mind."

"Sit!"

This time the order came from between clenched teeth, and with reluctance, Virtue complied. Tears welled in the backs of her eyes, and she fought with everything inside of her not to let them overflow.

"I know this isn't easy for you, honey, but you're doing the right thing." Beverly's tone had softened, and she reached across the table and placed her hand on top of Virtue's. "That's why we got here so early, so you could have the extra time to get yourself together. I told you I would help you through this, and I will. Okay?"

Virtue nodded, but she didn't feel the confidence that she needed. Two days ago she'd been sitting right beside Beverly when she made the call to Mitchell's office and set up the Saturday meeting. It was obvious that Mitchell had been surprised to get the call, but it was even more apparent that Beverly had been happy to make it. Virtue had sat quietly and listened while all the plans were made. Flights were more expensive during the Christmas season, but he'd said that he'd rather pay the elevated ticket price than make the long drive.

The meeting among the three of them had been set for eleven thirty. Virtue glanced at her watch and noted that there were at least ten minutes of agonizing waiting left. And if he was the same Mitchell she'd married, they could easily add fifteen more minutes to that. She remembered Mitchell as being a man who ran late for everything. The only time he'd been early for any important appointment was on the day of their wedding. Mitchell had gotten to the church an hour before the scheduled time. He'd told Virtue that the day was too important for him not to have been there. He said the knowledge that he'd be walking away from the wedding with her on his arm was all the incentive he needed.

"Good morning."

Both Virtue and Beverly flinched in their seats. Neither one of them had noticed Mitchell's approach, and both of them were unprepared for his early arrival. Virtue turned her head away and used her unrestricted hand to dab at the corners of her eyes in an attempt to erase the tears that had begun pooling. Beverly pulled her hand from on top of Virtue's and slowly stood. Virtue heard the exchange between the two as they made their initial introductions, but she couldn't get herself to look directly at them.

"Hi." Mitchell's voice was softer than Virtue remembered. He almost sounded apprehensive as he spoke. "Mitchell Andrews."

"Nice to meet you, Mitchell," Beverly responded. "I'm Beverly Oliver."

"The pleasure is mine. Thank you for calling and setting this up. I mean that."

"I hope your plane ride was good."

"It was uneventful," Mitchell said. "That's always a good thing."

"I agree."

As the talking subsided, Virtue's insides quivered. It had been traumatic enough seeing Mitchell for that brief moment in Dallas. Now he stood within arm's reach of her, making small talk with her closest friend as if all were right with the world. The moisture inside Virtue's mouth evaporated, and her tongue adhered to the top of it. Her lips began to feel as though they were becoming parched and cracked. It was a feeling like none she'd ever experienced before.

"Excuse me," Beverly said.

Mitchell took a step back and gave Beverly the additional space she needed to move from the side of the booth where she'd been sitting and to relocate so that she would be sitting beside Virtue. She literally had to force Virtue over in the seat to make room for her wide hips.

"Please sit," Beverly offered, pointing to the opposite side that she'd just vacated.

"Virtue . . . thank you for meeting me." Mitchell said the words to her as soon as he sat, but Virtue had no words for him.

The first few moments were awkward, to say the least. Nobody spoke, and any noise that could be heard came from the tables nearest them. The thick layer of tension was only cracked when the waitress approached to take their orders. Beverly gave her order, but when it was Virtue's turn, she sat in the same position she'd been in since Mitchell's arrival—her eyes glued to the menu. She didn't even acknowledge the server's presence. Beverly nudged her, but Virtue's only response was the release of a soft gasp accompanied by a lone tear.

"Bring her the Piatto Chicken," Mitchell said, drawing the waitress's baffled stare away from his ex-wife. "As a matter of fact, make that two orders of Piatto Chicken with the lemon butter sauce on the side, please. Also, bring the lady a cup of hot chocolate, with marshmallows if you have it. A cup of hot water will be fine for me. Thank you."

"I'll bring those out for you in a moment." The waitress tossed Virtue one last look of bewilderment and then left the three of them alone once more.

Mitchell still knew her well, and Virtue was uneasy with having to admit that truth to herself. Seafood had always been her favorite, but when they'd been together, they had dined Italian often. Mitchell couldn't have known that the specialized grilled chicken dish was what she'd had her mind set on ordering, yet he'd ordered it on her behalf without even being given a hint. Virtue was left a bit confused by his request for hot water, but she hadn't overlooked the fact that he remembered her favorite hot beverage. With all of that, she still never took her eyes from the table in front of her.

"It's okay, Virtue," Beverly said as she placed a comforting arm around her friend.

Virtue wanted to look in her mentor's eyes for additional confirmation, but she couldn't. If she brought her eyes up from the table, she'd not only see Beverly, but she'd be forced to look at Mitchell as well. She wasn't ready to do that. The persistent quiet was getting to be too much to suffer, though. Virtue was just about to pick up her purse and demand that Beverly let her out of the booth when Mitchell spoke.

"I'm sorry, Virtue."

Her body tensed at the words that Beverly had presumed he'd say. Those were the words, Virtue had been told on more than one occasion, that would give her closure and at the same time allow Mitchell the reprieve he needed in order to move forward. They were the words that would set him free, the words that would allow her to release him. Another tear dropped from her eyes onto the table.

"You don't have to say anything," Mitchell told her. "Just let me talk. Let me get this off of my chest, and I promise I'll never impose on you again."

Virtue shifted her eyes for the first time since Mitchell had taken the seat across from her. Her stare traveled from the table to Beverly's hand, which rested a few inches from Virtue's original focus point. Her own hands were locked together in her lap, and Virtue squeezed her fingers together, hurting her hands as she tightened her hold. Mitchell spoke again.

"I don't deserve anything from you, but there are some things that I need to say, things that I desperately need you to hear, so I thank you for being here. I know it wasn't an easy decision."

Virtue's body felt cemented in its position. She was grateful for the napkin that Beverly used to absorb the tears that continued to stream from her eyes. More would be spilling soon, but for the moment Virtue was able to see the table more clearly.

"I made a mistake," Mitchell said and then quickly corrected himself. "*Two* mistakes. When I finally owned up to my problems, I sought help for both my drinking and my anger. During my therapy, I was told that many times the victims in situations like ours blame themselves in some way for what happened. I'm not saying that you blamed yourself for anything, but if you do or if you ever did, I need you to know that none of what happened was your fault."

Oh, I know it wasn't my fault. If you think I've blamed myself in any of this, you couldn't be more wrong! That was what her insides screamed, but Virtue knew that she couldn't voice it. Not with Beverly, the woman who had been her counselor for a year, sitting right beside her. Virtue had told Beverly *everything*; and even now, as her former therapist nodded her head at Mitchell's words, she'd already given Virtue's one-time sense of guilt away.

Their waitress returned, bringing with her three plates of food that teased the nostrils. As delicious as it smelled and as hungry as she was, Virtue knew that she wouldn't be able to eat hers. Her stomach had begun tying itself in knots the moment Mitchell joined them at the table, and it hadn't stopped since.

Carefully balancing the large round tray in one hand, the waitress used the other to distribute the dinners and beverages to their owners. After she'd successfully dispersed the meals, the waitress tucked the tray under her arm and looked at each of them.

"Can I get you anything else?"

"You can go ahead and bring us a couple of carryout boxes," Mitchell said. "I doubt we'll be able to eat all of this."

Virtue blinked. He'd read her thoughts again.

"So, three carryout boxes, then?" the waitress offered.

"Oh, uh-uh, honey," Beverly said, shaking her head for emphasis. "Just bring boxes for the two of them. There won't be nothing left on my plate to carry nowhere."

Virtue didn't look up, but she heard Mitchell release a soft laugh. Imagining the expression on Beverly's face as she spoke to the server, Virtue probably would have laughed too. But just like the knots in her stomach wouldn't allow anything in, they also wouldn't allow anything out. She continued her silence while Mitchell reached across the table and beckoned for Beverly's hand. Beverly didn't hesitate, and in turn, she placed her unoccupied hand on top of Virtue's.

In the entire three years that they'd been married, Virtue couldn't recall one time when Mitchell had graced his food. In fact, she couldn't remember a time when she'd ever seen him pray in any form. She was astonished that he so freely did it in an open place such as this. When the blessing ended, Beverly wasted little time cutting into her steak. In a way, Virtue felt betrayed. The comforting arm that had been around her for the duration of Mitchell's spiel had now left her to help feed its owner a ribeye. Virtue made no attempt to eat, and neither did Mitchell. But Beverly didn't seem affected by their decisions.

"You never deserved it, Virtue," Mitchell said while retrieving a packet of apple cider mix from his pocket and emptying it in his cup. "All you ever were to me was good. I couldn't have asked for a better wife, and I certainly couldn't have asked for a more beautiful one."

His latest words caused Beverly to pause from her meal but not for long. The words had a different effect on Virtue. The skipping of her heart irritated her. As far as she was concerned, nothing Mitchell said should affect her in a positive manner. She *knew* she had been good to him. She didn't need him to validate what kind of wife she'd been.

"I know none of what I say means much to you now," he said. "But it means a lot to me that you'll allow me say it. I loved you, Virtue. I still . . ."

Everything seemed to be placed on pause. Mitchell stopped his sentence. Beverly stopped in the middle of her newest cut. Virtue's heart stopped . . . but ironically she could still feel it pounding in her ears. When Mitchell spoke again, he'd chosen to leave his last thought dangling.

"Seven years is a long time. Every Christmas I think of another year that my stupidity cost me. Now here it is again. Christmas is just days away. Our tenth anniversary, or what would have been, is just days away. And instead of being able to celebrate it the way I should have, I'm forced to once again look the man I used to be right in the eye and see what a fool he was."

Beverly finally began eating again, but her movements had become slower. She had managed to keep her feelings to herself, but Virtue knew that as soon as they were alone, Beverly would have a lot to say. Probably more than she wanted to hear.

"I need you to know that I'm not that man anymore, Virtue," Mitchell continued. "I'm sorry for everything he did to you. For those two years of having to hear him rant and rave about things that didn't make sense. For the curses that he yelled at you and for the times that he told you that you would never succeed as a dancer. For the day he even thought in his drunken mind to draw back his hand to hit you . . ."

The steadiness in Mitchell's voice broke, and for the first time Virtue was tempted to look up at him. Maybe she just wanted to see if the genuineness that saturated his voice showed any signs of itself in his eyes. She didn't know the reason, but she now struggled to keep her eyes staring at the table. Mitchell cleared his throat in an attempt to keep his emotions in check, and then he spoke again.

"I'm sorry for everything he did to you." His voice was barely above a whisper. "For what it's worth, I've been clean for quite a while—three years, actually. Betty Ford opened my eyes, but it was God who gave me the sight to see."

Virtue looked out the corner of her eye and saw Beverly place her knife and fork on her plate. She'd lost interest in her food just as the waitress brought the requested carry-out boxes. Noting that neither Mitchell nor Virtue had touched their food, the woman became concerned.

"Was everything all right with your meals?"

"The meals are fine," Mitchell answered, tossing her a look of appreciation. "We just decided to take them with us, that's all."

"All right then," she replied with a satisfied smile. "Will these be on separate checks?"

"No," Mitchell said, overriding Beverly's nod. "A single check is fine."

Once the waitress was gone again, Mitchell slid his plate to the side and used the empty space in front of him as a prop for his elbows. "As much as I know that God has forgiven me, I wanted to ask your forgiveness too, Virtue. You don't have to answer me now. You don't have to answer me ever. But I needed you to know that I am sorry and that I'd take it all back if I could. If you don't find it in your heart to forgive me, I can't exactly say that I blame you. But I hope that you can see beyond the man who hurt you and see the sincerity in the man sitting across from you now. I promise you, they're not the same people."

⁓ Seventeen ⁓

*E*funsgun Fynn had never considered himself to be a jealous man, but today he wrestled with the green-eyed monster in a way that was foreign to him. He should have been putting the finishing touches on the dramatization that the youth department would be performing next Saturday. Instead, he stood at the window of his office, looking at the world outside and wondering what had become of the meeting that his chosen bride had had with her former husband.

In hindsight, Fynn hoped he hadn't been too harsh in the delivery of his words to Virtue. He truly did love her, but in his attempt to draw her close to him, he felt that he may have pushed her away.

"It's a shame what the white man's beliefs have done to the mentality of our people," Fynn said aloud. His father had taught him early in life that a weak mind made a man more susceptible to deadly disease than did a weak body.

"Sick bodies are far easier to heal than sick minds," Obatala had said on many occasions while his sons sat at his feet. "You must never relinquish your place as a man. The Creator made you to be the strongest and the highest of any other. People may strip you of many things as you grow older, but never allow them to strip you of your manhood. Sometimes it's all you've got."

No one knew better than Fynn about how his people defined marriage. Realizing that she was born and raised in this foreign country called America, to parents who identified themselves as Americans, he even understood Virtue's ignorance. The weak minds of Blacks in America had been instilled with worthless information that was intended to rob them of the principles of their motherland. Little girls here had been raised to believe that education was the key to get them to the places in life that they wanted to be, but Fynn had been taught differently.

Education belonged to the leaders of the family. Men were the ones who needed the wisdom that came in textbook form. This was especially true in the United States. Black men needed to be educated so that they could know when they were being lied to and manipulated by those who thought of themselves as superior.

"An ignorant man is a dead man," his father had often said. "And a dead man is worth nothing."

Although Obatala was only a toddler when his family migrated to the United States, he had always held strong to his roots and passed the importance of doing so on to his children, particularly his boys. Fynn's grandfather, Bomani (meaning warrior), spoke only French, but managed to be successful at bringing his family to the States in search of a better life for them. Conditions in Niger had been very poor, even worse than today. Life expectancy was low, and there was little adequate work to be found. Although Bomani had left his native land, he too remained true to many of the traditions he'd grown up with. While attending the public school systems in America, Obatala and his siblings were taught English, and although his children were exposed to English all of their lives, Obatala made sure that all of them were fluent in their native language as well.

Fynn had made Obatala proud of the name he'd given him. Bestowing him with the name Efunsgun put Fynn in a place of honor that was far above his brothers. He had always been taught that more was expected of him than of any other of his father's seventeen children. Fynn was the first of his father's family to pursue a higher education, breaking the cycle of dependency that had kept them limited, even in their own country. He had attended one of the most prestigious universities in the United States and had earned a degree that accredited him to practice law, but Fynn never sold out to the unspoken principles of society. Success was required of him by God because he needed to be in the position to provide for his family. All that his wife needed—all that *any woman* needed—to do was care for her husband and bear the children he planted within her. That's what his mother had done up until the day she died giving birth to her fifth child in four years. That was all any of Obatala's wives had done.

In many ways, Fynn's values and beliefs mirrored those of his now-deceased father. But in other ways, he felt that they had drastic differences. Religion was probably their most profound point of divergence. Like many people born in Niger, Obatala followed the traditions of Islam. Fynn remembered crying for many days after he buried his father six years ago, but now he found himself thankful that Obatala's short bout with colon cancer had ended with the disease being the victor. Christianity hadn't become Fynn's way of life until a year after his father's demise. As proud as Obatala had been of his firstborn all of his life, Fynn knew that his father would have all but disowned him had he still been living when Fynn accepted Christ. As much as Fynn believed that he'd made the right choice when he opted to follow the ways of Christianity, he knew that the decision to do so would have been much harder, perhaps even impossible, to make during his father's lifetime.

"Knock, knock," Elder Bradley interrupted while simultaneously hitting the frame of the open door with his knuckles.

Fynn turned and smiled. Elder Bradley was the man who had led him to Christ. Over the past few years, he had become like a father to Fynn, just as the pastor was to many of the members of Temple of Jerusalem Church. Just like, as a child, Fynn had wanted to be like Obatala, now he wanted the same with Elder Bradley. He hoped that one day his ministry would flourish so that thousands of people would respect him in his calling and be captivated by his ability to translate biblical knowledge. The seasoned pastor was a man in his seventies, but he remained in good health and had a mind as sharp as any man who'd only lived half his years.

"I'm surprised that you're still here," Elder Bradley said as he stepped inside. "I saw your light on from down the hall and stopped by to say hello."

"I'm glad you did," Fynn said, motioning toward an empty chair where he hoped his pastor would sit. "I think our youth are about ready for the Christmas gala."

"That's good to hear," Elder Bradley remarked. Sinking slowly onto the soft seat that the sofa chair provided, he grunted and then relaxed. "I spoke with Sister Virtue yesterday and told her that it might be a good idea for the two of you to get together and compare notes. She's doing a special solo performance, you know. It's been awhile since we've been blessed with one of her praise dances. I'm looking forward to it."

Fynn had chosen to sit in a chair that faced the one his pastor occupied. His eyes dropped to his lap during Elder Bradley's talk, and that didn't go unnoticed.

"Is something wrong, Fynn? She did call you, didn't she?"

Fynn nodded as he raised his eyes to look directly at

Elder Bradley. "Yes, she did," he said. "I spoke with her early this morning. She told me of her routine and where on the program she thought it would fit best."

"Good, good," the pastor said.

"I thought it would be a good idea if we met so that we could put both our heads together to map the program out from beginning to end."

Elder Bradley smiled at the idea. "Two brilliant heads are certainly better than one. Do you have something in writing that I can look over?"

Getting up from his chair, Fynn strolled back to the window and turned his back to the preacher. "She had other plans," he reported. "She couldn't meet with me."

"Oh?"

Fynn knew that Elder Bradley was aware that he and Virtue had gone out on a couple of occasions, and he was sure that his wise old pastor also had some inkling of his continued affection for the leader of the church's praise dance team. It would be no great surprise if Fynn told him why the meeting that she was in today didn't sit well with him. He turned from the window and faced Elder Bradley.

"Because of my schedule today, I needed to be able to meet with her this morning at eleven o'clock. She told me that she had plans and couldn't be accommodating." Fynn said the last word of his sentence as though it was distasteful to his mouth. The unconscious grimace that followed displayed his irritation that she'd labeled her meeting with Mitchell more important than her meeting with him.

"Couldn't you set your meeting on a different date?"

"I needed to meet with her at eleven o'clock *today*."

The sudden sternness in Fynn's voice caused Elder Bradley's eyebrows to raise and him to sit forward in his seat. It appeared to catch Fynn by surprise as well. He immediately cleared his throat and threw an apologetic look toward his pastor.

"I'm sorry, Elder Bradley. I didn't mean . . ."

"You're angered by her inability to meet you on the date and time that you set in place?" The preacher's question cut Fynn's apology short.

Fynn turned back to the window and took a moment to gather his emotions. He'd already spoken too soon once; he didn't want to disrespect his pastor any further. However, Fynn did want to be totally honest. He was certain that his pastor would understand. He'd watched Elder Bradley be a leader in both the church and his home. He'd been a staunch disciplinarian to his children, and his wife showed him nothing but the utmost respect. Elder Bradley didn't come from the same place that Fynn did, but Fynn could see the African roots in him. He would understand and agree.

"Virtue wasn't *unable* to meet with me this morning," Fynn explained. "She *chose* not to."

"And that disturbs you. Why?"

His slowness to grasp the symbolism surprised Fynn until he realized that he'd failed to tell the pastor who it was that Virtue had chosen to meet instead. "Her meeting this morning was with Mitchell Andrews."

A look of confusion covered Elder Bradley's face as he tried to put the pieces together.

"He's her ex-husband," Fynn explained. "She chose to meet the man who beat her years ago rather than to meet with me."

The newfound information warranted that the pastor change his position. He rocked back and forth twice before releasing another grunt that brought him to his feet. Fynn watched him pace the length of Fynn's office once before coming to a stop and facing him.

"I wasn't aware that she knew of his whereabouts," he said.

"Apparently he found a way to contact her and wanted to meet with her in person. She didn't want to give me the details at first, but when I kept insisting that she meet with me this morning over breakfast, she finally told me the truth."

Elder Bradley spoke again. This time it was as if he was speaking to himself more than to Fynn. "I remember the time when she was so adamant about never wanting to see or hear from her husband again. I wonder what he could have had to talk about that was important enough to change her mind."

"*Ex*-husband." Fynn made a noble attempt to hide his brewing anger at his pastor's passive behavior, but exasperation could be detected in his words. "And what does it matter what he wanted to discuss? She should not be meeting with him for any reason, and she certainly shouldn't have chosen to meet with him over me."

Elder Bradley took several steps to close some of the space that separated him from Fynn, who continued to stand in front of his window. The pastor came to a stop directly in front of Fynn's desk. When Fynn turned from the window, their eyes locked. Elder Bradley's narrowed eyes told Fynn that his pastor was not pleased.

"You can't say who she should and should not meet with, Fynn. That's not your decision to make. Perhaps her meeting with her *ex*-husband was warranted. The matter that they had to discuss may have been time sensitive. And even if it was just a leisure meeting, there is no law against it."

"You cannot be serious," Fynn said in disbelief. "Would you feel the same way if *your* wife chose to meet a former lover over giving you the time with her that you asked for?"

"It's not the same thing."

"But it is, Elder Bradley. You and I are both men, and we should both be able to expect the same level of respect and consideration. How can you be for one situation and against the other?"

"Because the scenarios are very different."

"Why?" Fynn challenged. "Because one involves you and the other involves me?"

"No," Elder Bradley said. "Because Lillian is my *wife*."

"And Virtue is *my* . . ." Fynn stopped himself this time.

Elder Bradley tilted his head, and confusion was in his eyes as he glared at the youth pastor of Temple of Jerusalem. Fynn read his body language well. He knew that Elder Bradley was just a moment away from declaring him incompetent for the position that he held. He had to somehow break through seventy-four years of non-ancestral beliefs that had, no doubt, been drilled into his pastor's non-African brain. Fynn had to get him to understand his plight.

"Elder Bradley," he began. "You have to understand that I'm a proud man, preceded by generations of proud men. The things that we are taught to accept as normal in the United States aren't truly normal to our people. I understand that Sister Bradley is your wife under a law that for years our people have been forced to live by. I understand that, I respect that, and I honor her as such. However, in our true culture, such rituals as are carried on here are not necessary to make a man and woman one. In Niger, men can pick their brides without the years of courtship and the waste of thousands of dollars on ceremonial rubbish that has no real meaning, even in the eyes of God.

"No, Virtue is not my wife in the way of American custom. But in the ways of our fathers, she has been spoken for. I have loved her for two or three years now. I spoke with her just a day or two ago, and I think I was finally able to get her to see another way. Now this demon from her past has resurfaced, and I feel in my heart that he has come to deceive her and to once again do her harm."

"Fynn, I understand the ways of Niger," Elder Bradley said. "But Virtue doesn't live in Niger, and neither do you."

"But I honor my homeland, Pastor."

"If you want to uphold the traditions of Niger, that's fine," Elder Bradley emphasized. "But don't expect those around you to do the same. Your spoken claim on Virtue has no merit unless she accepts your claim as a valid proposal."

"As I said, I believe she understood better following our last conversation."

"I don't think so, Fynn," Elder Bradley said. "If she now saw the world through your eyes, would she have kept her appointment with her ex-husband, realizing that you wanted to meet with her?"

Fynn folded his arms and once again turned his back to his pastor. He wanted the conversation to end, but Elder Bradley kept talking.

"You are in a leadership position wherein you are trusted to be an example to many impressionable youngsters. Many of them are boys who are looking to you to be a role model. I've never known you to be anything but upright, Fynn, but I must tell you now that I cannot allow you to plant such unacceptable seeds in the hearts and minds of our church's children. I won't tell you what you can and cannot do with your own life. As long as I know that you are living by God's Word, I won't impose on your traditions. However, you must be able to separate your tribal or homeland beliefs from those that you know are widely practiced among the members of this congregation."

For several moments, it seemed as if silence had become a permanent fixture in the room. Fynn thought it best to remain quiet. He had never tried to impose his cultural traditions on the young members who served in the ministry that he headed, and he resented the fact that Elder Bradley felt the need to hint of an ultimatum. But the pity that he felt for his pastor and all people of African descent overshadowed his anger. In a sense, he felt sorry for the widespread ignorance that had taken hold of Blacks in America, and it made him all the more thankful that he was counted among the few who knew better.

~ *Eighteen* ~

*T*he Hyatt Regency Houston, conveniently located near the airport, had been Mitchell's choice of hotel for his short stay. The complimentary shuttle that provided transportation to and from the airport, which was one of its offers that swayed Mitchell to choose it, had also been the offer that almost made him late for his lunch appointment. Almost immediately after he'd checked into his room, he had realized his dilemma. Most of his weekend trips were business-related conferences that took place in hotels, and for them, using the hotel shuttle was the practical thing to do. But as soon as Mitchell put his belongings in his suite, he'd become conscious of the fact that for this trip he needed to have reserved a rental car.

For a moment, he had gone into a mode of panic. Mitchell had planned the trip down to the painstaking details, or so he'd thought. His morning flight to Houston had arrived at eight o'clock. He had no luggage to get from the baggage claim area, so all he'd have to do was call for hotel transportation to meet him at the pickup area outside the airport. He'd take advantage of the option for early check-in that the reservations desk had given him during Thursday night's phone call to the hotel. Then he'd get a shower and change into fresh clothing and still be able to get to the restaurant before eleven o'clock, more than a half hour ahead of schedule.

Once Mitchell realized his mistake, he'd been forced to create a Plan B. He took a quick bath and changed into the clothes he'd packed in his shoulder bag. The iron provided in the room wouldn't heat fast enough, so Mitchell could only hope that Virtue wouldn't see the wrinkles that his quick pressing job had left behind.

The airport shuttle ran once every half hour, so he had to wait ten minutes before he could catch a ride back to the same place he'd left just thirty minutes earlier. He felt both blessed and fortunate that Hertz had cars that were immediately available for rental. Not all that familiar with Houston, he'd had to get directions for the twenty-five-minute trip that eventually got him to Piatto Ristorante with only a few minutes to spare.

It was nightfall by the time Mitchell got back to his Houston hotel room. The meeting with Virtue and Beverly had ended hours ago, but he'd spent most of the afternoon riding around the city, killing time, just so he wouldn't have too much idle time to think about what had happened. All these years, he'd only been able to presume how his ex-wife had been affected by the anguish and abuse he had inflicted on her. Today, at the restaurant, it had become all too clear, and it was worse than he'd imagined.

The three of them had sat in the booth together for two solid hours, and not once did Virtue speak to him. Not once did she even look up at him or acknowledge his presence. The thought that she couldn't even bear the sight of him was heartrending. Had Beverly not been there, Mitchell would have had no one to interact with. At first, he'd been disappointed when the woman called him and said that she would be accompanying Virtue to the meeting. Mitchell had hoped to have some private time with his former wife to say the things he'd been forced to hold inside of him for years. But after sitting with them and seeing Virtue's hurt materialize itself in the form of unending, silent tears, Mitchell was grateful for Beverly's presence.

Beverly had tried to get Virtue to talk to Mitchell, but she remained quiet and unresponsive. It was Beverly who thanked him for owning up to his mistakes and being brave enough to admit to them and ask forgiveness. Through Beverly, Mitchell found out that she'd been more than Virtue's friend; she was the professional who had gotten Virtue through the roughest time following their divorce. Beverly was selective in her revelations, but she'd disclosed enough for Mitchell to know that both his and Virtue's paths to healing had led them down a road wherein they'd found Christ.

Even now, when he recalled the moment that Beverly had told him, Mitchell smiled. In the end, that was the most important part. He understood that Virtue was still working through remnants of the pain, and although she hadn't voiced whether or not she accepted his apology or was willing to forgive him, Mitchell found comfort in knowing that Virtue didn't have to face her fears alone.

He could point fingers and say that if she truly knew Christ, she should have no problem getting over the ugly past that he'd put her through. But Mitchell could relate to her struggles. He still fought the demons of his past too. He hadn't had a drink in years, and he knew that God had delivered him from the evils of alcoholism. But every now and then something happened that reminded him that the battle was not completely over. Back then, drinking the vodka would temporarily free him from having to think of his failures. His newest temptation happened just hours ago, when he had seen the eternal tears that fell from Virtue's eyes. At least for a little while, a glass of vodka on the rocks could have rescued him from the image that seemed to want to etch itself in his mind, but Mitchell knew that drowning himself in the strong drink wasn't the answer.

Removing his coat, he sat on the edge of his bed and released an exhausted sigh. Mitchell kicked off his shoes and then eased his back onto the firm mattress and stared at the ceiling above him. Fresh memories of Virtue's anguish were eating at him like hungry piranhas. As tired as his body was, Mitchell knew that he wouldn't be able to sleep anytime soon. In times like these, there was only one person who Mitchell knew would know just what to say. Fishing for the clip that was attached to his belt, Mitchell pulled out his phone and dialed the memorized number. One ring followed another with no answer.

"Man, where *are* you?"

The last time he'd spoken to Chris was Thursday, shortly after he'd left work. Mitchell had called to tell him about the incident with Lisa, but at the sound of Chris's voice on the phone, he lost his nerve. They chatted for a while, and Chris told him that he had a follow-up doctor's visit scheduled for Friday morning. He explained that he wouldn't be in the office again until Monday, but Chris calmed Mitchell's growing anxieties when he ended the sentence by informing him that Barbara would return on Friday. That meant that Mitchell wouldn't have to deal with Lisa again, and it gave him a few more days to get up the nerve to tell Chris the painful truth about his bride-to-be.

"Well, you must be feeling better—that's for sure," Mitchell mumbled to himself as Chris's voice mail picked up.

He'd already left one message for him on Friday afternoon, letting Chris know that he'd be out of pocket for the weekend. Mitchell didn't give him any details of where he was going and why. He had been very uncertain about how the meeting with Virtue would pan out; and as far as he was concerned, if it had turned into a nightmare, the fewer people who knew, the better. Now that it was over, though, he needed to share his day with his best friend.

"Hey, Chris, it's Mitch again," he said after the beep had signaled. "I had something on my mind and just needed to talk to you about it. All I'll say right now is that guilt ain't nothing to play with. I'm in Houston right now, and something happened that has guilt lying right here in my hotel bed, taking up more space than another human would." Mitchell stopped to laugh at his own analogy and then continued. "My flight back to Dallas is tomorrow afternoon, so I won't be at church in the morning. If you get this message anytime before midnight, hit me back. I'm sure I'll be up until then."

He had just ended the call when the telephone beside his bed rang. At first Mitchell stared at the piece of equipment as though it were foreign. He'd not given anyone back home his room information and hadn't at all expected to receive any calls. After a moment's thought he reasoned that it must be a guest-services call to see if everything in the $180 per night room was to his satisfaction.

"Hello?"

"Mr. Andrews?"

"Yes."

"This is the front desk calling," the woman said. "You have a visitor here who would like to see you."

Mitchell paused. "A visitor? To see me?"

"Yes, sir," the attendant said.

Mitchell could hear the muffled voice of the woman asking his visitor for a name. He tried to strain to hear through what seemed to be the operator's hand over the mouthpiece of her telephone, but Mitchell could not hear the response. A split second later, the attendant's voice returned.

"Dr. Beverly Oliver?" She said the name as if she was unsure that the person waiting had given an honest identification.

Mitchell paused again. A flood of questions rushed through his mind, but he had no answers to any of them. "I'll be right down," he told the caller. "Thank you."

Among the questions that bombarded him was whether Beverly was alone. From the limited time that he'd spent with the two of them today, Mitchell had gathered that Beverly had taken on the role of a guardian. She attended Virtue in such a motherly manner that Mitchell was left to speculate that his ex-wife had latched on to Beverly after her parents moved from their home in Detroit.

Virtue and her mother had been extremely close. Peggy Monroe was an eye-catching woman who was defying quite well the signs of aging. Even approaching her mid-forties, she and Virtue looked more like sisters than they did mother and daughter. Peggy was the parent who had given Virtue her defined beauty and her shapely figure. Walter, Virtue's father, had never really made Mitchell feel like one of the family. He had always seemed to carry a chip on his shoulder about the man he'd given his daughter to marry. But on most visits, Walter had been cordial enough that Mitchell hadn't felt like a complete outcast.

Peggy had been different. She had embraced her son-in-law and never failed to greet him with warmth and love. Mitchell loved Peggy's hugs. They were snug and heartfelt. In return, Peggy enjoyed it when Mitchell would lift her from her feet during their embrace and spin her into a full circle before putting her back on the floor. She had been like a second mother to him before everything started going awry. Mitchell felt a twinge of depression as he thought of how disappointed Peggy must have been in him for turning into a monster. She must have been crushed when she found out he'd struck her daughter.

Smoothing out his shirt and tucking it securely into his slacks, Mitchell stood in front of the full-length mirror to be sure that he looked presentable. Walking into the bathroom, he opened his shaving pouch and pulled out his mouthwash, swishing the mint-tasting liquid around from jaw to jaw until he was satisfied enough to release it down the drain of the sink. Taking a brush, Mitchell groomed his low-cut hair and then he retrieved a personal-sized bottle of lotion and proceeded to moisturize his clean-shaven face, paying special attention to the high cheekbones he assumed he'd gotten from his father. When Mitchell looked at his image again, he almost laughed.

"What are you doing all this for?" he asked himself and then paused as though waiting for his reflection to answer. "Even if Virtue is down there with Beverly, she's not going to care one way or the other about your appearance. She couldn't stand to look at you at 11:30 in the morning, and she won't be able to stomach looking at you at 8:30 at night."

Mitchell's shoes felt as if they were made of metal as he made his way to the elevator that would take him to the first floor. His body wasn't overly exhausted, so he could only gather that it was mounting guilt that was weighing him down. When the elevator reached its destination, he took a moment to breathe before stepping out into the sparse lobby. A few people stood around chatting while others were just arriving and checking in at the front desk.

"Hi, Mitchell."

He turned to the voice that called from behind him and hoped that his disappointment didn't show as he greeted Beverly, who approached him all alone.

"Hi, Beverly. Is everything okay?"

Her smile relieved his forming fears. "Everything is fine, hon," she assured him. "Is there somewhere we can go and talk for a minute?"

Mitchell took a second to search her face. He looked for signs of whether he should doubt her claim that all was well. When he saw none, he scanned the lobby for an area where they could sit in private. Nothing looked promising.

"Are you hungry?" he asked. "The restaurant here is closed on weekends, but the lounge is open. We could go there for a bite to eat if you like."

Beverly beamed. "Well, that lunch we had earlier is gone from me now, so I could eat with no problem."

The simple exchange made Mitchell think of his carry-out plate. It was still in the backseat of the car where he'd placed it seven hours ago. The hunger that he'd been too preoccupied to notice, all of a sudden made its presence known. "Yeah, I could use a bite to eat too," he said.

Very few words were traded between the two as they made their way to Derrick's Saloon, the hotel's popular sports bar. Several television screens were positioned in strategic areas throughout the place, delivering images of different sporting events. Once Mitchell and Beverly were seated, they were quickly waited on and then left to themselves after they'd placed their orders. A bit on edge as to why she'd come to see him at this hour, Mitchell was tempted to say something to give the conversation a jump start, but Beverly beat him to the punch.

"Are you comfortable with talking about our meeting today?" she asked.

"Sure," Mitchell said, glad that she wasn't the kind to beat around the bush.

"I guess I should also ask whether or not you're comfortable about talking about your past with Virtue," she added.

Mitchell nodded slowly. "I don't think I have any secrets that I'm not willing to share."

"Good," Beverly said before propping her elbows on the table and looking directly at him. "I know that I don't have to try and convince you of how much you hurt Virtue."

"No, you don't."

"Please," Beverly said, holding up her hand to stop Mitchell from saying anything further.

They paused while the waiter placed their glasses of water in front of them, but Beverly began again as soon as she knew he was out of listening range.

"First, let me say that I'm not telling you any of this to hurt you. I honestly don't think I can inflict any more guilt, misery, regret, or shame on you than you've already endured."

Mitchell nodded in agreement but said nothing.

"As Virtue's therapist, I'm going to try and share as much of this with you as I can without breaking my code of ethics." Beverly took a thoughtful breath and then continued. "I have to tell you that I was very impressed with you today. Virtue has never shared much about you other than the details surrounding the breakup of your marriage. Sometimes even when we professionals hear such disturbing stories, we create mental images of the antagonist that fits the wrong that they are accused of doing. You don't at all match the illustration that I'd drawn in my head."

Accepting her words as a compliment, Mitchell smiled. But again, he remained quiet.

"It's been about five or six years since Virtue first visited Temple of Jerusalem. When I first met her she was, at best, a basket case. Still is, sometimes," Beverly added with a shrug. "I've come to love that girl like my own daughter. In a way, she *is* my daughter. I just didn't give birth to her.

"I know her not being able to get herself to even look at you today was a bit unexpected from your perspective. It was unexpected from my perspective too. I had to convince her to accept your meeting invitation, and it wasn't easy. She fought it tooth and nail, but she was no match for Beverly Jane Oliver." The smile that Beverly flashed was filled with triumph. Mitchell smiled too.

"Virtue has often told me about you, and most times she's in tears when she does. You hurt her, Mitchell. You hurt her real bad."

Swallowing hard to relieve his drying mouth, Mitchell turned his eyes to the table. He knew he'd hurt Virtue. The reccurring visions of the blood streaming down her face mingling with the tears that ran down her cheeks were visualizations that he would carry to his grave.

"I don't mean just physically," Beverly said, reading his thoughts with accuracy. "I mean in *here*." She tapped the left side of her chest as she spoke. "She wants everybody to think that the physical scar that she still carries on her head is the one that keeps her remembering the day you hit her. But I know that it's the one you left *here* that breaks her down."

Mitchell turned away. It wasn't news that he was unaware of, but it wasn't information that he wanted to hear either. Beverly reached across the table, placed her hand on his, and then resumed her speech.

"I'm so glad that you sought professional help. Lots of men are too proud to see that they need help, so I know with all that testosterone and ego that you got in you, seeking help was a big step for you too. But most of all, I'm glad that in the midst of it all, you found salvation. Ain't nothing too hard for the Lord," she said. *"Nothing."*

Mitchell forced a smile and nodded for the third time.

"I've asked Virtue a lot of questions about you over the years, Mitchell," Beverly revealed. "I've asked her if she's still hurt, whether or not she's still angry, if she thinks she'll ever fully trust again. . . . I've asked her everything, and you know what? She's always been able to give me an answer. Her most recent meltdown came after she saw you in Dallas. She sat right in my office and cried like a baby. Sometime during my talk with her, I asked her if she still loved you."

Her words captured Mitchell's full attention, and he looked straight into Beverly's eyes, not caring whether the hopefulness he felt inside showed on his face.

"She didn't give me an answer," Beverly said. "Every other question I'd asked up until that day, she'd had no problem giving a response. But that one was different."

"You think she still loves me?" Mitchell finally broke his silence.

"Do you still love her?"

"Yes," Mitchell said with no hesitation.

Beverly smiled. "One thing I have never done in my life is encourage a woman to go back to the man who abused her. When I sat across from you at the table this morning and listened to you speak your heart to a woman who wouldn't even look at you, you won me over. Do I think she still loves you? Yes, I do. If she didn't, it wouldn't still hurt her *here*," she said, tapping her chest once again.

They quieted again as their trays of food arrived. Reaching for Beverly's hand, Mitchell said grace; and when the short prayer ended, Beverly gave his hand a tight squeeze.

"It's not going to be easy, honey," she said. "As long as she has that scar to remind her, Virtue is always going to be fearful. But I want you to know that I'm in your corner, and God has been known to answer more than a few of my prayers."

"Thank you," Mitchell said as she released his hand. "Another chance with Virtue is something I've prayed for for a long time. I think I started praying for that even before I found a personal relationship with God. After awhile, after about a thousand prayers with no result, I accepted the fact that she was gone forever. And I told myself that I didn't deserve to get that prayer answered anyway. I didn't deserve Virtue. So I stopped praying for that and started hoping for just the chance to tell her how sorry I am that I screwed up both our lives."

Beverly picked up a french fry and twirled it in ketchup before bringing it to her mouth. "One thing I know for sure," she said, still chewing her food. "We ain't never deserved anything that God has ever given us. It doesn't matter how good or how bad we think we've been. Everything God gives us is done out of His mercy and grace, not because we deserved it. So, no, you don't deserve Virtue, but she don't deserve you either, Mitchell."

Having never heard it put like that before, Mitchell pondered her words.

"And you know something else I know for sure?" she said, adding more food to her mouth. "I know that sometimes in life we give up on God too quickly. Just when He's about to bless us, we give up. Sometimes it's prayer number one thousand and one that gives us our miracle. Don't you ever give up on God, Mitchell, 'cause sometimes what you're asking for is just one prayer away."

~ Nineteen ~

*O*nly six days were left until Christmas, and signs of the holiday could be seen all around the city of Dallas. There had been hints of the approaching festive day ever since Halloween ended nearly two months earlier. The city, as usual, had skipped right over Thanksgiving and gone from being decorated with ghosts and goblins to being covered in trees and tinsel. Blinking lights were everywhere, not to mention rows of stores that displayed signs to lure in gullible shoppers who would buy now and pay for the rest of their lives.

For Mitchell, Christmas had gone from being his favorite holiday to the one he dreaded the most. Now the day was a constant reminder of what he'd lost, but years ago, he'd eagerly counted down the days. When he was a child, Grandpa Isaac and Grandma Kate would use the little money they had and turn their house into one fit for the North Pole. Colorful lights could be found in every corner of their property, including in the hedges, on the rooftop, in the trees, around the pillars on the porch, and throughout the inside of the house. Every year his grandfather purchased a live tree from one of the local sellers. Once they set it up inside, the entire house smelled like fresh pine. Then on Christmas Eve, his grandmother would begin the task she enjoyed the most: cooking. Kate had always baked a large turkey and ham to match. There would be candied yams, macaroni and cheese, collard greens, cranberry sauce, yellow rice, and enough cakes, pies, and banana pudding to feed a small army.

None of it went to waste, though. All of his grandmother's busybody friends would stop by to trade the latest gossip and to eat. And Isaac's stogy-smoking, card-playing friends who lived in the neighborhood would pay their visits as well. Mitchell often wondered if any of them actually cooked for the holiday. With the mounds of food they ate at his home, they couldn't possibly have room to eat again when they returned to their own. He didn't mind, though. When the neighbors came by, so did their children and grandchildren. On Christmas, Mitchell felt like he had dozens of friends, although most of them he only saw one time of each year.

Even as he'd grown into adulthood, Mitchell favored Christmas over other holidays. Being that he hadn't been brought up in the church, Christmas was never about the birth of Jesus. Mitchell was a grown man and had given his life to Christ before he really knew the true Christmas story. Up until then, Mitchell had always thought that *Little Drummer Boy*, the touching animation that he'd seen many times on television, was factual. Every now and then, Chris would still bring up the story for a good laugh when people who hadn't heard it before were around. As embarrassing as it was then, sometimes Mitchell laughed too when he revisited the day that he flipped feverishly through his Bible to try to prove to his new best friend that the little boy carrying the drum really had gone to Jesus the night He was born to play music for the Savior.

When he had met Virtue and, for the first time, had someone he loved with all his heart to buy gifts for, Mitchell's appreciation for Christmas increased even more. He'd bought gifts for girlfriends before Virtue, but when he looked back, he could only label them as "flings." None of them came close to capturing him like Virtue had. Buying for her brought him joy. It was only befitting that they get married on Christmas Day. That year, she was the only gift he needed. And unwrapping her . . .

A car blew its horn and snapped Mitchell back to himself. The traffic light in front of him had turned green, and he'd been too engrossed to notice that he was holding up the people behind him who were trying to get to their Monday morning meetings and to the jobs that awaited them. Looking at the clock on the dash of his Tundra, Mitchell realized that he needed to be in a hurry as well. It was already ten minutes past opening time for Jackson, Jackson & Andrews.

Parking his truck, Mitchell felt a flutter in his stomach, and the mixed emotions he'd been battling since Thursday resurfaced. Yesterday he'd mustered up the courage to tell Chris but couldn't find him. Apparently Mitchell hadn't been the only one who decided to get away for the weekend. When he had arrived back in Dallas yesterday afternoon, he stopped by Chris's house, only to find him gone. Church services would have long ended before then, so Mitchell figured that Chris must have gotten away to celebrate his return to full health. And in doing so, he must have left his cell phone behind. That was the only explanation he could figure as to why Chris hadn't returned any of his phone calls.

"Good morning, Barbara," he said as he stepped into the warmth of the foyer and removed his jacket. "How was your weekend?"

It was the way he always greeted the faithful secretary on Monday mornings. Although he hadn't met most of her family, Mitchell knew the names and ages of each of Barbara's children. She spoke often of how disappointed she'd been in the way they'd turned out. Her oldest son was unwilling to work, so he'd formulated an on-the-job accident and had himself declared permanently disabled so that he could stay home and still collect a monthly check. Barbara's second son was a professional thief. He stole from store warehouses and then sold the items at a discount rate out of the back of his truck to patrons at hair salons, nail shops, in mall parking lots, or wherever he could unload them. Her only daughter enjoyed the finer things in life, but did so by using her body and her children. She made it a point to only date wealthy, married men. She had three children from three different relationships, and she collected a nice sum of hush money every month from each of their fathers. Generally, on Monday mornings, Barbara was glad to unload the burden of whatever new drama had unfolded over the weekend. But today Mitchell's question got a different reaction.

Standing quickly from her desk, Barbara put her finger to her lips and gestured for Mitchell to keep quiet. Her pace was fast as she rounded the counter and stood next to him. When she spoke, her voice was a low, frantic whisper.

"Mitchell, what did you do?" The panic in her face startled him.

"Me?" he asked, pointing to himself in confusion. "What do you mean?"

"I've just never seen him like this; he's furious."

"Who?

"Chris."

Mitchell followed the direction of Barbara's gesture and noticed that his partner's office door was closed. That was very uncommon. Both of them kept their doors open unless they were in a private meeting with a client.

"Why?" Mitchell asked, still unsure of what Barbara

was talking about. "Does he have someone in there with him? Did they upset him?"

Shaking her head vigorously, Barbara answered, "No, Mitch. There's no one in there. He's angry at *you*. The door has been closed ever since he slammed it a half hour ago."

Mitchell turned his attention to the closed door once more. Rewinding the weekend in his mind, he couldn't think of any reason why Chris would be angry with him. Although Mitchell had taken the unscheduled trip out of town, he'd still taken the files with him and had used his laptop computer and the hotel's complimentary high-speed Internet service to work on the accounts. What he didn't get done in Houston, he'd stayed up late last night and worked on. But Chris wouldn't know about the delay in him working on the files anyway. He'd not spoken directly to his partner since Thursday night.

"Let me go put my stuff down in my office," he said to Barbara. "Then I'll see what's up."

"No," Barbara said, catching him by the arm. "He told me to tell you to come in his office as soon as you got here. He wanted that to be your first stop."

This was more than bizarre. Mitchell had never seen so much fear in Barbara's eyes nor heard so much terror in her voice. He took a quick review of the past few days once more. It suddenly dawned on him that he hadn't checked behind Lisa when she went through the files in Chris's office. If she threw something away during the purge project that she shouldn't have, it would be too late to salvage it. The trash had been picked up on Friday, and it would be extremely embarrassing if Chris had to go back to a client and ask for information to replace what he'd already been given. It would make him appear incompetent, and professionalism in the company that Willie James Jackson had founded wasn't up for discussion.

"Okay," Mitchell said as he released his belongings in Barbara's hands.

Taking slow, hesitant steps, he walked toward Chris's door and stood in front of it for a moment. Mitchell was surrounded by an eerie feeling. He would exchange his pounding heart for the stomach flutters he felt just moments ago any day. He turned to take one last look at Barbara and saw her standing quietly, clutching his leather jacket in her hand as if whatever was behind the door he stood in front of might eat him alive once he entered.

"This is crazy," he whispered to himself, barely moving his lips.

It couldn't be as bad as Barbara had described. Even if needed files had been destroyed, Mitchell was willing to take the blame and accept the responsibility to personally make it right. The embarrassment would be great, but he could handle it. Balling his tingling fingers into a fist, Mitchell knocked, not having any idea what to expect. He heard a delayed silence and then the scuffle of a chair. The voice that finally invited him to enter didn't sound much like Chris's, but it was.

Mitchell stepped inside and immediately caught his partner's glare. Chris stood behind his desk. His fair skin had a reddened appearance, but not like the look it had had when he battled the flu. This one came across far more like raw anger.

"Hey," Mitchell said. He tried to keep his voice steady, but it wasn't easy. "Barbara said you wanted to see me. What's up?"

At first his words got no reply, but when they finally did, it wasn't a return greeting.

"Close the door."

Mitchell was full of questions, but he obeyed and then walked toward the empty chair where Chris's clients sat when they came in to meet him.

"Don't even bother," Chris said, stopping Mitchell before he sat. From behind his desk, Chris kicked a box that slid out into the middle of the floor and came to a stop not far from where Mitchell stood. "I took the liberty of packing all of your personal belongings from your office. I want you to get the box and get out."

Chris's tone was uncharacteristically low, and his words were slow and threatening. Not knowing what to think about what he'd seen or heard, Mitchell stood silent, looking from the box on the floor to the man who looked like his best friend, but couldn't be.

"Wha . . . ?"

"Get out!" Chris ordered in a raised voice.

His anger was seething, and Mitchell could see it well. With every heated word he spoke, Chris's voice trembled with fury. But Mitchell couldn't just conform to the orders he'd been given. He needed answers as to why he was being treated so badly.

"What . . . what . . . what do you mean, get out?" he stammered. "What's going on, Chris? What are you doing?"

"I'm trying to save you from what's gonna happen if you don't get out; that's what I'm doing," Chris growled. "Now get your junk and get out of my place of business. Do you understand me?"

The lines in Mitchell's face deepened. "No, I don't understand you," he replied, getting more irritated with each passing moment.

"Well, let me put it like this. You're fired!" Chris screamed. "Did that break it down far enough for you?"

"Fired? Why? Man, we've been through too much. You can't do this." Mitchell felt his body trembling, but anger had little to do with it. He felt desperate, like a man who had just been evicted from his home and had nowhere else to go.

"Don't tell me what I can't do," Chris barked. "I can, and I just did."

"But I own a third of the company. You can't just . . ."

"Read the fine print," Chris interjected. "I can buy you out at any time if I deem it necessary. I do, and I'll have a check in the mail to you by the end of the week. The paperwork outlining the reasons for termination of partnership is in the box with the rest of your belongings."

"You're not making sense, Chris. Don't I at least deserve some kind of explanation?" Mitchell's body tensed, and he instinctively took two steps back as Chris rounded his desk. Every movement that his now-former partner made mirrored the hostility of his voice.

"*Deserve?* If I gave you what you deserved, you'd need a coroner to take you out of here. And how do you come off asking *me* for an explanation?"

All of a sudden, Mitchell wasn't sure whether he wanted one or not. But it was too late. And for what he was about to hear, he had in no way prepared himself.

"How about you give me one," Chris proposed. "How about you explain to me what happened with you and Lisa on Thursday?"

Mitchell's heart plummeted. He stared at Chris in silence and then said the only word that came to his mind. "What?"

It sounded foolish, even to him, but he honestly didn't know what else to say. Even so, Mitchell didn't think that his dumbfounded one-word reply warranted Chris's fist across the side of his face. For a brief time, Mitchell knew what it was like to be one of the cartoon characters he'd grown up watching on television. The world around him spun, and he saw stars and heard the chirping of birds. The next thing he knew, he had toppled over the chair that he was standing near and was on his back, looking up at three blurred images of Chris looking down on him.

Lying there for a while until he got his clear vision back seemed like a good decision, but Mitchell soon found that the choice wasn't his to make. Chris reached down, grabbed him by his shirt and tie, and pulled him to his feet before slamming Mitchell's back against the wall. Still dizzy from the first blow, all Mitchell could do was grunt from the force that now had him pinned against the wall.

"So you like hurting women, do you?" Chris said through clenched teeth.

"What?" Mitchell managed the one word again.

"My fiancée has a bruise on her wrist where you grabbed her when she tried to fight you off of her."

"What? No," Mitchell panted. He needed to explain himself. He needed to get it through to his friend that Lisa had lied to him.

"No?" Chris said in an almost-taunting manner. "Are you telling me that that bruise I saw was a figment of my imagination? That it didn't come from you? That you didn't grab her?"

Chris's grip around the collar of Mitchell's shirt got tighter with every question he posed. He felt his supply of air diminishing.

"No," Mitchell said, and then quickly changed his answer to, "Yes. I mean, I did grab her arm, but I didn't mean to bruise her."

"Just like you didn't mean to hit your ex-wife hard enough to bust a gap in her head?" Chris said as he pulled Mitchell from the wall and slammed him against it again, this time with more fury that drew a louder groan from his opponent. "How dare you try and make a move on my girl? I will *kill* you; do you understand that? I will kill you if you ever come near her again!"

Finally able to get his focus back, Mitchell looked Chris in the face. "Man, you know I wouldn't do that. You know me better than that. As God is my witness, I didn't try to force myself on Lisa. I grabbed her arm to keep *her* away when she tried to come on to *me*."

"Liar!"

This time Chris's fist found a home directly in Mitchell's rib cage. The impact sent him sliding down the wall and sinking onto the floor, doubled with pain. Mitchell tasted blood in his mouth, and he had an urge to vomit, but nothing came up, only pain.

"I believe this came with the job," Chris said as he reached down and stripped Mitchell's cell phone from the clip on his belt. "And since you don't work here, you won't be needing it," he added before stepping back from Mitchell's crumpled body.

From his fetal position, Mitchell saw the office door open. Barbara rushed in and immediately knelt beside the spot where he lay.

"Christopher!" she yelled as she looked up at her boss. "Stop it right now! Look what you've done. Your daddy would turn over in his grave if he could see how you've turned his office into a battleground." As she spoke, she pointed at the portrait of Willie James Jackson that was mounted on Chris's wall.

"No. What would make Daddy turn over would be for him to know what kind of maggot I hired to work in his office."

"Whatever this boy did to you, it can't be no worse than what you're doing to him," Barbara said. "Now stop it! Whatever it is, if y'all can't talk it out man-to-man, leave it alone."

"Man-to-man?" Chris said, curling his lips as if the idea of Barbara's words was absurd. "If we talk man-to-man, who's gonna speak for *him*? That ain't no man. A real man wouldn't try and mess with his boy's girl. That's about as low-down as you can get."

"I didn't do it, man; I didn't do it," Mitchell mumbled.

"You *did* do it!" Chris shouted. "Just like you beat up your wife and only God knows how many other women in your lifetime. You ain't nothing but a sick piece of trash that likes to beat on defenseless women who won't let you have your way. What? You need to beat on women to prove to yourself that you're a man? Is that it?"

Mitchell heard the hurtful, harsh words, but he could

say nothing in his own defense. The excruciating pains that shot through his entire body wouldn't allow him to speak. All of the energies that he could muster went toward breathing.

"You as much as admitted to doing it," Chris added.

Mitchell couldn't see him, but he heard Chris's footsteps. He must have gone to get his cell phone, because the next thing Mitchell heard was his own voice over the phone's speaker.

Hey, Chris, it's Mitch again. I had something on my mind and just needed to talk to you about it. All I'll say right now is that guilt ain't nothing to play with. I'm in Houston right now, and something happened that has guilt lying right here in my hotel bed, taking up more space than another human would.

Chris stopped the message there, and Mitchell could hear him slam his cell phone on his desk. "You gonna tell me that wasn't you? What were you going to do? Come clean with me over the phone like the coward that you are? Lisa had told me about it Friday night, so I already knew what was up. Did you really expect me to call you back so you could try to clear your guilty conscience over the phone? It don't work like that, fool. If it was the last thing you did, you were gonna face me. For once in your life, you know what it's like to pick on somebody your own size. This is what it's like to fight a man, punk."

Mitchell heard quick footsteps again, and he braced himself for the next round of punishment. Barbara rushed to her feet and stopped Chris from getting any closer. Feeling a bit of his strength returning, Mitchell pulled himself up to his hands and knees and crawled through the pain of his movements. If he could make it to the wall for support, he felt that he could bring himself to stand.

"There ain't gonna be no more fighting in here," Barbara said. Her voice was sterner than Mitchell had ever heard it. "Now, you touch that boy again and I'm going to call the police, Chris. I mean it. I'll call the police."

"I'm the one who should be calling the police on *him*," Chris said. "That's what I should do. I should have you locked up for assault and attempted rape for what you did to Lisa. Maybe being locked up in jail and getting raped a time or two yourself would be just the punishment you need. Or I don't know, punk, maybe you'd *like* that."

Chris's words cut to the marrow of Mitchell's bones. To think that Chris thought he was capable of attempted rape was almost as painful as the ache in his stomach. And for Chris to wish him such defenseless torture behind prison bars just added salt to the wounds. The last sentence, Mitchell found degrading. Finally on his feet, Mitchell tried again to defend himself, but Chris's voice cut him off before he could even form his words. Although there was anger in his voice, Mitchell could hear an overtone of hurt and betrayal.

"Man, I can't believe you played me like that. You know how I feel about Lisa. We're getting *married*, man! All the women in the world, and you had to go for mine? You were supposed to be my friend."

"I am your . . ."

"You ain't no friend of mine!" Chris interrupted, throwing a look that said he was insulted that Mitchell would even try to convince him otherwise. "You ain't never been my friend. Now, I'm gonna say this one more time. Get your stuff and get out. And I never—and the operative word is *never*—want to see your face again."

~∽ Twenty ∽~

*B*everly sat at her desk at the Houston Center for Women and stared at the beautifully decorated card in her hand. Had she known what it was before she broke the seal, she would have tossed the mail out, unopened. Now, instead of throwing it in the garbage beside her, Beverly couldn't stop looking at it. She'd read the words at least ten times, but ten times just didn't seem like enough.

"It's a shame that anybody could be so cruel," she said through a heavy sigh.

It was five days before Christmas, and after the time she'd spent talking privately to Mitchell on Saturday night, Beverly had been in a festive mood. She hadn't known the man for more than a few hours, but he'd found a place in her heart, and she could only pray that Virtue would give both of them a second chance at happiness. Beverly had gone out after work on Monday and purchased a few items to decorate her office. This morning, before any of her appointments had arrived, she set up her tabletop Christmas tree and hung the colorful wreath on her door. Everything was good until she sorted through the mail that had been dropped in her box while she was away for lunch.

The invitation was exquisitely adorned in silver script writing on purple metallic card stock. Beverly knew that Dondra and Lester didn't really want her at their nuptials. In fact, she had doubts that they'd even had knowledge that the invitation had been mailed to her. Her instincts told her that the receipt of the announcement of the upcoming celebration had been orchestrated by Renee Bell.

For the life of her, Beverly couldn't figure out why Renee was so hateful toward her. Any altercation they'd ever had had been initiated by Renee, and Beverly had made it a point not to let the young twenty-something-year-old get under her skin. At least, she didn't let Renee *know* that she was succeeding in doing so anyway. Beverly had to admit that there were times when she wanted to grab the little troublemaker by the throat and squeeze until Renee's eyes bulged out of their sockets. But one thing Beverly's late mother had told her was never to reduce herself to the level of an idiot. And in Beverly's eyes, Renee personified Webster's definition. Sending her this invitation, Renee had reached her limit. Beverly didn't think she could take much more.

Finally loosing her fingers from the corners of the invitation, Beverly allowed the expensive paper to fall to her desk. She hadn't quite mastered the art of taking her eyes away from it, though. Beverly continued to stare at the words and the date that was set for Christmas Eve. Since Lester and Dondra had been seeing each other for quite some time with no marital plans, Beverly supposed that the pregnancy was what had put them in the sudden rush. It was hard for her to believe that this was the same Lester Oliver who wooed her for months and then stole a suit from his uncle so that he could look good when he took her out on their first date. That Lester, the one she had fallen in love with more than thirty years ago, didn't seem capable of being so wicked and deceiving.

When Lester's sins had first been revealed and Elder Bradley stripped him of his ministerial collar, Beverly remembered how horrified she'd been. She wasn't just hurt by her husband's blatant disregard of their marriage vows; Beverly was drowning in humiliation. She was ashamed for many reasons. For Lester to leave her for another woman was one thing. But for him to leave her for a child was another. Legally, Dondra was an adult. But compared to Lester, she was still a baby. Not only that, but many times Beverly had opened her house to Dondra.

When she thought about the many times that she'd gone so far as to feed her when she'd come over for one of the "meetings" that she needed to have with Lester, it almost made Beverly sick to her stomach. Lester had been the preacher who headed the activities ministry at the church. With her being over the dance ministry, Dondra's need to periodically meet privately with him had raised no red flags with Beverly. Now she had to wonder what had really gone on behind the closed door of Lester's office when Dondra was inside.

Beverly sighed. It was water under the bridge now, but that didn't stop her from wondering what had pushed Lester to step outside their marriage for satisfaction. *Could it really have been about my barrenness?* This wasn't the first time she'd mulled over that thought. Renee's malicious remark had struck a tender chord with Beverly, but she refused to let the woman know it. That would have been just what Renee wanted, and Beverly wouldn't dare give her the satisfaction.

That was one of the reasons she'd been so forgiving of Mitchell. He hadn't wronged her personally, but as close as her relationship with Virtue was, it had felt like it. It had taken him a while, but Mitchell had come back to Virtue and apologized. In Beverly's eyes, the cases of Mitchell and Lester were very different. Not only had Mitchell not claimed to know Christ during his time of wrongdoing, but he hadn't even gone to church. All of his abusive behavior had taken place during a course of time when he was a dysfunctional alcoholic.

Lester, on the other hand, wasn't under the influence of any type of controlled substance. He had put on a suit every Sunday morning and taken his place in the pulpit among the ministerial staff as though all was well with his soul. Lester had preached several times during the course of his lengthy affair, teaching on the evils of sin when he himself was entangled in a web of deceit in its worst form. And he'd never made the attempt to apologize. Mitchell's apology would have come earlier had he known of his ex-wife's whereabouts. Beverly still lived in the same house that she and Lester had shared for more than twenty years. He knew exactly where she was and had made no attempts at asking her forgiveness.

Now, he was about to marry his mistress and have a baby who would no doubt be mistaken for his grandchild. When Beverly thought of it, she almost laughed. *By the time that child grows out of diapers, Lester will be wearing them.* It was an exaggeration, but the image in Beverly's mind made for a good pilot for a comedy series. Her smile faded when she looked down at the invitation again. She took in a deep breath and then slowly exhaled. Believing that God had allowed her to endure the failure of her marriage so that she could counsel the women of the HCW with the compassion that they needed was what kept Beverly going. Before her own abusive situation, she'd only had textbook knowledge to use when she counseled them. Now she was living proof that experience was the best teacher.

A knock at her door tore her eyes from the invitation once again. Ripping the card in half, she disposed of it in the can beside her desk. Then she stood to greet her early arriving client.

"Come in."

"Hey," Virtue said as she opened the door and ducked her head inside. "You're not busy, are you?"

"Not for another twenty minutes," Beverly said with a grin. "Come on in."

Beverly knew the purpose of Virtue's visit even before she began speaking. She had no doubt that God had answered Beverly's only constant prayer when He placed Virtue in her life. She'd almost given up on the hopes of having a daughter when she met Virtue. It hadn't been in God's plan for Beverly to give birth in the traditional sense, but she'd gotten her daughter anyway. And just like natural mothers and daughters, she and Virtue had their quarrels from time to time. Last night had been one of those rare occasions when it had turned from a heated disagreement to an all-out war of words.

"Would you like something to drink?" Beverly offered as she walked in the direction of her water cooler.

"No, thanks."

She filled a cup for herself and then carried it back to her desk, where she drank a few swallows and then took her seat. The stillness that covered the office for only a few seconds felt much longer.

Beverly was tempted to speak first, but she chose to wait so that she could get a feel for what was going through Virtue's mind. She'd been quite upset last night, and Beverly understood why, but she still disagreed. She'd told Virtue the details of her private meeting with Mitchell, or at least she'd tried to. Virtue had become so irate at the very onset of the conversation that Beverly had little opportunity to explain anything. The short but overly heated confrontation had ended with Virtue storming out of the house. She had returned at some point during the night, but Beverly had long since lost her battle with trying to stay awake to wait for her. Now was the first time she'd seen Virtue since the argument ended.

"How does he look?"

189

Thrown by Virtue's peculiar question, Beverly didn't immediately understand. "How does who look?"

"When I ran into him in Dallas, I saw him, but I didn't really *look* at him. I was so caught off guard and frightened; plus everything happened so fast that I can't even remember what he looked like. Then last weekend, I couldn't force my eyes off of the table. There were a couple of times that I actually wanted to look at him, but I couldn't. So I feel like, although I've been in his presence twice in the past few weeks, I still haven't seen him in seven years."

Beverly's lips parted in a broad smile. "Well, I don't know what he looked like as an alcoholic, but he cleans up real good," she said.

Virtue's eyes wandered, scanning the wall of the office and coming to a stop, fixed on a potted green plant on a stand in the corner behind Beverly's desk. When she spoke, she kept her eyes locked there as if she could see a slide show of her past.

"He used to be a handsome man who wore his hair in the neatest fade that I'd ever seen. He went to the barbershop early every Saturday morning and got it trimmed. He was clean-cut and had the darkest eyes and the brightest smile around." She paused and wrung her hands together, but she didn't break her stare. "Then when he started drinking, he stopped caring about everything, including his appearance. He lived for his next drink. Even his skin reeked of liquor. After a while I couldn't stand for him to touch me, not that he was trying to anyway. At least not in a good way. His hair grew thick, and he hardly ever combed it. Just covered it with this dingy old baseball cap that I would have thrown away if I wasn't so scared of what he might do. He grew a beard, and before long, he was looking much older than he was. He looked like an old drunk."

Beverly could detect the sadness in Virtue's eyes, but at least this time she wasn't crying. It was a small victory, but it was a definite sign of strength. When Virtue didn't offer any further information, Beverly assumed that it was her turn to speak.

"That was the old Mitchell, Virtue. None of us is built of stone. No matter what shape or form a person is in, God is able to remold them and make them into someone new. That's what He's done for Mitchell. That's what He did for all of us who, at some point in our lives, chose to walk with Him. We were all sinners who deserved nothing but death and eternal damnation. There aren't any good sinners and bad sinners. A sinner is a sinner, and the same destruction that awaits one, awaits all those who reject Christ. The Bible tells us that when we come to God, old things are passed away and all things become new. No matter how offensive, downtrodden, or even violent a person may have been at one time, God can forgive him and turn his life around. Mitchell has come a long way, Virtue. You want to keep envisioning him as that unkempt, intoxicated abuser who you left behind. But who he is now is far better than even the clean-cut man who you remember marrying.

"Do you really want to know what he looks like?"

Virtue nodded, and Beverly was more than willing to tell her.

"He's as handsome as he can be." She grinned. "He dresses well, he's clean-shaven, and his face is very youthful, just like yours. He still has those dark eyes that you remember, and I believe that smile of his could charm a cobra. If I was a few years younger, I might try to net him for myself; but since it's you he said he loves, I'll leave him be."

Barbara saw the look that covered Virtue's face when she not-so-discreetly disclosed the last bit of information. Knowing that Mitchell had openly declared his love for her meant something to Virtue, whether she admitted it or not. She stood from her chair and took a few steps across the floor. At first, Beverly thought that she was headed for the window, to look through the open blinds. But Virtue made an about-face and came to a stop at a small bookcase in the back of the office, where Beverly kept hardbacks of some of her favorite novels. Virtue ran her hands across the wood frame and then spoke with caution.

"How do you trust after what I've been through, Beverly? Not just the Mitchell thing, but you know my whole story. How am I supposed to just forget everything that happened and open my life up to something like this again?"

While Virtue was clearly torn, Beverly heard and saw even more signs of growth. The hostility that was in her voice as late as last night, when they'd argued, had dissolved. She still sounded confused and hurt, but Beverly couldn't detect the anger that had always been so prevalent in their past discussions.

"Don't let anything that anyone has done in your past make the decisions for your future. Don't give anybody that kind of power over your life, Virtue."

"I'm scared, Beverly."

"I know. But like I told you the first day we talked, I'm with you every step of the way. More important, God is too."

Virtue turned from the bookcase. "I want to tell Mitchell that I forgive him. I don't know if I'm doing it for my sake or his, but I want to do that. Beyond forgiving him . . . I can't make any promises."

"And I don't think he expects you to," Beverly said as she flipped through her Rolodex and picked up her telephone and began dialing.

"What are you doing?" Virtue asked.

"I'm calling Mitchell."

"Right now?"

"Yes," Beverly said with a smile as she listened to the telephone ring. "It will be easier this way than in person, don't you think?"

On the third ring, a woman's voice answered.

"Jackson, Jackson & . . ." She paused and then continued. "May I help you?"

"Yes, please," Beverly said. "I'd like to speak with
Mitchell Andrews."

There was another pause.

"Mr. Andrews is not in. Would you like to speak to
Mr. Jackson?"

"No, thank you. Can you tell me when Mr. Andrews
will be in?"

This time the pause lasted longer, raising Beverly's
suspicions.

"Uh . . . Mr. Andrews no longer works here, ma'am,"
the receptionist said. "Mr. Jackson is handling all of his accounts. I'll switch your call to him."

"No," Beverly quickly said. "This is a personal call.
When did he stop working there? I just spoke to him from
his office last week."

"His last day was Monday, ma'am."

Beverly grimaced and looked at Virtue in confusion.
"Did he go to another office?" she probed. "Can you tell
me how I might be able to reach him?"

"I'm sorry, ma'am. I've given you all the information
that I can. Thank you for calling."

Before Beverly could say another word, she heard the
dial tone that indicated her call had ended.

"What's the matter?" Virtue asked.

Beverly hung up the phone and stared at it for a moment before looking at Virtue. "Did he leave you any more
numbers besides the one to his office when he left the message on your voice mail that day?"

"No, that was the only one. Why, Beverly? What's the
matter?" she repeated.

"I'm not sure, but when I find out, I don't think I'm
gonna like it."

~∽ Twenty-One ∽~

*T*he hands on his desk clock told Rev. Inman that he only had a few minutes left in his final premarital session with Chris and Lisa. And since he had another meeting immediately following theirs, there would be no time to linger afterward for small talk or to say the things that he hadn't said during the ninety-minute appointment. As with all of the meetings before, Chris and Lisa had sat hand in hand like any couple in love would. But something was different about this meeting, and the signs hadn't escaped Rev. Inman's notice.

There were times when Chris's mind seemed to venture away from their conversations, and every now and then, his countenance reflected unhappiness. He participated and even laughed during their interactions, but Rev. Inman could see through many of the orchestrated smiles. Several times during their meeting, Lisa used her unoccupied hand to stroke the back of Chris's. It was a subtle change from the previous sessions, but Rev. Inman took note of that as well. Her strokes were more than touches of affection.

The pastor defined them as a means of comforting Chris. The question in his mind was: *Why does he need comforting?*

With the final minutes ticking away, Rev. Inman decided that it was time to address his concerns. Even after all of their meetings and all of the textbook answers he'd been given for the questions he'd asked, Rev. Inman was still uncertain about the pending union. He wouldn't be able to perform the ceremony if he didn't clear his own conscience.

"Are both of you ready for this gigantic step in your lives?" He smiled as he looked across the desk at them and took note of their nods.

"February tenth," Lisa announced as if he didn't already know the date. "You do have us marked on your calendar, don't you?"

"I do indeed. What a way to usher in Valentine's Day, huh?"

"Yes," they replied in unison.

"We have a few minutes, so I want the two of you to hear from my heart. We've gone through the steps that our church bylaws require, but I want to step outside of the handbook and speak to you outside of the role of a pastor. I want to speak to both of you as your friend, and after I've heard what you have to say, I'll share some things from my heart with you. I'd like to start with you, Lisa."

When she nodded in agreement, he continued. "We've talked about your past marriage and why it failed. What do you believe it is about this pending union that will be different?"

"Well, first of all, Felander was a fool," she said without hesitation. "He was always so jealous. Every time I left the house, he needed to know where I was going, who I was with, what I was going to do, and when I would be home. Christopher is way more confident and trusting," she said, tossing her fiancé a loving smile. "With Christopher, I feel like I come first and that I won't have to worry about him being insecure. I feel like I can go anywhere and do anything and he'll support me. I feel loved."

Rev. Inman looked toward Chris. "It'll be hard to beat that, won't it?" he teased, drawing laughter from the couple. When they calmed, Rev. Inman continued. "What makes you so sure that she's the right one for you, Chris?"

"I think I fell in love with her when I first met her," Chris began. "Lisa's the whole package. She's beautiful, she's smart, she's honest, and she loves the Lord. I can't ask for more. All of those things are important to me, but especially the latter two."

Rev. Inman nodded and then waited as Chris readjusted himself in his seat and seemed to struggle with what he would say next.

"You know, when Lisa first walked into the church a while back, she caught every eye in the building," Chris said. "There were brothers who tried to win her even before I got up the nerve to ask her out. But as beautiful as she is, I respected the way they all backed off when they knew the two of us had bonded. At least, I thought they had anyway."

Rev. Inman sat up straight. "What do you mean?"

"Sweetie, let's not talk about that, not today," Lisa urged.

"If it's an issue, it needs to be addressed," Rev. Inman said.

Lisa disagreed. "It's not an issue. It's just some trifling mess that never should have happened, and I think that if Christopher talks about it, it's only going to make him angry all over again. I don't want him upset. What's done is done. He did what he had to do, and now we're moving forward."

Rev. Inman looked from Lisa to Chris and hoped that this wouldn't be the end of the discussion. They only had five minutes of meeting time left, and Rev. Inman felt that they'd tapped into something that needed to be exposed.

Only a moment of quiet lapsed before Chris spoke again.

"No, babe," he told Lisa as he kissed the back of her stroking hand. "I want to tell this. I want Rev. Inman to know what kind of scum is mixed in with the good people of Living Word Cathedral."

Once again, he had his pastor's full attention. "Go on," Rev. Inman urged.

"I just had to break off my relationship with the closest thing that I've ever had to a replacement for my brother Jonah."

In slow motion, Rev. Inman reached up and removed his glasses from his face before placing them on top of his desk and looking back at Chris. "Mitch? You ended your friendship with Mitch? Why?"

"Because of this, that's why," Chris said as he lifted Lisa's arm and then rolled back her sleeve to reveal the bruise that still hadn't completely faded.

Rev. Inman got up from his desk and walked around for a closer look. "What does this have to do with Mitch?"

"He did it." There was returning anger in Chris's voice. "While my secretary and I were out of the office sick last week, I made the mistake of sending Lisa there to help him keep up with the workload. I guess he thought what was mine was his. He tried to make a move on Lisa, and when she refused his advances, this is what he did."

Rev. Inman looked at the bruise again and then back at Chris in disbelief. "I just find that so hard to believe."

"Well, he did," Lisa said accusingly.

"It ain't that hard to believe, Rev. Inman," Chris said. "See, what I know that you *don't* know is that Mitch used to be married. He was a sloppy drunk, and he used to lay into his wife all the time. He's got a history of battering women, Rev. Inman. It ain't so hard to believe once you know the facts."

"I've known about that for years," Rev. Inman said, catching Chris off guard. It could clearly be seen in his expression that he had no clue that the pastor had known all along what he'd just found out weeks ago. Rev. Inman continued. "Mitch told me about his past in the early days of his joining our ministry. I'm well aware of the two times that he struck his wife, but that was then."

"Well, *this*," Chris rebutted while simultaneously holding up Lisa's arm, "is now."

"And you *know* that this happened?" As soon as Rev. Inman had spoken the words, he could feel Lisa's eyes burning into his skin.

"I told him that it happened; so, *yes*, he knows that it did."

Never taking his eyes off of Chris, Rev. Inman rephrased his question. "Did you confront him about this?"

Chris released a short, frustrated laugh. "I did more than confront him; I clobbered him."

"You hit him?"

"No," Chris said. "I *beat* him. I should have killed him, so he got off easy."

Wiping his hands over his chin, Rev. Inman took several slow breaths and walked back around his desk. The clock on his desk said he had less than sixty seconds, but he knew he needed more time. His next appointment would just have to wait. He turned back to face Chris.

"Did he admit to doing this?"

Chris grimaced and shook his head. "Of course not! It takes a man to admit to being wrong. Mitch is not a man; he's a sleazeball. He admitted to hurting her arm, but get this: He tried to tell me that Lisa was trying to come on to him, so he had to grab her like that to keep her off of him."

Rev. Inman's eyes immediately shot to Lisa, and in an instant, she turned hers away from him. He restrained himself well, but the preacher felt a level of annoyance brewing in his stomach. He had no doubt that what he believed to be true, was. Lisa had used deceptive tactics to tear two friends apart, and love had put shields over Chris's eyes, causing him to be blinded to what had really happened.

"Perhaps it would be a good idea to get the three of you in a meeting together to see if we can . . ."

Chris cut into his pastor's sentence with words that were drenched with rage. "I'm not meeting with him!" he said. "And I'm not asking Lisa to have to stomach being in the same room with a man who would do to her what Mitch did. No. We're not meeting with him."

"Chris, we have to find a way to work through this. You can't avoid Mitch forever. We have to worship together each week. You don't want that kind of tension looming."

"I ain't worshiping with him either," Chris said. "In my opinion, a man who is hurting women ought to be banned from the church. I can't believe you're going to let him still come here. What? You're gonna keep this all under wraps like you did with knowing that he had beat his wife?"

"That's enough!" Rev. Inman said, raising his voice for the first time. "If Mitchell Andrews did this to Lisa, then it will certainly be addressed . . ."

"What do you mean, *if*?" Chris asked. "I just told you that he said he did."

"I don't mean the bruise," Rev. Inman explained. "I mean the attempt to force himself on her."

"What? You don't believe me?"

Avoiding Lisa's question, Rev. Inman spoke again. "As his spiritual leader, it is my obligation to hear what he has to say before passing judgment. I cannot listen to one side of the story and draw a conclusion without giving the other party the same courtesy of a listening ear. Knowing about Mitch's past isn't a reason to hand down a verdict. The testimony he's lived since being a member at this church doesn't match what you are accusing him of. It's the testimony in *this* case that decides *this* verdict. Not the one from nearly a decade ago."

Chris rose from his seat and pulled Lisa up with him. "Well, you know what, Rev. Inman? With all due respect, if you're going to associate yourself with the man who basically tried to rape my fiancée, then I'm not sure you're the right man to perform this wedding."

Rev. Inman stood in silence for a moment, and then conceded with a slow nod. "Our reasons for saying so are quite different, Chris, but our conclusions are the same. But I hope that you will allow yourself to release this anger so that God can deal with you. Truth sometimes hurts, but ignoring it hurts worse. Lisa, I wasn't there, so I can't accuse you of being dishonest; but as God has given me the spirit of discernment, I can, with confidence, say that *something* is not being revealed. Whatever you need to tell your fiancé, it is only fair that you tell him before the wedding."

Rev. Inman saw a look of concern gloss over Chris's face, and he knew that he wasn't the only one God had been dealing with. Chris had his own misgivings, and Rev. Inman could see it in the brief moment of silence that followed the advice he'd just given Lisa. But in spite of Chris's doubts, Rev. Inman watched as he headed toward the door, pulling Lisa with him.

As they exited, the bride-to-be looked over her shoulder and caught Rev. Inman's eyes. Turning away quickly as if his stare frightened her, she closed the door behind them.

Rev. Inman shook his head in regret—not for the stand he had taken, but for what he knew was going to be the biggest mistake of Chris's life. As he walked around his desk to prepare for his next conference, Rev. Inman flipped through the pages of his calendar and then picked up a pen from his desk. With a slow stroke of his hand, he drew a single line through the words "Performing the Jackson wedding."

∽ Twenty-Two ∾

Mitchell couldn't believe that his life had come full circle. But as he lay in his bed and thought of how he'd once again lost the person closest to him, lost his job, and was now looking at a full bottle of vodka, contemplating whether it would help him make it through the agony, he realized that it had.

He'd finally gotten some relief from his physical pain. Monday morning, Mitchell had managed to drive from the office to his home after his altercation with Chris, but it had taken him an hour just to climb from his car and walk from the garage into his house. The pain seemed to worsen with every step. Once inside the house, he collapsed on the living room sofa, unable to go any farther. For hours he lay there aching from his head to his toes and feeling like he was slowly dying. Not even able to get up and go to the restroom, Mitchell endured the humiliation of reliev-ing himself on the fibers of his couch. He kept telling him-self that the pain would ease with time, but it never did. To Mitchell, it felt as if his ribs had been shattered and the broken pieces of bones were lodged throughout his body, piercing his insides every time he dared to try and become mobile.

Around nine o'clock he heard his doorbell ring. Lying still and pretending he wasn't home wasn't a problem. In fact, at the time, it didn't even seem optional. Mitchell wasn't expecting any company, and he knew that there was no chance that he could get up from the sofa to let them in anyway. He thought that if he said nothing, the person would soon leave. Instead, the visitor went from ringing the doorbell to an insistent knocking.

"Go away. Please go away," Mitchell remembered whispering over and over again.

"Mitch? Are you in there?" It was Barbara. "I see your car in the garage, and I just wanted to stop by and check on you. If you're in there, please let me in. I'm alone, and Chris doesn't know I'm here. I promise."

Mitchell almost became tearful. He couldn't believe Barbara had come to check on him. He'd figured that Chris had filled her in on all the details, and by now she would be just as angry with him as his friend had been.

"Mitch?" she called again.

"I can't open the door, Barbara," he said as loudly as his pain would allow him. Mitchell was glad that he'd decided to lie on the couch that was nearest the door.

"You can't open the door?" Barbara repeated. "Why?"

"I can't get up," he admitted. "I can't move. I'm hurt."

"You stay right there," she said, sounding almost as panicky as she had when he'd first entered the office that morning. "Don't you move at all, Mitch. You hear me? I'm gonna get you some help."

All Mitchell could think about was the fact that his slacks were still wet with urine. "No, Barbara. I'll be all right."

"No, you won't," she called back. "You stay right there."

It had been an embarrassing episode, but Mitchell had survived it. An ambulance, a fire truck, and a police car all arrived at his home in no time. With lights flashing and sirens blaring, they had brought half the neighborhood out to watch them pry the door open and load Mitchell onto a stretcher to transport him to the hospital. Barbara had followed in her car and stayed with him until he was admitted.

Mitchell had refused to give the policeman any details surrounding his injuries. He only told him that he'd suffered a fall. It wasn't the whole truth, but it wasn't a lie either. X-rays showed that there were no broken bones, but Chris's blow and the slams against the wall had left him quite bruised. The doctor told him that a little more force would have resulted in a fracture to his ribs. The damage from the blow to his head near his eye was more severe than the small bruise made it appear. It was the root of the throbbing headache that wouldn't go away. The force behind Chris's fist had been enough to damage Mitchell's iris. The doctor called it iritis and prescribed steroids and anti-inflammatory drops that Mitchell would have to administer daily until his follow-up visit. For precautionary measures, the doctor also advised him not to wear his contact lenses, so Mitchell was forced to wear his eyeglasses for the next few days. The medical staff had bandaged him up, given him some medicine to ease the pain, and then kept him overnight for observation. Barbara had been kind enough to use her lunch hour yesterday to pick him up from the hospital and transport him back home.

During those few hours away, while he was confined to a hospital bed, the stench from his earlier accident had built up in his home. He had thanked Barbara for removing the cushions from his couch and placing them outside on his deck so that they could air out until he was able to get them cleaned. While there, she had sprinkled a carpet-freshening agent throughout his house and then vacuumed before leaving to go back to work. Not once did she ask him whether he was guilty of what Chris had accused him of. On one hand, Mitchell had hoped for an opportunity to explain the truth of the matter to Barbara, but on the other, he didn't care anymore.

When he awakened this morning, Mitchell found that he was able to move with much less pain. He moped around the house for a while and then became depressed when he picked up his daily paper from his front door and flipped to the classified ads. The thought of losing the job he loved and having to find a replacement was too much for him to deal with. It was then that he dressed himself, climbed into his car, and drove to the nearest package store. The medicine had helped the physical pain diminish, but now Mitchell needed something for his mental anguish.

From his bed, Mitchell could hear his doorbell ringing. He could make it to the door today if he wanted to, but he didn't. So he continued to lie flat on his back, allowing his eyes to scan his surroundings. On a normal day, his room was kept neat, just like he'd kept his office space at Jackson, Jackson & Andrews. But today, clothes were piled in a heap at the foot of the unoccupied side of his bed, and the blue drapes that he normally kept pulled back to allow the sunshine to enter his home were closed shut, making his room dark and dreary, like the feeling he had inside. He didn't want to be bothered. Mitchell had seen the way the neighbors across the street had eyed him when he'd pulled out of his driveway earlier today. They all knew something was wrong, but he wasn't about to give any details. They'd never visited him before, and he didn't want them to start now. To his contentment, the ringing stopped.

As he sat up on his mattress and stared at the bottle that lay on the bed beside him, it was as though Pearl was reminding him of how much she'd helped him before. The bottle was clear, and so was the liquid inside. She looked beautiful and harmless, but they needed no introductions.

Mitchell had lived with her for years. Pearl had cost him everything. She'd cost him his wife. The thought of the price he had paid for the temporary fix infuriated him.

"Nooooooo!"

He'd heard his own voice resonate around him before hearing the bottle shatter into smithereens as it came in contact with the ivory-painted wall in his hallway. Mitchell had picked up the still-unopened bottle of expensive liquor and hurled it with all of his might through his bedroom's open door. Tears broke from his eyes, and Mitchell buried his face between his knees, weeping in a way that he hadn't in years. Several moments passed before he raised his head again, but when he did, his eyes focused on his pastor.

Thinking that he was imagining the figure in front of him, Mitchell grabbed his glasses from the nightstand beside him and put them on, being careful not to disturb the bruise on the side of his eye. "Rev. Inman?" he said, using his sleeves to wipe the moisture from his face.

"That's a pretty good arm you've got there," Rev. Inman spoke. "I'm glad I was just a few steps behind."

"I didn't drink any," Mitchell said, like a little boy who had been caught in the act. "I didn't. See?" he added as he grabbed the dry glass from his nightstand and held it up for his pastor to see.

"I believe you, Mitch," Rev. Inman said through a faint smile before taking the liberty to sit on the side of the bed. "That's a pretty nice bruise. Did Chris do that?"

Mitchell looked at his pastor and nodded in silence. He should have known that Chris would make the battle between the two of them public knowledge. Before long, everybody would turn against him, just like his family had done once his uncle had broadcasted Mitchell's blame for the death of his grandparents.

"My final session with him and Lisa was yesterday," Rev. Inman explained. "He told me everything. He was quite angry."

Mitchell shook his head in frustration and fought the onset of more tears. He was tired of defending himself . . . tired of being called a batterer . . . tired of being called a liar . . . and tired of being labeled by his past.

"I know you didn't do it, Mitch."

Quickly raising his head, Mitchell looked at his pastor. Rev. Inman continued.

"I saw the mark on her wrist and I heard the story, but I know you didn't do it."

"I didn't," Mitchell said with a whisper as he shook his head once more. "He wouldn't believe me, but I promise, if God was standing right here in front of me, I'd tell the same story. I didn't try to have sex with her. I didn't try to make a move of any kind on her. Lisa lied to him, Rev. Inman. She was the one who was coming on to me."

"I know," Rev. Inman said.

"I mean, I'm not all innocent," Mitchell said. "For a minute, I felt like I was melting right into her hands, but I beat it. It wasn't easy, but I won the battle over the weakness of my flesh. But she kept trying, so I grabbed her wrist as hard as I could to let her know that I meant what I said. I knew I hurt her because she yelped. But I didn't know my grip was tight enough to leave a bruise. I'm sorry for hurting her, but I didn't try and take advantage of her."

"Mitch," Rev. Inman said, raising his voice slightly. "I said I believe you. You don't have to convince me."

Turning his body so that his legs dangled off of the side of the bed like his pastor's, Mitchell winced. It was nearing time for him to take his second dose of antibiotics for the day.

"Head hurts?" Rev. Inman asked.

"Not as much as this." Mitchell rolled up his shirt so that the pastor could see the dark spot that Chris's fist had left behind.

"Ouch," Rev. Inman whispered.

"You're telling me," Mitchell said. "I can't believe he thinks I'd do something like that."

"Sometimes love really is a blinding force, Mitch. I think at some time in all of our lives we are misled by one emotion or another. God has a way of bringing us back, but many times we have to learn our lessons the hard way. I'm almost certain that Chris believes you; he just doesn't want to believe you. He wants to believe that Lisa is telling him the truth, but I saw something in his eyes yesterday that indicated that he might have had his own reservations about her. But I fear he'll choose to give her the benefit of the doubt. Unfortunately for Chris, since he's unwilling to listen, he'll probably have to learn of Lisa's true self after he's married her."

"Like her first husband probably did," Mitchell mumbled.

"That's my guess as well," Rev. Inman agreed. "When he told me about the brawl in yesterday's meeting, I decided to stop by to see you last night, but no one was home."

Mitchell sat quietly. He didn't want to tell his pastor that he had been home but just hadn't answered. Yesterday, he was still dealing with the pain. He'd heard the doorbell but ignored it.

"When I rang the doorbell today," the preacher revealed, "I didn't get an answer either, but when I turned the knob, I found that your door was unlocked, so I let myself in."

"I must have left it unlocked when I came back from picking up my package," Mitchell said, pointing in the direction of the shattered glass that was now filling his house with the smell of vodka. "I'm right back where I started, Pastor," he suddenly said, shifting Rev. Inman's attention away from the broken glass and back to him. "No family, no friends, no job. That's why I stopped by the store and bought that stuff anyway. It only seemed right. It was all that was missing from the original equation."

"That's where you're wrong on all accounts," Rev. Inman said. "You've not returned to your starting point at all. You may not have a natural family surrounding you, but you have a spiritual one, and you also have friends. Your job situation is temporary. You're very marketable, and some-one else will see that in you."

Mitchell nodded and tried to look hopeful, but start-ing over wasn't something that he looked forward to.

"And let's not even talk about equations," his pastor added. "You have Someone in your life now that you never included in the original equation, and He is all powerful. That's why you were able to throw that bottle out the door. Nothing in any equation is a match for the power of God."

Before Mitchell could respond, the sound of his door-bell interrupted them.

"Are you expecting anyone?" Rev. Inman asked as he stood.

"No. And I really don't feel like much company."

Mitchell was certain that his pastor had heard him, but only seconds after Rev. Inman left the room to answer the door, Mitchell could hear a woman's voice nearing his bed-room door. It sounded very familiar, but Mitchell strug-gled to place it. Only wearing a T-shirt and boxer shorts, he pulled his legs back on the bed and covered them with his comforter.

"Is that liquor that I smell?" the woman demanded. "What on earth happened here? Look at all this glass."

"Yes, ma'am," Rev. Inman replied. "It happened in a moment of victory. Watch your step."

In the next instant, Mitchell could see Beverly Oliver standing in his doorway and Rev. Inman towering over her from behind. Beverly took one look at Mitchell lying in the bed and rushed to his side.

"Are you all right?" she asked as she cupped his face in her hands and examined the discoloration on the side of his face.

"I'm fine, Beverly. What are you doing here? Where's Virtue?"

"Don't you worry about Virtue. She's fine. It's you that had me driving two hundred and forty miles in the middle of the week. I'm here because I heard about what happened."

"You got the word about this all the way in Houston? How?"

"That scared rabbit that that rascal's got working for him down at your old job told me," Beverly said as she set her large tote bag on the side of Mitchell's bed and began searching it. "At first she didn't want to tell me what was going on, but that number was the only one I had; so I kept calling, and I told her I wasn't gonna stop calling until she told me what I needed to know. I had just talked to you a few days ago and heard how much you loved your job, and it just didn't make sense that you'd just up and leave it. When I called up there yesterday afternoon for the umpteenth time, I told that woman that if she didn't tell me the truth, I was gonna hunt her down like a mangy dog."

Mitchell tried to join his pastor in a hearty laugh, but the soreness in his rib cage stopped him.

"You're hurting there too?" Beverly asked when she saw him cover the area with his hand. "I ought to find that boy who did this and give him the whipping of his life."

"He's thirty-two, Beverly," Mitchell said.

"And?" she challenged as she removed his glasses from his face and nudged at him so that he would lie down flat.

"What's that?" Mitchell asked as she dipped her hand in a jar of something that looked like Vaseline but smelled like grapefruit and peppermint. He closed his eyes while she carefully smoothed the cream on the bruised area.

"Something my mama taught me to make. Whatever the doctors gave you is fine and good, but most of what we need for the healing of the body, God gave us in nature."

"Amen," Rev. Inman agreed. "That's true."

Mitchell grasped at his covers when Beverly reached for them and attempted to pull them back.

"Boy, you don't have nothing under here I haven't seen before," she said, prompting another moment of entertainment for Rev. Inman to laugh at.

Mitchell released his grip, and Beverly peeled the comforter back so that it only covered him to his waist. Then, slowly lifting his shirt, she examined the larger, more tender wound. Mitchell flinched when she touched it, and Beverly shook her head in disgust.

"This is a God-in-heaven shame," she mumbled just before dipping her hand in the jar and pasting the concoction on him.

The salve, whatever it was made of, felt cold to Mitchell's skin and seemed to relieve some of the discomfort upon contact. He couldn't recall the last time someone had cared for him with such maternal tenderness. The times when Grandma Kate would massage Vicks VapoRub on his chest was the closest thing to it.

"You came all the way here to take care of me?" he whispered, looking up at the woman who nursed him as if he were her son.

Beverly chuckled. "Had to," she said. "From what I heard, you were half dead. I didn't know if you had anybody here to see about you, and when I told that woman that I'd hunt down all of her children if she didn't give me all the details, she started giving me their addresses."

This time, Mitchell laughed through the soreness. He imagined Barbara being glad to finally find someone who might be able to scare her children straight.

"Your number is private, so I couldn't get it from information or the phone book," Beverly said. "I had to make sure you were okay. I'm glad to know you weren't all by yourself, though," she concluded, looking toward Rev. Inman with a look of gratefulness.

The preacher returned her smile and then began approaching Mitchell's bedside. "I wish I could stay longer, but I have an appointment in my office shortly. Mitch, I think I'm leaving you in good hands," he said, placing his right hand on Beverly's shoulder. "But before I go, I'd like to pray with you."

Twenty-Three

There were still two days before the night of the Christmas banquet, but the decorating committee at Temple of Jerusalem had already done an excellent job of transforming the fairly simple dining hall that they used during periodic fellowship dinners into an elegant space that looked like something straight out of *House Beautiful* magazine. All of the tables were covered in red cloths, and silver candelabra were aligned in a neat row down the center of all of them. More candles stood on tall stands lining the walls. The plan was to dim the overhead lighting so that the white lights that would be twinkling from the Christmas tree would stand out. Since the overhead lighting would be lowered, the candles on the table would add to the ambience. There was still more decorating to be done, but to Virtue, it already looked like a showstopper.

The altered space almost looked too good to use as a rehearsal hall, but Virtue's routine was at the stage of development where she needed to practice her moves in the place where she would actually perform them. She needed to get a feel for the available space and be sure that every sweeping move would be perfect. Ducking into one of the back rooms, Virtue changed into an outfit that would allow her the comfort she needed to move freely. It wasn't the dress that she would wear on Saturday, but it was a worthy substitute. As usual, she bowed her head and said a quick prayer before beginning. The next step was to insert her CD into the stereo system. She chose track number thirteen and took her place on the stage.

Virtue could never understand the power that music had in her life, and she'd given up trying to figure it out years ago. For as far back as she could remember, ever since she was a child, it had been that way. Whenever she felt sad, frightened, or even angry, she'd lock herself in her room and turn on the radio for comfort. She didn't know then that music would become such a pertinent part of her life, but it had, and it continued to be a source of strength. The sounds of beautiful instrumental music or music that was accompanied by meaningful lyrics took her to another place. That was the reason that gospel music was her favorite. In her mind, there was nothing like it; and when she danced to songs of worship, she lost herself in the freedom that they offered.

As BeBe Winans's rendition of *My Christmas Prayer* streamed through the stereo speakers, Virtue moved with flowing grace. It was only rehearsal, but she danced as if the guests who would take part in the Christmas Eve fellowship were already in their seats and being blessed by her interpretation. It was her first time practicing the entire routine, but Virtue was almost flawless. She'd been trained to keep dancing even if she forgot a step. That was what she and her fellow dance majors were taught at Hope College, and remembering that instruction often came in handy. Today, she'd missed her cue for a turn, but she danced through it, remaining absorbed by the artist's uniquely gifted voice and the perfect melody of the piano and the stringed instruments that played along with her. As the music faded and she made her final move, Virtue's concentration was broken by the sound of slow hand claps.

Bringing herself to a full standing position, she looked out into the chairs and saw Fynn leaning against one of the walls beside one of the standing candleholders. Walking to the CD player, she turned the music off and then turned back to face his direction. He walked toward her.

"Very good, my love. The pastor will be very pleased with what you've created."

"Thank you," Virtue said as she caught her breath.

Fynn stopped a few feet from the bottom of the stage. "I hadn't heard from you since your lunch with the ex. I was hoping that he hadn't killed you and stuffed your dismembered body in the trunk of a car."

He laughed, but Virtue didn't share his amusement. She ejected the CD and blew away imaginary dust particles before inserting it again.

"It was nothing like that," she said, maintaining her composure and wondering why she even responded at all.

"Did you go alone?"

"Beverly went with me."

"Then that's probably what foiled his plans."

"Speaking of plans," Virtue said, thinking it best that they change the subject, "how are the youth coming along with the skit that you mentioned they would perform in the program?"

"They are doing well. They will also be singing, but you would know that had you met with me last Saturday as I wished."

"Good," Virtue said as she wiped beads of perspiration from her forehead and continued to ignore his insinuations. "I'm glad they're doing well. Since they are singing, do you want the program to end with the youth performance or with me?"

"Does it really matter what I want, Virtue?"

In frustration, Virtue propped her hand on one hip and quietly looked down at him from the elevated flooring. There was a lot that she wanted to say, but none of it seemed worth getting into an argument. She took a calming breath and then spoke again as she unnecessarily fiddled with the knobs on the sound system, creating the illusion that she was adjusting them.

"I believe Elder Bradley said that he wanted half of the performances to be before dinner was served and the second half after his message. He never mentioned which performances should go where, so maybe we should just let him make the decision on that."

By the time she turned back to him, Fynn had chosen to sit in one of the chairs on the floor. His presence was not only beginning to make Virtue uncomfortable, but it was becoming annoying. More than anything, she wanted him to go back to doing whatever he'd been doing before he walked in so that she could go through her dance routine once more before heading home. But Fynn seemed to be in no hurry. As she walked about the stage doing nothing in particular, he sat in the chair and watched her every move.

"Is there something more that you wanted to discuss?" Virtue asked, keeping her voice steady. "I do need to get back to my rehearsal."

"Am I stopping you?"

"I like to be alone when I rehearse, Fynn."

Standing from his chair, Fynn shoved his hands in the pockets of his tweed coat and took a few steps toward the stage. "That's your problem right now, Virtue. You've been alone too long."

"Excuse me?"

"You're thirty years old, my love. No fertile woman as beautiful as you are should be alone at thirty."

"But a thirty-year-old barren woman should?" Virtue challenged.

"A barren woman is good for very little," Fynn said. "That's why, even in the Scripture, women like Hannah cried out to God to give them the ability to have children. They knew that without that ability, their value lessened. Medical findings have proven that the older you get before starting your family, the harder it is to conceive. There is a reason why God made the woman's body in that manner, Virtue. He intended for them to be fruitful and multiply. At your age, you should have many fruit by now."

Virtue felt nauseous. "Fynn . . ."

"No," he said, holding up a hand to silence her. "You asked if I had more to discuss, so listen as I discuss it."

His commanding tone was almost too much. The muscles in the side of Virtue's face twitched as she forcefully held her tongue. She was in no mood to hear anything more of Fynn's archaic beliefs concerning marriage and children, but she withheld the outburst that would have told him so.

"You've been alone too long," he repeated. "Not just because of the children you must bear, but I find that those of you who are alone far past your teenage years begin to take on the mind-set of a man. Because you've had to do so much on your own, you begin to think that you don't need a man to lead you. You become what you call independent, but what I call loose and beyond control. No woman should be running free with no restraints. God never meant for it to be that way. That is why He created Adam first, and that is why He used Adam's rib to then create the woman. Without Adam's rib, there would have been no Eve. Without a man, a woman is nothing, but with him she has all that she needs."

"Is there a point to what you're saying, Fynn?"

"See, that is what I mean," he pointed out in an accusing tone. "It is because you are alone and because you have allowed yourself to be raped by the cultures of this foreign society that you are so untamed. You should never interrupt me while I'm speaking, Virtue. How can I get you to understand how much you not only disrespect me, but you disrespect yourself? When the head is bruised, the body suffers."

"Who are you calling untamed?" Virtue said, finally giving up on her fight to remain calm. "Wild animals need taming, Fynn, not women. Furthermore, you are not my head. You are always talking about what a man deserves and what a woman should do. If you—or any man, for that matter—want respect, you have to *earn* it. Not only that, but you have to *give* it as well. No self-respecting woman wants to be referred to in such antiquated terms as the ones you often speak. It's you who are disrespecting me right now by trying to force me into a place that I have no desire to be."

"It's only because you are unaware of what is best for you, my love. How can I convince you of this?"

"And how can I convince you that I'm not interested in a relationship with you? I don't *want* to be your wife. Despite your put-downs of our country, I'm proud to be an American. I thank God for every one of my African ancestors, Fynn, but I don't have to prove my heritage to anybody, and I certainly don't have to do it by agreeing to marry a man that I don't love."

Fynn's body stiffened. "This has something to do with the meeting with your batterer, doesn't it?"

"I have forgiven Mitchell for what he did to me, Fynn, but what I'm saying now has nothing to do with my meeting with him."

"Of course it does," he accused.

"He doesn't even know that I've released my anger, Fynn, so my words to you have nothing to do with him. In that meeting I never said a word to Mitchell. I couldn't even look at him. But since the meeting, I've come to realize that I've been wrong for trying to hold on to my grudges and refusing to believe that he could have possibly changed. Mitchell has changed a great deal. He stopped tormenting me years ago. I was tormenting myself, and I had to forgive him not just for him, but for me as well. But that has nothing to do with what I'm saying to you."

"But I had gotten through to you before you met with him, and now you are so defiant. Someone has poisoned your heart against me."

"*You* have poisoned my heart against you, Fynn," Virtue said. "I may have never had a romantic connection to you, but I honestly used to enjoy your company, and talking to you would be something that I looked forward to. But because you took that and tried to forcefully turn it into something else, I can hardly stand to see you coming. You can't just lay a claim on another human being and expect that person to automatically become submissive to whatever you say. At least, not when that person is me. Now, I would appreciate it if we never visited this topic of conversation again. You say you love me, Fynn. Well, if you truly do—if I mean anything at all to you—if I can request that your love grants me one wish, it is to stop pursuing me. I don't love you, and I will never agree to marry you.

"You're standing there in judgment of Mitchell for what he did to me in the past, but you are the abuser now, Fynn. Every time you approach me on this subject, you become the batterer. You may not use your hands to touch me, but there is such a thing as mental abuse too, and it can be just as tormenting. Mitchell was man enough to see his mistakes and to apologize. Maybe one day, with all the man that you proclaim to be, you'll be able to do the same."

Fynn stood quietly, gazing at Virtue for what seemed like hours. Finally, still having said nothing, he took several steps backward and then turned and walked through the same doors that he'd entered.

Virtue's mind raced. She didn't realize the level of tension that Fynn's presence had brought on until he was gone. She walked to the CD player and pressed the button that would skip forward to track thirteen. As the music played, she began moving again; and with every sway, she felt the stress drain from her body.

Fynn stopped suddenly as he walked through the doorway that separated the fellowship hall from the corridor that led to the sanctuary.

"Minister Fynn. We have to talk."

Fynn swallowed. He'd had no idea that Elder Bradley was in the building, and he certainly didn't know that he was within listening range of him and Virtue. "Can it wait? I have some paperwork to complete for the youth ministry's part in the Christmas program."

"No, Fynn. It can't wait," Elder Bradley said.

Shoving his hands in his pockets, Fynn leaned his back against the wall behind him. Music could be heard on the other side, and he imagined Virtue dancing masterfully to it. Why a woman so graceful and so beautiful had to be so rebellious, he didn't know. Fynn knew that she would be the perfect mate for him and the perfect mother of his children—if only he could amend her way of thinking.

"I heard your conversation with Virtue," Elder Bradley said.

"I guessed as much."

"Why do you continue to harass her, Fynn? I thought we'd cleared the air on this matter."

"What matter, Elder Bradley? I am not harassing Virtue. I'm schooling her and molding her back into the lady she was intended to become from birth, before society cursed our women with this devilish feminist way of thinking. This is not of God, and I am disappointed in you as a man and as a pastor that you would condone such atrocities among the sisters here at the church. You should be back-

220

ing me, Elder Bradley, not chastising me. If we, as men, don't stand up and be the leaders that God and our forefathers ordained us to be, then we are nothing but weaklings. And if we are weak, who will lead? There are times in our lives when we have to plant our feet firmly on the ground and remind those who are out of line where their places are. Like Virtue, they may not immediately like it or appreciate it, but in the long run they will see the error of their ways and realize their place as the helpmates God designed them to be. Can you not see and understand that?"

"As a matter of fact, I do," Elder Bradley said, bringing a smile to Fynn's lips. His grin, however, was abbreviated. "I can see and understand that you are determined to hold on to the ways of ancestors who knew not God. Your father and grandfather, proud men though they may have been, were not men of the almighty God, Fynn. They worshiped other gods and followed other traditions, religious and otherwise, that were never directed or orchestrated by our Lord and Savior. You are trying to live for their gods and for Christ, and the two don't mix. Matthew 6:24 tells us that we can't serve two masters, Minister Fynn; you have to hate one and love the other. I placed you as the youth pastor of this church because I believed you were steadfast and unmovable in your work for God. Now I feel inadequate as a pastor for entrusting you with such an office."

When Fynn replied, his voice was stern. "I serve only one God, Elder Bradley. Just because I hold to the teachings of our forefathers does not make me any less of a man of God than you. I chose not to allow myself to be violated by a European society. I don't think God frowns upon me for that. In fact, I think it is men such as you who He frowns on for becoming weak under the pressure of a world that has long forgotten Him."

Fynn watched as Elder Bradley's eyes saddened. The pastor shook his head and exhaled and then said, "Minister Fynn, as of this moment, you are relieved of your duties as youth pastor of this body of Christ. I am not asking that you leave the church. I'm only removing you from your current office. I pray that it is only temporary. But until you go through some much-needed counseling and educational training . . ."

"I will *not* be treated with such disrespect! You have allowed yourself to be brainwashed and Americanized to the white man's way of thinking, but I won't let you strip me of the dignity and honor that my grandfather and father instilled inside of me. There are too many other churches that would love to have a man of my caliber working with them for me to surrender my self-respect just to be called youth pastor of your organization.

"I am sorry that it has come to this, Elder Bradley. Not only do you lose, but so does Virtue and many others who would have benefited from having me be a part of this ministry." Fynn pulled his key ring from his pocket and removed two keys, placing them in Elder Bradley's hand. They were the keys to the church and to his office.

Without another word, he walked away, leaving Elder Bradley still shaking his head. This time, it was out of pity for the man who would forever walk with a distorted vision of what God's plan was for his life and the lives of those around him.

Twenty-Four

For a whole year, Chris had waited for this day to arrive. It had seemed perfect to receive the love of his life for Valentine's Day, but accepting her as a Christmas gift was even more inviting. He'd had to find a new best man, hire a preacher he really didn't know, and use the facility where Lisa's family attended worship services, but he didn't mind. Chris didn't even think twice about moving the date and putting their plans on fast-forward. Lisa said that they should get married early, just to show all the naysayers that they wouldn't be swayed by their doubts and lies. Chris agreed. The bridesmaids' dresses had already been hand-made, and it took no time for him and his groomsmen to find their wedding gear. There was no better way that Chris would have chosen to celebrate Christmas.

The preacher, a short, stocky, older man with a receding hairline, smiled at the groom as he and Lisa's brother took their places at the altar. Chris couldn't believe how nervous he was. This was the day that he'd prayed for—the day when he would finally make Lisa his bride. But as many times as he had stood in front of his home mirror and rehearsed the debonair pose that he would strike while standing at the altar on this day, Chris felt as though someone had moved one of the church's heating vents and placed it directly over his head. Using his handkerchief, he wiped beads of perspiration from his forehead and face. The palms of his hands were sweating too, and it felt as if he had a dripping fountain under each of his armpits. Every once in a while, his heart would pound with such intensity that he thought the people sitting on the back row of the church could hear it.

Glancing around, Chris was amazed at how quickly Lisa's family had been able to pull it all together. No one would ever know that the church decoration was a rush job that had been taken care of in a single afternoon. There had been no time for the standard rehearsals, but Lisa said they didn't need one. All but one of the soloists that had been set to perform in their original plans were members of Living Word Cathedral. Since the pastor of that church had been removed from their program, it only seemed proper to do the same for anyone else who was linked to what was now their former church. If Lionel Inman or anyone else thought that their actions would stop Chris from marrying the woman he loved, they couldn't be more mistaken.

As a matter of fact, their doubts gave him additional determination to not only marry Lisa, but to be the absolute best husband she could ever dream of. He would shower her with love and affection. Even if he never saw his former pastor or the members of Living Word Cathedral again, they would hear talk of the blissful life he shared with the woman whose integrity they'd doubted. Like his father, Chris would be a strong family man who loved God and provided for the family they would create together.

The processional music finally began, and one pair at a

224

time, the well-dressed groomsmen and bridesmaids walked arm in arm up the church's center aisle. Flashes from cameras belonging to the well-wishers who had come to celebrate the day with them served as additional lighting for the sanctuary. With the wedding officially underway, Chris's anxieties eased.

As he watched the honored witnesses make their entrance, Chris scanned the crowd, and most of the faces he saw belonged to people he'd never met. Because of their sudden rescheduling of plans, even his mother and sister had been left out of the most important day of his life. His sister had been angry and his mother had been hurt by the news, but Chris promised to send them a copy of the video and to get multiple sets of his photos developed so that each of them could have her own treasured memorabilia of his day. Chris's promises had done little to pacify them, but he couldn't worry about that now; it was his and Lisa's moment, and the love of his life was about to make her grand entrance.

At the cue of the music, the audience stood, and all eyes turned to the back of the church. Within seconds, the wooden double doors that had been hiding his bride swung open, and audible gasps ran up and down each row of pews. The gown was certainly breathtaking, but Chris couldn't determine if they were awed by the dress's majesty or by the fact that Lisa wore white and had layers of netting that formed a thick covering for her face. Chris's smile broadened because he remembered the day Lisa had told him about her chosen gown.

"The saleslady at the bridal shop told me that because I'd been married before, it was improper for me to wear white and even more inappropriate for me to wear a veil," she'd told Chris. "But I told her that I wasn't even thinking about traditions and superstitions. You are the first man to really love me like a woman should be loved; and in my heart of hearts, you'll be the first man to know me in every way. That's what my white attire is going to represent."

Chris loved the idea, and he watched with renewed love while Lisa's father escorted her across the petals that the little girls had already thrown down. Chris anxiously tried to see through the veil, but he couldn't. And he couldn't help but be touched when he saw Lisa's father take a tissue and reach under the covering to dab at each of her eyes. Chris was glad to see that he wasn't the only one who was overjoyed about this day.

The ceremony proceeded, but Chris hardly heard a word of it. He just wanted to skip forward to the moment when they would be declared husband and wife. As far as he was concerned, all the rest of the ceremony was just age-old tradition. If Lisa had agreed, he would have settled for a courthouse wedding. But she'd done that when she married Felander. This time Lisa wanted a day filled with pomp and circumstance, and Chris was happy to oblige.

For a fleeting moment, he was thrown when he turned to his chief usher to get the ring for Lisa's finger. Just that quickly, he'd forgotten the sickening deed that Mitchell had done to disqualify him for his position as best man. Chris wasn't naive or unreasonable. He could understand any man being attracted to his bride; there was good reason for him to be. But Mitchell had gone way past an innocent attraction, and Chris would never forgive him for what he'd done.

Repeating his vows and placing the ring on Lisa's finger, Chris almost kicked himself for wasting any part of his special day thinking of Mitchell. He certainly wasn't worth it. There had to be a special place in hell for people like Mitchell Andrews. For men who hurt women, hell's fire had to be hotter.

As they held hands and knelt down to pray while the organist played *The Lord's Prayer*, Chris realized that it was almost over. He could barely contain himself, prompting him to squeeze Lisa's hands from across the prayer bench.

226

She squeezed back, and that sent his heart soaring. She was just as ready to get started on their new life as he.

The moment had finally arrived. "By the power that is vested in me by God and the state of Texas, I pronounce you husband and wife. Christopher, you may salute your bride."

Pulling back her veil, Chris was finally able to see Lisa in all of her beauty. She'd always been a sight to behold, but as Mrs. Lisa Jackson her beauty was beyond words. Stepping closer to her, Chris lifted her chin and pressed his lips against hers. He could hear the audience cheering them on and hear the snapping sounds of the cameras that captured the moment, but his total focus was on his wife. Lisa wrapped her arms around his neck and parted her lips to deepen the kiss. For a moment, Chris felt as though he was in heaven, but just as soon as the pleasure of the kiss reached its peak, something went awry.

Chris didn't know what was happening, but suddenly he found himself struggling to pull away. Lisa wouldn't let go. She wrapped her arms tighter and continued to do whatever it was she was doing that was inflicting so much pain. Chris tried to scream, but he couldn't free his lips to do so. It felt as if Lisa were gnawing away, eating his flesh. The people continued to cheer as if nothing was wrong, but Chris could feel warm fluid streaming from his face and mouth as his new bride sucked the life out of him. Using all of his might, he tried one last time to release himself from what had become a kiss of death. Chris managed to break from the torment, but when he did, he screamed in the resulting pain and fell backward onto the floor. The front of his white tuxedo was being decorated with blood that streamed from the open lacerations on his face. He tried to wipe the blood away, but it was no use. Every drop that he wiped away was quickly replenished by more.

"What are you doing?" he screamed as he looked up at his wife, standing over him.

Lisa's face had transformed. Her face was bloody too. And the red fluid that dripped from her mouth fell onto the fibers of her once-beautiful white gown. It wasn't her blood, though. It was Chris's blood. She knelt beside him and cradled her arms around his body. Chris tried to pull away, but the heavy loss of blood had sapped his strength.

"Come on, sweetie," she cooed in the voice that he used to love. "Kiss me."

Awakened by his own screams, Chris sat up in his bed and tried to gain control over his trembling body and quick, shallow breaths. With widened eyes he looked around in the darkness, trying to identify his whereabouts as moisture dripped from his face onto his covers. Frantically, he jumped from his bed and turned on his overhead light. Terrified of what he might find, Chris took frightfully slow steps to his mirror and was overtaken by relief when he found that the wetness that fell from his face was perspiration. It was the same dream he'd had during the time he'd been ill—the same dream he'd blamed on his body's heightened temperature. But there was no fever now, and this time Chris recalled every horrible detail of the nightmare. He wished he didn't, but he did.

Stumbling across the hallway and into his bathroom, Chris splashed several handfuls of cold water on his face, trying to wash away the images that were still very vivid in his mind. With his eyes blinded by water, Chris used his hands to feel for the towel rack. Finding it, he buried his face in the cotton and held it there until the water had soaked into the thickness of the fabric. Chris was still shaking when he walked into the kitchen to get a glass of water to hydrate his dry throat.

For ten minutes Chris just stood in the kitchen, listening to the quiet of his house that was interrupted only by the sound of his heavy breathing. He now knew that it was all a dream, but Chris touched his face once more just to be sure that there were no signs of blood. With the cup of water still in his hand, he managed to get his weak knees to carry him to the living room where he sat on the sofa and stared into the darkness.

He couldn't go back to bed. Not tonight. So Chris sat in the chair, refusing to allow his eyes to close for fear of what he might see.

Twenty-Five

*E*arly Friday morning, Beverly was awakened by the smell of breakfast and the sounds of Christmas. *O Holy Night* was one of her favorite Christmas carols, and it sounded beautiful as it played from a radio somewhere inside the house. Beverly climbed out of the bed that she'd slept in for the past two nights and slipped on her robe before walking out into the hallway. Mitchell's bedroom door was open, but she saw no sign of him inside. To know that he felt well enough to be up and about so early in the morning was comforting. Beverly had to head back to Houston today, and knowing he was returning to his normal self made her feel better about leaving him alone.

Virtue had called her on her cell phone last night. She said she was calling to see how Beverly was doing, but Beverly knew that it was really Mitchell that she was concerned about. She had played along, though, telling Virtue how she'd spent her day. Beverly made sure to add that Mitchell's bruises were slowly healing. Although Virtue hadn't said so, Beverly knew that the report gave her some relief. Both she and Virtue had been upset when Beverly got the details of the fight between Chris and Mitchell. Beverly had tried to get Virtue to come with her to Dallas, but she wouldn't hear of it. She had forgiven Mitchell, but she wasn't about to give him any hints that she wanted any kind of relationship with him. Beverly chuckled when she thought about it, because she knew that deep down inside, Virtue did.

"Mitchell?" she called as she walked down the hallway into the kitchen.

On the stove was a covered pot of grits that bubbled from the heat of the low flame beneath it. Opening the oven, Beverly saw one pan that was filled with sausage links and another that held what looked like a casserole made of eggs. The whole kitchen smelled good enough to eat, and her stomach rumbled, indicating that it was ready whenever she was.

"Mitchell?" she called again, with still no reply.

Beverly stepped into the living room and looked around. Yesterday she'd called a carpet-cleaning company and had them come by and give the cushions of Mitchell's sofa a good cleaning, as well as cleaning the carpet that covered the floor of his hallway. It seemed like a simple task, but it had taken them two hours to rid the house of the dangerous particles of glass and the smell of vodka.

"Mitchell?"

The music now sounded like it was coming from outside, but when Beverly looked out of the living room windows, she saw nothing. Opening a door that she'd thought belonged to a closet, Beverly was surprised to find a set of stairs. The music was coming from below. She walked down the steps and into a spacious den that she hadn't known existed until now. The room, covered in hardwood floors, looked large enough to be a second home. One end of the space was set up like a living room. There was leather furniture, a coffee table, and a large entertainment center that consisted of a wide-screen television and a stereo system. In the middle of the floor, there was a Ping-Pong table, a sit-up bench, and a set of free weights. But it was what was on the far end of the basement that captured her attention the most.

Beverly stood in amazement while she watched Mitchell play with the skill of an expert pianist. Every few moments, his eyes would close and his upper body would sway as though he could feel every note that his fingers demanded from the instrument. She wanted to move closer, to get a better view of his mastery, but Beverly was afraid that if he knew she was there, he would stop. When the song came to an end, Beverly broke into an applause that tested the acoustics in the large room. Wincing from the sudden loud noise, Mitchell turned around and broke into a grin. Standing from the piano stool, he took a playful bow.

"You're looking better this morning," Beverly remarked.

"I feel better too. I had a great nurse."

Beverly beamed at his compliment. "You're just full of surprises, aren't you?" she said. "That food up there smells like it was prepared by Emeril, and now you're in here playing like Little Richard. Where did all of this talent come from?" Beverly asked as she approached.

"I'm glad my grandfather wasn't around to hear your comparison." Mitchell laughed. "I guess I got all of my talent from my grandmother," he explained as he ran his fingers across the finish of the baby grand. "I picked it up from watching her, both cooking and piano playing. I can't remember the last time I played before today, though. It's been awhile."

"Well, I sure couldn't tell by listening to you," Beverly said. "May I?"

Mitchell stepped aside. "Do you play?"

Smiling, Beverly answered by sitting on the vacated stool, tightening the belt of her robe around her, and placing her fingers on the waiting keys. She looked up at

Mitchell as she began playing and saw an impressed grin on his face.

"I like that song," Mitchell remarked.

"Do you sing?"

Mitchell laughed. "Only to the dead . . . or maybe to those who are terminally ill and looking for something that will speed along the process."

Beverly laughed too. "You're so full of surprises; I just thought I'd ask. Where do you know this song from?"

"I have the CD," Mitchell said. "I bought it when it first came out and played it to death for the first few weeks that I had it. I haven't heard it in over a year."

"Well, that ain't my testimony," Beverly said with a laugh. "I've heard it so much over the last couple of weeks that it's etched in my brain. If I didn't truly love it, I'd hate it by now."

"They're playing it a lot on the Houston stations this year?"

Beverly stopped her music and turned to face Mitchell. "No. Virtue is dancing to it at our Christmas banquet tomorrow night. She's been playing the CD around the house while she's been choreographing her steps."

Beverly took note of Mitchell's change of demeanor. "I haven't seen her dance in ages," he said, filling the empty space on the stool next to her. "It used to give me chills to watch her dance. She would get standing ovations at her school performances quite often."

"She still gets standing ovations," Beverly said.

The two of them sat in silence. Beverly had left the door leading to the stairwell open. The alluring smell of the food was bouncing off the walls of the den about as loudly as the earlier music had.

"Be honest with me, Beverly," Mitchell said, pulling her mind away from the kitchen. "What do you feel are the chances that Virtue will forgive me and at least consider giving me another chance?"

"Do you really want my honesty, Mitchell?"

He hesitated but nodded his answer.

"Virtue has already forgiven you," Beverly told him. "She told me she had, so that part of your concern can be dismissed. Will she give you another chance? I honestly don't know. But with that same honesty, I will tell you again as I told you before when we met at the hotel—I believe that she still loves you."

"She still hasn't denied it?"

"Not to me she hasn't," Beverly said. "I think that every adverse emotion that Virtue has ever had toward you stemmed from love. I think she was so hurt by you because she loved you. Mitchell, nothing is more heartbreaking than having the person you love be the same person who caused you pain. I think she was angry because she loved you. Nobody really wants to love somebody who has hurt them so badly. She couldn't rid herself of the love, so she became angry at both you and herself. I even think she feared you because she loved you. Can you imagine how frightening it is to love somebody so much that even though they have put your head in stitches, you still have thoughts of them and dream about them? I think memories of you have tortured Virtue for years. Not because she's hated you, but because she's never stopped loving you."

Mitchell closed his eyes and sighed. "How do you know so much, Beverly?"

"Because I've lived, and I know what it's like to be hurt. I never told you this, but I'm divorced too. My husband never raised a hand to hit me, 'cause if he had, he knew I would have cut it off at the wrist."

Mitchell grimaced at the thought of her threat.

"But what I found out is that there are a lot worse things than being hit. I think I would have preferred that Lester hit me than for him to have been unfaithful. It was something about him leaving me for another woman that cut all the way to the center of my heart. I think infidelity is the worst kind of deception, and then when you find out that it wasn't just a mistake caused by a moment of weakness, but a full-fledged relationship, that just makes it worse."

"Do you still love him?"

Beverly let out a short laugh and then folded her arms in front of her. "I wish I could answer with an emphatic no, but I honestly think there's something about true love that just never completely goes away. Even if you want it to go away, it stays, if only to remind you of just how powerful it is. I don't love Lester in the same manner that I did for all those years that we were married, but I have to admit that there will probably always be a place in my heart for him."

Mitchell tossed her a grin. "I wonder if he's sitting somewhere just like me, trying to figure out a way to win you back."

"I doubt it," Beverly said. "Last I heard, he was sitting somewhere planning out his wedding. He's getting married tomorrow."

The smile that Mitchell displayed earlier faded quickly. "I'm sorry, Beverly."

"Don't be," she said as she tapped him on the knee. "At this point, I wouldn't take him back whether he was getting married or not. He's got his day coming for all the wrong he did. God promised that what we sow, we have to reap."

Mitchell stared off into the distance. "You know, when I was lying up there in the living room on my sofa, unable to move for all those hours after Chris attacked me, I started thinking that maybe God had finally decided to give me my due punishment for what I did to Virtue. I mean, Chris is a strong dude, but so am I. I should have been able to fight him back, but each blow I took basically paralyzed me."

"Everybody loses a fight in their lifetime, Mitchell."

"Oh, don't get me wrong," Mitchell quickly said. "I've lost more than a few fights in my lifetime, but any other time it happened, you'd best believe I went down like a man, and my opponent *looked* like he'd been beat up whether he won or not. Monday morning, I went down like a wimp wearing a tutu. I didn't even get in a small punch. I dragged myself home, barely avoiding a black eye and broken ribs. My body felt like I'd been in a car wreck with me riding on the hood at the time of impact. If anything was black or broken on Chris, it was his knuckles from all that Mitch bashing."

Beverly laughed.

"I was rescued by a grandmother in her *sixties*, Beverly," Mitchell continued. "It don't get no more humiliating than that. Now, tell me God wasn't sitting up in heaven going, 'Now how 'bout that. I bet you won't hit Virtue no more.'"

Doubling in laughter, Beverly slipped her arm around Mitchell's body and gave him a quick squeeze. "I don't think what happened between you and Chris had anything to do with God's punishment," she told him. "But it *is* said that He has a sense of humor, so who knows?"

After all of the conversation that had just been exchanged between the two of them, Beverly noticed that Mitchell seemed to shut down without warning. He sat with his eyes cast toward the floor as if he'd suddenly been entranced by the pattern in which the flooring had been laid.

"What is it, hon?" she pried.

"Grandma Kate used to say that," he whispered. "She didn't do much church, but she always said that God had a sense of humor."

"You still miss her, don't you?"

Mitchell nodded. "I miss both of my grandparents. It gets worse at Christmastime."

"I imagine so," Beverly said. "What're you doing for the holiday? You need to surround yourself with friends."

"Chris and Lisa are going to visit Chris's family in California. I was supposed to go as well. I hadn't checked with them, but I'm almost sure that I've been scratched from that deal."

"Fine then," Beverly said as she rose to her feet and began walking toward the stairs. "I'm going to go upstairs and get some clothes on; then when I come back down, we're going to eat breakfast together and then pack so we can head out to Houston."

"Houston?"

"Uh-huh," she said through heavy breaths. It had been much easier coming down the steps than it was going back up. "Make sure you pack a nice suit to wear to the Christmas banquet tomorrow night."

Twenty-Six

Virtue never ate before dancing, so when Elder Bradley told her that he wanted her to be the closer for the Christmas banquet, she knew that she'd have a long wait before being able to satisfy the hunger that the smell of the buffet-style meal had activated. The wait also put her on edge for another reason. When Beverly had walked into the house yesterday afternoon and immediately announced that Mitchell had come with her and was staying at a hotel near the church, Virtue literally had to catch her breath.

"I couldn't let him spend Christmas by himself, Virtue," Beverly had defended. "He just lost his best friend, and he doesn't have any family to speak of. I wasn't going to leave without inviting him to come. Now, if you don't want anything to do with him, fine. You don't have to interact with him at all. He's staying in a room that's miles away from our house, and he's coming to the banquet as my date, not yours. So you don't have to do anything; you don't have to say anything; you don't even have to look at him if you don't want to. I hear you're pretty good at that."

Virtue had given Beverly a look of warning for her sarcasm. After a moment of thought, she said, "Did you just call him your *date*?"

"That's right," Beverly had said.

"Mitchell is a thirty-one-year-old man, Beverly," Virtue had made the mistake of pointing out.

"And what am I?" Beverly challenged. "A fifty-five-year-old mattress? I'm a woman. I'm a mature woman, and he's a man who happens to be just a few years younger. Umph," she grunted. "That sweetens the pot, if you ask me."

Virtue had known that Beverly was pulling her leg, but at that moment it felt as if she were using both hands. Virtue felt a twinge of jealousy but hid it behind a melodramatic laugh.

She was surprised that she hadn't seen Fynn at all. Virtue expected to at least see him in passing as he prepared the youth ministry for the part they would play in the banquet. Virtue felt relief in not seeing him. She didn't need the added pressure before her performance. She hated that they couldn't at least remain friends, especially with both of them leading ministries within the same church, but Beverly had been right. Virtue had to take charge, put her foot down, and be firm. Fynn's personality wasn't the flexible type, and he wasn't one who could be convinced that his way of thinking was warped. The only way to deal with him was to *not* deal with him. Being his friend wasn't important enough to Virtue for her to have to suffer through his useless lectures.

She'd chosen not to mix and mingle with the people who packed out the decorated dining hall. Just knowing that Mitchell was somewhere out there in the crowd made her more nervous than ever. Virtue knew that no matter what Beverly said, she wouldn't be able to realistically avoid Mitchell for the entire night, but for now, she needed to. From the room where Virtue waited, she could hear the goings-on that took place on the other side of the wall. Right now, Elder Bradley was bringing the Christmas message for the year. Virtue knew that she only had a few more minutes to calm herself. Her cue to enter would come directly after the sermon ended.

Mitchell sat beside Beverly and enjoyed his meal while exchanging small talk with the others who sat with them. All eyes seemed to turn toward him and Beverly when they walked into the building together. It was clear that everyone wanted to know the identity of the strange man who escorted her and the status of their relationship. The stares made Mitchell uncomfortable, but Beverly was enjoying every minute of it.

Despite the age difference, even Mitchell had to admit that they made an eye-catching pair. He wore a navy single-breasted blue suit, and Beverly looked smashing in her floor-length silver gown that caught reflections of the soft light provided by the candles. As Elder Bradley began winding down his message, Beverly excused herself. When Mitchell stood with her as a show of respect, he unintentionally added fuel to the flame of gossip that had started the moment they walked in.

"I just want to say thank you and God bless you to everyone who bundled up on a night of record low temperatures and came to spend your Christmas Eve with us. Whether you are a member of Temple of Jerusalem or a friend of the ministry, we thank you. There is plenty of food left and a few more hours left in the night. We are coming to the end of our program, but by no means do you have to be in any hurry to leave. I encourage you to stay and fellowship with your brothers and sisters in Christ for as long as you wish. As we end our program we have a special, special treat for you."

As Elder Bradley said the words into the microphone, Mitchell heard Virtue's name spoken from the mouths of several of those in the crowd, and many of them had already begun to clap in anticipation. He couldn't help but feel proud knowing that she had made such an impact.

"I call her God's angel of praise," Elder Bradley said. "You call her Virtue. Please give her a warm welcome as she interprets for us this evening."

Mitchell felt a million butterflies take flight in his stomach as he stood with the others while Virtue walked gracefully onto the stage. She struck a pose and stood as still as a mannequin as the audience members returned to their seats. The music started, but as soon as Virtue was about to make her first move, the music stopped, the banquet room darkened, and everything was brought to a standstill. The electrical power had gone out. Had it not been for the dozens of candles still illuminated throughout the building, they would have been in complete darkness. But because of them, they had a beautiful low-light setting. Elder Bradley took the stage and tinkered with the sound system, but nothing happened.

"Well, the weatherman did tell us that tonight's low temperatures might cause some electrical problems," he said, his voice echoing through the open space. "But God is still good."

"Amen," the crowd responded.

"Is Beverly Oliver in the building?" the pastor called. "Our church organist isn't here tonight, but God always has a ram in the bush, and Sister Beverly can be our ram tonight. We need to see Virtue dance."

Mitchell looked at the empty seat beside him. Beverly hadn't yet returned from her restroom break.

"She stepped out," someone took the liberty of announcing to the pastor.

Mitchell looked toward the stage and saw Virtue standing there fidgeting. He remembered from their days of courtship and in the early stages of their marriage how important Virtue said it was for a dancer's concentration not to be broken. He could tell that hers already had been, but the longer she had to wait, the worse it would become. Standing from his seat, he took a deep breath and buttoned his suit jacket as he headed to the front of the room. He could hear murmurs around him as he passed the strategically placed tables.

"Do you play, young man?" Elder Bradley asked.

"Yes, sir," Mitchell responded.

"Wonderful," Elder Bradley said as he walked to the side of the stage to greet him as he ascended the stairs. "What's your name?" he whispered.

As soon as Mitchell answered the question, he knew that his name was not foreign to the pastor. The two men locked eyes for a moment, and then Elder Bradley turned and looked at Virtue as if seeking her approval. She stared at Mitchell for a moment and then gave her pastor the nod that he needed.

"Let's give Brother . . . Brother Mitchell a hand," Elder Bradley said. As the thunderous applause resonated through the building, he stepped off the stage and took his seat on the floor at the head table.

Mitchell adjusted his frames on his face and waited for Virtue to strike her pose. This was a first. In all the time that they'd spent together, Mitchell had never provided the music for one of her routines. The butterflies in his stomach were still in full flight, but he placed his fingers on the keys and began to play a soft introduction. And as if they had rehearsed together, Virtue began dancing. Mitchell was sure that his version wasn't the exact one on the CD, but Virtue moved in perfect sync to his melody. Halfway through the song, it felt as if his fingers had disconnected themselves from his body. Even in Mitchell's opinion, the song had never been played with more power or meaning than he now provided.

It had been years since he'd observed Virtue in her element. Mitchell hadn't forgotten how beautiful she was or how well she moved across a stage, but even with the years that had lapsed, she'd never been lovelier, nor had she ever danced more gracefully than she did right now. Seeing Virtue in a setting such as this one and performing to a song that was brought to life by his gifted fingers almost brought Mitchell to tears. A glow about her could be seen as she swayed and gestured, so much so that Mitchell believed they could blow out the candles and he would still be able to see her in spite of the darkness.

Sporadic outbursts from the crowd could be heard throughout her presentation. When Mitchell heard one loud, high-pitched female voice shout, "Boy, you betta play!" he realized that not all of the accolades were for Virtue. The song ended with Virtue on her knees with her hands cupped together under her chin and the crowd on its feet clapping and rendering verbal worship as though they'd just been delivered a second sermon.

The standing ovation sounded like the onset of an earthquake. The young people who had performed earlier banged on the tables, causing forks and plates to clank together under the vibration. The handclaps sounded like thunder, and cheers were deafening. Mitchell clenched his jaws together and swallowed back his emotions as he watched Virtue make several curtsies. Then, to Mitchell's surprise, she gestured an arm in his direction, making him the center of attention. The cheers that had begun dying down found new life, and Mitchell stood from the piano seat, placed his right hand over his heart, and ducked his head in appreciation.

As the pastor made his reentrance on the stage, Mitchell walked down the stairs and then turned to assist Virtue. There were only six steps, and he knew she didn't need his help, but offering it would give him a chance to touch her for the first time in seven years. She hesitated, but placed her hand in his and made her descent. At the bottom of the stairs their eyes met, but only for a fraction of a second before Virtue turned and exited through the side door. Turning in the opposite direction, Mitchell took the long walk back to his seat at the table near the rear.

Following the official benediction, the crowd dispersed, many trying to get home to see if their neighborhoods had fallen victim to the power outage. Mitchell shook countless hands that belonged to the unfamiliar faces that he'd seen throughout the evening. Several of them raved about his craft, and while Mitchell appreciated all of the kind words he received from the strangers, he searched for a more familiar face. Thirty minutes passed, and then an hour. Mitchell had spoken at length with the pastor and his wife, and now almost half the crowd had gone and Virtue still hadn't emerged from the other room.

"Hi."

Mitchell turned to the owner of the unfamiliar voice behind him. He returned the greeting and accepted her extended hand. She was a rather average-looking girl, but the white gown she wore was lovely. The way she held his hand longer than necessary immediately reminded him of Lisa. Mitchell pulled away.

"I'm Renee Bell," she said.

"Mitchell Andrews," he said, immediately wishing he could withdraw the second half of his response.

"Andrews?" She quickly picked up on the similarity. "Are you related to Virtue?" She pointed to the empty stage as she said the name.

Mitchell's mind raced at a speed quicker than light. "No," he answered, glad that he was being truthful.

"Well, you were amazing up there," she said. "You've had some classical training, haven't you?"

"No. I learned to play from my grandmother," Mitchell said while flashing an appreciative smile for the compliment she'd given him.

Renee tossed a look in Beverly's direction and then looked back at Mitchell. "So what's the deal? You two can't be a couple."

Mitchell looked across the room where Beverly stood next to the coffeemaker, sipping from a cup. She gave him a brief glance, but although she showed no outward emotion, Mitchell detected that there was friction between the two women. Before he could respond, two of the male teenagers who had participated in the earlier theatrical production walked up to him and began talking, exchanging brotherly pounds with Mitchell as they complimented him on his piano skills. The manner in which they interrupted was rather discourteous, but Mitchell was glad that they did.

"Come on, hon," Beverly said, walking up as soon as the boys dispersed. "I'm ready."

Renee continued to stand nearby and watched as Mitchell helped Beverly slip into her coat before putting on his own.

"The wedding was beautiful," she suddenly said.

Mitchell turned to look at her. He didn't know what she was referring to, but the look on Beverly's face indicated that she did.

"My boyfriend was the photographer. The photos are still on his digital," she said as she pulled the camera out of her open purse. "I'll bring them to church next Sunday for you to see." Setting the purse on the table beside the place where Mitchell stood, Renee proceeded to use both hands to spread the skirt of her gown and make a full turn, as if she were modeling before a crowd of buyers. "See the dress that the maid of honor wore? It was so expensive that I thought I'd get double my money's worth by wearing it twice before having to return it on Monday."

Mitchell began recalling his chat with Beverly yesterday, and the fog in his head began to lift. His first thought was to step in and rescue his friend, but as he considered,

Mitchell thought of another way that he could help that might be even better.

Beverly blew lightly into her cup and took a sip before responding. "Renee, I have no interest in your dress or the wedding."

As if she hadn't heard Beverly's response, Renee said, "Lester said he had never been happier, and Dondra was so beautiful, she was glowing. But between you and me, I think hers came more from the baby. I did tell you she was pregnant, didn't I? Hope that doesn't ruin your Christmas."

"Come on, let's go," Mitchell said as he stepped in front of Renee and escorted Beverly toward the door.

They made their exit, but it soon became clear that they were not going to get away so easily. Renee had grabbed her coat, draped it over her shoulders, and continued her taunting. Beverly mumbled something under her breath and attempted to turn, but Mitchell wouldn't let her.

"Keep walking, Beverly," he said.

"Lester said that you and your family were so poor that y'all had to get married in your mama's living room, and there weren't but eight people there to see it. Do you want to know how much money they spent on today's wedding?"

This time, Beverly turned before Mitchell could stop her. "No, Renee, I would not like to know how much the wedding cost. But it would be rather interesting to know how much the bridal shop will charge you for ruining their gown."

Renee quickly looked down at herself, trying to find what Beverly was referring to. Mitchell looked too, but both their questions were answered when Beverly took the top off of her near-full coffee cup and splashed the contents on the front of the expensive dress. Renee's eyes bulged, and she screamed in horror while the stain expanded, creating a large ugly scar.

"Hope that doesn't ruin your Christmas," Beverly said, mimicking Renee's own words before climbing in the driver's seat of her car and starting the ignition.

Mitchell raced around the car and got in just in time, before Beverly began backing away. Once they pulled out onto the street, Mitchell and Beverly exchanged glances and burst into laughter. When they began talking, it seemed as though they'd made an unspoken pact. Neither of them discussed Renee or what had just taken place. For the first few minutes, while they rode down the darkened streets, they chatted about the banquet, and Mitchell told her how much he'd enjoyed talking to Elder Bradley. When Beverly turned the conversation to Mitchell's playing and Virtue's dancing, the conversation fizzled when Mitchell didn't seem interested in keeping it going.

"Good night," he said as they pulled into the hotel's drop-off area.

"I'll be by bright and early to get you in the morning. If the power comes back on in time, Christmas dinner should start at noon. But I'll come and get you around nine."

"I don't think that's the best idea, Beverly. I think it's clear from tonight that Virtue doesn't want to see me. She's not ready for this. I've caused enough problems for her, and if she doesn't want me around, then I'd rather just not come. Thanks for everything, though," he said as he picked up her hand and placed a small object in it.

"What's this?" she asked, turning on the car's overhead light and then looking at Mitchell with her jaw dropped open.

"Yours," Mitchell said. "That's what it is."

Beverly looked again at the photo card that he'd removed from Renee's camera and then broke into a grin and pulled him over for a hug. "Thanks, Mitch," she said.

"Merry Christmas," he said with a laugh before stepping from the car and closing the door behind him.

Mitchell zipped his coat up to his neck and watched Beverly circle the driveway in preparation for heading back toward the street. As he turned away to walk through the hotel's entrance, a horn blew, and he stopped and turned.

"Nine o'clock," she said through her open window. "And I know your room number, so don't make me have to come up and get you."

Twenty-Seven

The two-carat diamond looked flawless to the naked eye. No one would know that it had a small chip in it that the jeweler had cleverly hidden beneath one of the prongs that held the diamond in its place. The chip was the reason that Chris had been able to purchase the diamond at such a good price. It looked perfect, but in reality it wasn't. The irony of it all made him shake his head.

Finding out the truth made Chris angry. He was angry both at himself and with Lisa, but he was angrier with her. Even with hard-core evidence pointed directly at her, Lisa wouldn't come out and tell the truth. Chris wanted to believe that Lisa was the one who was being honest, but even before he'd heard yesterday's message with his own ears, he had begun to doubt her. Since her first accusation of Mitchell, her story had changed twice. In the original account that made him release Mitchell of his duties and then attack him physically, Lisa had told Chris that his partner caused the bruise while he held her down on the top of his desk in an attempt to force himself on her. In version number two, which he'd overheard her telling her mother in a telephone conversation on the day after his horrific nightmare, Lisa said Mitchell had her arms pinned above her head while he held her against the wall of his office, trying to kiss her. The bruise resulted from her fight to get away. In her most recent explanation, the one that had been conveyed to Chris by Barbara, Lisa insisted that the mark resulted from Mitchell grabbing her by the wrist and jerking her back to him when she tried to walk away following his inappropriate advances.

The story had changed too many times. The flag that Lisa's inconsistencies had raised was so red that Chris felt as if he lived in China. Initially, he'd lied to himself and said that Lisa had been so traumatized by what had happened that she couldn't accurately recount the details. He'd heard that trauma could cause that kind of memory loss, and that was Chris's desperate diagnosis. To explain away the nightmare, he convinced himself that it was just a result of what Mitchell had accused Lisa of doing combined with the negative vibes he got when Rev. Inman refused to outright believe Lisa's story. Mentally, Chris wasn't ready for both his best friend and his pastor to take sides against him. Their doing so had weighed heavily on him, and when he drifted off to sleep that night, those were the thoughts that were heavy on his mind. To justify the dream, Chris kept recalling the Scripture that defined dreams as "a multitude of thoughts." Blaming the dream on the thoughts that were in his head as he went to bed that night gave him temporary comfort.

Then came the message. Because both he and Mitchell used their cell phones for business as well as personal matters, they used the same access codes to retrieve messages. They kept very few secrets from each other, and neither of them minded the other knowing their codes. Since he'd confiscated Mitchell's phone, Chris checked his messages every day to be sure that he didn't lose any clients while he searched for a capable replacement to handle Mitchell's former accounts. Yesterday, while he was listening to the messages, he was shocked to hear one from Lisa, who was oblivious to the fact that Mitchell's phone had been taken away.

"Hi, Mitchell, it's Lisa. I know you're angry at me right now, and you have every right to be. Believe it or not, I feel very bad about what happened between you and Chris. I knew telling him that you had tried to force yourself on me would upset him, but I honestly didn't know that it would turn into a fight or make you lose your job. I guess I wasn't thinking. I'm sorry about that. I'm sorry about this whole mess, but when you threw me out of the office that day, I knew that you were going to tell him what happened, so I had to get to him first. I couldn't let you talk first, because then he would be angry and probably would have ended our relationship. I didn't want that.

"I really do love Christopher, but there's just something about you and your mixture of sexy and saved that turns me on. Christopher has been a church boy all of his life, and sometimes a girl likes a man who is a little bit rough around the edges. You know what I mean? I want to spend the rest of my life with Chris, but I wanted to have just one time with you.

"You're my fantasy, and I thought that just maybe I could be yours too. I know your relationship with Christopher has been ruined forever, and knowing that most of that is due to me and what I told him makes me feel bad. But I think that it's better this way. Knowing the way I feel about you, it's probably not a good idea that the two of you be friends anyway. Since we're getting married, that would make for a very awkward situation, especially if you and I are ever left alone. I just wanted to call you and let you know that I'm sorry, and I hope you can find it in your heart to forgive me. If you're too angry at me to accept my apology, I understand. But if you want to keep in touch . . . or whatever . . . I'm game for that too. Bye."

Yesterday, Chris had been so torn and so angry that he chose to say and do nothing. He had already spoken with Lisa that morning, so it wasn't unusual for him not to contact her again later in the day. He'd come straight home from work and listened to the message at least three more times before going to bed. For most of the night, he lay awake, wanting to cry, but he couldn't. His first plan was to let the holiday pass and then confront Lisa, but that would mean that he would have to pretend that nothing had happened while he took Lisa to California with him to spend the day with his mother. Not only had he decided not to take her with him, but Chris decided that he wouldn't go either. His mother wasn't happy to hear of his sudden change of plans, but when he filled her in on the details of what had taken place over the last few days, her emotion changed from sadness to disappointment.

Chris lost count of how many times she said, "I am ashamed of you, Christopher!" and he understood why. He was ashamed of himself. His mother tossed aside the issue with Lisa, saying that she was never fond of her anyway. Her only regret that the marriage was going to be called off was that she knew that Christopher loved Lisa and that his heart would suffer because of her deceptions. Her main concern, though, was the manner in which he had carried on with Mitchell. Christopher's mom loved Mitchell. He had become like a part of their family, and her disappointment was about the way Christopher had chosen to handle the matter. For Chris, few things were more disheartening to him than having his mother tell him that she was ashamed of him.

As soon as he ended the call to his mother, Chris got dressed and headed to Lisa's apartment. The grin she displayed when she opened the door disappeared when he pressed the speakerphone button on Mitchell's cell and allowed her to hear the message. Even after hearing it, she swore that it wasn't her.

"Mitch must have had some girl call his phone and say all that stuff so that he could bring it to you and make you think it's me."

When he heard her absurd defense, Chris just shook his head and looked at her in disgust. That's when things turned messy. Accusations were tossed between the two of them. Their voices rose to a level that caused Lisa's nosy neighbors to come to their doors to see what the commotion was about. Chris couldn't believe it when Lisa gathered the nerve to accuse him of being unfaithful. She said that his desire to be with another woman was the driving force behind him believing Mitchell over her. She screamed at him, saying he was no better a man than Felander, and proceeded to call all men "cheaters."

Chris didn't take her verbal abuse lying down, though. His mother would have been ashamed of him for the way he carried on, but he refused to let Lisa's neighbors think that he was the reason for the breakup. He'd loved her too much and been too trusting of her to allow her to make him look like the unfaithful one. He loudly announced her infidelity, and for emphasis, he replayed the message on Mitchell's phone for those closest to them to hear. It was like a never-ending scene from Jerry Springer.

"Hey . . . hey!"

Chris turned around to see a man approaching with a bouquet of flowers in his hand. It was apparent from the look on Lisa's face that the man's visit wasn't a scheduled one. But what was more apparent to Chris was that this man's visit was not a *first* one.

"Fool, what you doin' all up in my girl's face?" the man asked as he stood toe-to-toe with Chris with an expression on his face that made it clear that he had no problem with coming to blows.

Realizing that he'd been played even more than he'd been aware, Chris took several steps away from the man and looked at Lisa with repulsion. A part of him was so angry that he could have spit in her face, and another part of him was hurting so deeply that he wanted to curl into the fetal position and cry like an infant. But Chris chose not to do either one. Lisa seemed too shocked by her surprise visitor to say anything more in her defense. Chris took several more steps away from the man who still stood in a threatening pose.

"That's right, baby, she ain't worth it," one of the older neighbors called to Chris as she stood in her doorway, two doors down. "You deserve better anyway."

Chris determined that as painful as it was, the old lady was right.

"Christopher . . . ," Lisa said.

"God help you, Lisa," Chris responded as he began backing away. "If I never see you again, that'll be just fine by me. But God help you."

Chris hadn't asked her for the ring back, but when she tearfully snatched it from her finger and threw it at him, saying that she deserved someone better than he, Chris agreed. She immediately had second thoughts about the jewelry and demanded the ring back, calling it a gift that he could not repossess. If he didn't give it back, she threatened to sue him. Chris thought of the price tag that had come with the ring and the number of monthly payments he still had to make before it would be paid off and decided that he'd take his chances. He made his exit from the apartment hallway before Lisa's *other* boyfriend could get any ideas on ways to get the expensive jewelry from him.

Now, snapping the box shut, Chris tossed it onto his bed, fell back onto the mattress, and stared up at the ceiling. He began recalling things that he'd purposely ignored over the past two years. There were times when he'd caught glimpses of Lisa's "friendly" exchanges with Mitchell when she thought he wasn't around. He even remembered a time when he'd almost brought it to her attention. But then he thought about the first heart-to-heart talk that he and Lisa had had when their relationship began to get serious. She'd told Chris about Felander and his jealousies. Chris didn't want her to see him as a man with the same insecurities that her first husband had, so he never said anything, believing in his heart that all of her flirtations were harmless. Chris felt like a certified fool.

He was embarrassed just thinking about the lengths he'd gone to in his fight to defend Lisa's honor. He had mistreated people who cared about him and ousted the man who had been nothing but a friend to him since Chris had hired him on as a business partner. Mitchell had helped him salvage his father's business when the work that had accumulated during those months when he'd tried to do it alone threatened to swallow him. Chris still remembered the all-nighters that they'd pulled to catch the business up to date. Through it all, Mitchell never complained. He worked as if it were his own father who had laid the foundation for Jackson, Jackson & Andrews.

This afternoon, after rehearsing his apology in front of the same mirror he'd used to practice his wedding vows, Chris had taken the drive to Living Word Cathedral to talk to Rev. Inman. Chris was certain that he would find Rev. Inman at the church, and although he knew going in that his pastor would forgive him, the knowledge of it didn't make admitting his awful mistake any less embarrassing. Now, as he lay still staring at the ceiling, Chris knew that talking to Rev. Inman had been the easy part.

For three years he and Mitchell had been inseparable. Their bond was so solid that they'd been able to work together day in and day out and still be friends both on and off the clock. They knew how to separate business dealings from personal matters. Chris couldn't have been prouder of the man that he'd chosen to help him fulfill his father's dreams. Mitchell had never been anything other than honest and dependable. His biggest fault was running on a clock that was fifteen minutes slower than everyone else's, but that was minor. Chris knew he could trust Mitchell with his life. He was his ace, his sidekick, and his right-hand man. He had known Mitchell longer than he'd known Lisa, but when the cards were laid on the table, he'd chosen the queen of hearts over the ace of spades, and it had been the worst gamble of his life.

Disrespecting a man was one thing, but demeaning him was another. Although Chris's disrespect for his pastor and his friend had been on different levels, what he had done to Mitchell was far worse. He had accused him of being immoral, openly referring to him as a rapist and a chronic abuser of women. He had brought up Mitchell's past, things that had been told to him in confidence; and he threw them back in his face in front of someone who had no prior knowledge of it. His rage against Mitchell for what he thought he'd done had him using his powers as two-thirds of the partnership to strip Mitchell of his livelihood and to drive him from the office literally battered and bruised.

"How do you apologize to a man after all of that?" Chris spoke aloud.

When he thought of how he'd even put Mitchell's manhood in question, it made the possibility of being forgiven drop even lower on the percentage chart. Rev. Inman told him that whether Mitchell accepted his apology or not, it was Chris's God-ordered duty to seek forgiveness. Right off the top of his head, Rev. Inman quoted at least a half-dozen Scriptures to back his findings. There was no getting around it.

Twice today he'd called and left messages on Mitchell's voice mail. To no surprise, he'd not yet received a return call. As a last ditch effort and with the hopes that he'd at least come out of it alive, he'd driven to Mitchell's place. Chris had just yelled at Mitchell a few days ago, accusing him of being a coward, and Mitch had been trying to apologize to him over the phone. Now here he was, doing the same thing. But the attempt to visit came up empty too. Chris had knocked on the door and rang the doorbell, but got no answer. He'd looked through the window on the garage door and saw Mitchell's car parked in its usual place. Chris knew then that Mitchell wanted nothing further to do with him. He'd been left with no choice but to return home with his tail between his legs. Perhaps the worst part of it all was that Chris couldn't blame him. If the tables had been turned, he was sure he'd react the same way that Mitchell was reacting.

Shortly after his father passed, Chris remembered hearing his mother say, "You don't really know how much you love somebody until they're gone."

She was right.

Twenty-Eight

Mitchell had been in bed for three hours, but sleep had totally escaped him. The hotel's emergency power source saved him from being in the dark like most of the city. The digital clock beside his bed reminded him that it was already Christmas morning, and he only had a few hours to try to get some rest before he'd have to get up and be ready to meet Beverly downstairs. Mitchell was still grateful for her invitation to join her for the holiday, but he had to admit that a big part of why he'd agreed to the four-hour drive and to paying the high cost of the one-way airline ticket back to Dallas on the twenty-sixth was because he hoped it would give him some time to spend with Virtue. So far, nothing could be further from the truth. He hated to think that he'd have to go back home with only the memory of touching her hand to help her down the steps of the stage.

Just like he did every night that he knelt at bedtime, Mitchell began his prayer by thanking God for another day and ended it with a plea for Virtue. After not being able to get the song that he had played for Virtue out of his mind, Mitchell gave his prayer a twist, telling God that *this*—another chance with Virtue—was his Christmas prayer. He got up feeling like the little gap-toothed boy that he'd seen years ago, dancing around and singing, "All I want for Christmas is my two front teeth." If Mitchell could have an "all I want for Christmas" wish, Virtue would be it. He'd prayed the prayer for so long that it seemed senseless to give up now. Every time he thought about giving up, Beverly's words rang in Mitchell's ear.

Sometimes what you're asking for is just one prayer away.

The thought that he might give up when the prayer was so close to being answered wasn't a chance that he wanted to take. Virtue was worth every prayer he uttered. Without a morsel of sleepiness inside of him, Mitchell sat up in the bed, put on his eyeglasses, and flipped through the channels of the television. The suitcase that sat in the corner caught his eye. As was customary for him, he had never unpacked it. When he traveled, all of his clothes remained in his bags unless they needed to be hung in the closet. That way, he never made the mistake of leaving anything behind, and he didn't have to get up any earlier than necessary to catch his flight on the day of checkout. Right now, the only clothing items that were outside of his bags were the ones he'd already pressed in preparation for Christmas at Beverly's.

He settled on a program to watch, cranked up the volume, and sat with his back against his pillows for comfort. At home when he couldn't sleep, the sound of the television sometimes helped. Forty-five minutes later, he was watching the credits scroll up the screen from an old episode of *In the Heat of the Night*. The show had long ago been out of production, but it was still one of his favorite TV series.

All the measures that normally worked during the rare times when Mitchell was faced with symptoms of insomnia had been exhausted. He'd read a few passages of Scripture, drunk a cup of hot apple cider, and watched television. Short of driving to a convenience store and buying some over-the-counter sleeping pills, he didn't know what else he could do. He hadn't been so sleepless on the night before Christmas since he was a little boy anticipating the arrival of all the fair-weather friends who would stop by for some of his grandmother's cooking.

What at first he thought to be a sound coming from the television turned out to be knocks on his hotel room door. Mitchell turned down the volume. Oddly enough, when he had trouble sleeping, the louder the volume was, the better the chances were that he'd drift off. He slipped on his bathrobe and headed for the door, prepared to give an apology to the neighbors in the next room for his lack of consideration.

"Hey." The word was barely capable of being heard when it escaped his lips. The last thing Mitchell expected when he opened the door was to look down into Virtue's eyes.

"Hey." Her voice was even less audible than his had been, and even though she'd just gotten there, Virtue already looked like she was close to tears.

"Come in. I mean, would you like to come inside?" Mitchell wanted to be careful not to say or do anything that might make her feel threatened. She had come alone, and he didn't want to give her a reason for regrets.

Nodding slowly, Virtue brushed past him when he stepped aside to give her clearance.

"Would you like something to drink?" he offered as he closed the door.

Mitchell watched Virtue's head shake in slow motion as her eyes locked on the Bible that still lay open on his bed.

"Would you like to sit?" He pointed in the direction of the round table in the corner near the window.

"Why are you here?" she asked suddenly.

Mitchell paused. "Because Beverly invited me. Didn't she tell you?"

"Yes. But why are you *really* here?"

Her inquiry didn't exactly surprise him. Virtue was a smart woman, and she knew him well.

"Because I love you." He saw no reason to continue hesitating. He'd prayed for time, and God had delivered. Mitchell felt that it was best that he make the most of it.

The tears that were pooling when she'd first knocked at his door had now begun to trickle down Virtue's cheeks. She shook her head as though his answer were unacceptable, or maybe it was just that she didn't believe him.

"I do love you, Virtue," Mitchell said. "I know I hurt you in unimaginable ways, but . . ."

"There are no acceptable excuses for what you did to me or what you did to us. You lied to me, Mitchell. You said you'd love, honor, and cherish me; but instead you broke my heart and did all you could to break my spirit. There are no 'buts,' Mitchell. There are no excuses."

"And I'm not trying to give you any." Mitchell started to step closer to her but didn't. "I was wrong, period. No reasons are good enough to explain away what I did. I meant every word of my wedding vows, Virtue; you have to believe me. I let alcoholism take over and turn me into somebody that I wasn't. But just like I told you when I met you and Beverly for lunch, I was a different person then. I was a drunk, a fool, and, worst of all, I was a sinner.

"I didn't know how to handle Grandpa Isaac's death nor Grandma Kate's. I hated myself and everything about me. You were the sweetest wife a man could ask for. I just took out on you what I felt about myself. I treated you like trash because that's what I felt like. I hurt you because I was hurting. I knew I was wrong when I did it, but it took God to bring me to the place where I could accept responsibility for it. I can't take away the turmoil, sweetheart; if I could I'd do it in a New York minute. All I can do at this point is say I'm sorry and beg your forgiveness."

Virtue shook her head. "You don't have to do that any-more, Mitchell. I've already forgiven you, but I still wanted you to know how I felt. The day you met us for lunch, I had a million things that I wanted to say, but I couldn't say them. I had all these questions to ask, but I couldn't ask them."

"You didn't even look at me."

"I *couldn't* look at you. All of that hurt and anger from seven years ago resurfaced that day. Even when you said that you had given your life to Christ, I was angry. God dealt with me heavily on that. I felt like it wasn't even fair that He would accept you. I wanted Him to punish you, not save you. I thought you should hurt the same way I had been forced to hurt."

"If it's any consolation, I think my ex-partner took care of that for you," Mitchell said while pointing at the fading bruise on his face.

"Oh, yeah," Virtue said. "I'm sorry about what hap-pened. Beverly said you were still in a lot of pain when she got there."

Mitchell smiled. "She took care of me well. You're very fortunate to have her in your life. I guess when you're this far away from your mother, having a person like Beverly is an extra blessing."

Virtue didn't respond. Instead she wrapped herself in her arms as if a sudden draft had entered the space.

"It was great to see you dance again," he said, breaking the silence. "You did it beautifully, as always."

"Thank you," she said, looking up at him momentarily before turning away. "I had forgotten that you could play the piano so well. Thanks for doing it for me."

"I'd do anything for you, Virtue," he whispered. "I know you don't want to hear this, but I love you so much, and all I want is a chance to prove it."

At his words, she turned and walked in the direction of

his window. The curtains were closed, but she stared at them as though she could see through the fabric. "It's been seven years, Mitchell," she said with new tears spilling from her eyes. "It's too late."

"No, it's not too late. It's been seven years; so what? Look at how we've both changed during those years. We needed those years, baby. We took two whole different paths during that time, but both of our journeys led us to God and then back to each other. I know I'm not the only one feeling this, Virtue. Can't we give this another chance? It's not even a chance," he added. "Chance involves risks. What we have, if you let me back in, is a sure thing. There are no gambles here, Virtue. You and me . . . we're a sure thing. Please, baby."

Even to himself, he sounded like a spineless, begging wimp, but Mitchell didn't care. There was no time for ego trips or masculine hang-ups. He remembered when he was a teenager in high school, bragging along with his friends that he'd never beg a woman for anything. If there was going to be any groveling in any of his relationships, *she* would be the one who would be pleading for another chance to be his one and only. All of that juvenile macho foolishness meant nothing right now. This could be the last time he would talk to Virtue, and he'd get on his knees if that would win her back.

"You hit me, Mitchell," Virtue whispered through trembling lips and increased sobs. "I swore that I'd never become my mama by letting a man hit me and still remain with him."

The words caused Mitchell to step backward. "Peggy?" His words reflected his shock. "Walter hit Peggy?"

"I grew up watching Mama get slapped around all the time," she blurted. "I loved my daddy so much, Mitchell. I was a daddy's girl if there ever was one. He never showed me anything but love, but he beat Mama on a regular basis. I tried to pretend it wasn't happening because she tried to pretend it wasn't happening, but I knew. I knew it all along, and I promised myself that I'd never live a life like that: lying to people about falling or cutting myself in the rose garden or slamming my hand in the car door. For years my mama got beat by a man who said he loved her. He was the same man who told me that he'd kill any man who touched his baby girl. And you know what, Mitchell? I believed him. That's why I never told him the truth about what happened with us—because I believed him. My daddy abused my mother for thirty years, Mitchell. *Thirty* years."

Mitchell recalled Virtue's mother's arm being in a sling on the day he had met her, and she'd been on crutches with a sprained foot on the day they got married. The abuse was a secret that Virtue had kept from him throughout the time that they were together. Mitchell wished she'd never told him. Knowledge of it heightened the magnitude of the shame he already felt for what he'd done.

"I'm so sorry," he said before proceeding with caution. "I know this doesn't make it any better, but you said thirty years. Did Peggy finally leave him? Did the abuse stop?"

Virtue accepted the box of tissues that Mitchell handed her from the dresser behind him. "Yeah, it stopped," she said. "It stopped three years ago today, on Christmas morning, when she ran from the house during one of Daddy's beatings. I was home visiting for the holiday, and I begged him to stop, but he wouldn't. In her desperation to get away from him, Mama darted blindly between two parked cars and right out into the street. I saw my mother get killed instantly by an oncoming vehicle."

Virtue's last words were distorted by a burst of tears. On impulse, Mitchell reached out and grabbed her, holding her close to his chest. He rethought his actions almost immediately, but she seemed to welcome his comfort. The tight hold that they had on each other drew pain from Mitchell's bruised rib, but having Virtue this close and returning his embrace felt too good to let go. Delivering a single kiss to the top of her head, Mitchell stroked her pinned-back hair until her sobs quieted.

"I'm sorry for not being there for you," Mitchell whispered. "I wasn't there for you then, sweetheart, but let me be here for you now."

"I can't, Mitchell," she said, slightly pulling away and looking up at him. "I can't forget the old memories. I have a scar on my head that won't let me forget the memories."

Although she'd forced a small gap of separation between them, her hands remained around his waist, and Mitchell saw a glimpse of the look that the Virtue he married would give him in her eyes. He never considered himself a gambler, a daredevil, or even much of a risk taker, but Mitchell would bet it all for this one chance.

"Baby, I'm not asking you to forget the old memories. I'm asking you to allow us to make some new ones. Please let me give you some new ones."

Before she could respond, Mitchell's mouth found hers; and for him, it was as though seven years of separation began dissolving. Initially, he was cautious, not wanting Virtue to feel overwhelmed by his heightening passion; but when she offered no resistance, Mitchell pulled her closer. Without letting go of her, he removed the clip from her hair and ran his fingers through her thick hair like he used to before his habit complicated their lives. Virtue moaned when his mouth traveled to her ear. Whispering words that he hoped would remove any doubt from her mind of how much he loved her and wanted to make things right between them, Mitchell placed more kisses on her cheeks, her forehead, her nose, wherever his lips landed. Ultimately, they found their way back to hers, deepening with every breath taken.

The telephone blared, startling both of them and prompting them to pull away from each other. Wiping the moisture from her lips, Virtue turned away. Mitchell watched her momentarily and then looked at the phone again when it rang for the third time.

"Hello?"

"Okay, it's time for Virtue to come on home now," Beverly said. "She don't need to be over there at that hotel with you for too long. Y'all might forget that you're not married anymore. Tell her I'll be waiting up for her."

~ Twenty-Nine ~

*W*hen Virtue walked in the door, Beverly was sitting on the living room couch waiting up for her just as she'd promised. Several large candles were lit and had been placed in different areas of the house. Fortunately for them, their heating was gas-powered and the house, although dark, was warm and comfortable.

"Did God tell me to call when I did, or did God tell me to call when I did?" Beverly asked knowingly when Virtue sank onto the love seat across from her.

"Mitchell wants us to get back together," she said, leaving the question unanswered.

"And this surprises you?"

"No," Virtue said. "What surprises me is that I want it too." Even in the low lighting, Virtue could see Beverly's toothy grin. "I didn't give him an answer," she quickly added. "I want to believe all of his promises, but I did that before and ended up hurt."

"There you go, dredging up the past again," Beverly said, throwing her arms up in the air and then allowing them to drop by her side.

"I can't help it," Virtue defended. "It's my past, and I have permanent scars that won't allow me to just pretend that nothing happened."

"Well, fine," Beverly said in frustration as she rose from the couch. "The boy is not going to wait around for you forever, and he doesn't deserve for you to keep throwing all that old mess up in his face; so if you're not going to be able to move on *with* him, then tell him that so at least he can move on *without* you."

Virtue sat in silence while Beverly rounded the sofa and headed down the hall. A few seconds later, she heard Beverly's bedroom door slam. Too tired to try to sit up and sort things out tonight, Virtue walked through the living room and began blowing out the candles. She picked up the two that stood on the dining room table and carefully carried them to the bathroom so that she could shower and prepare for bed. Virtue picked up her brush from the bathroom counter and began her one-hundred-strokes-per-night routine. It was a habit that she'd picked up from her mother. Peggy Monroe taught her that if she brushed her hair every night, using one hundred strokes, her hair would continue to grow. Virtue didn't know if it was true or not, but she'd always had a head full of hair that would at least challenge anyone who disputed it.

With the strokes complete, she put the brush down and began running her fingers through her hair in preparation of tying it back for the night. As she'd often done in the past, Virtue parted the hairs and looked at the scar that barely showed under the dim candlelight.

"That's just how it's going to be on the day of judgment."

Beverly's voice startled Virtue, and she winced before turning to face her. She hadn't heard Beverly emerge from her room, nor had she taken notice when she first approached the open bathroom door. Virtue said nothing. She only looked at Beverly and waited for the clarification that she knew was soon to follow.

"All kinds of folks who have been letting the devil wreak havoc on their lives and cause them to do foolish things are going to have to squint just like you're having to do in order to see that scar," Beverly said. "I can just imagine all the sinners looking at the devil and saying, 'This little thing? Is this the little thing that I allowed to make me miss out on eternal life?' Virtue, the devil knows how to make himself look a whole lot bigger than he is, and he knows how to make our problems look a whole lot bigger than they are too. You think about that and then ask yourself if that little scar on your head is worth you missing out on a good life with the man you love."

By daylight on Sunday, electrical power had been restored around the city of Houston, and once again, Christmas was in full bloom. Mitchell woke up at the sound of his alarm clock, but for several minutes he remained in bed. His first thoughts were of Virtue and the passionate exchange that he could still feel on his lips. Mitchell wanted to believe that it was the start of something new for them, but when he recalled the manner in which she'd rushed out after Beverly's call, he wasn't sure.

With less than four hours of sleep, Mitchell's body was tired, and it begged to remain under the covers of the comfortable bed. Even after Virtue left, Mitchell had continued to struggle with getting to sleep. He finally drifted just after the clock read 4:00. More than the kiss had him thinking about last night, though. He still couldn't believe that his former mother-in-law was dead. Knowing that Walter had been the cause of her death was even more astonishing. Mitchell had never had a clue of the abuse that was going on in his in-laws' house. But he was sure that there were many who would have said the same for his household during the time that he'd hurt Virtue.

The situation involving her family made Mitchell realize just how blessed he had been. All of the worst forms of what-ifs ran through his mind. He was sure that Walter, during his episode on that fateful day, didn't intentionally run his wife into the path of oncoming traffic any more than Mitchell had intended to hit Virtue so hard that it caused her to bleed from the impact her head made against the table. Mitchell realized that as bad as his situation was, it could have been much worse.

What if Virtue had fallen in a different direction? What if the table had struck her head in a more crucial place? What if she'd never gotten up? What if she'd died at the hands of his drunken rage? Mitchell would never have forgiven himself, and he knew that his whole life would have turned out differently. He definitely would have gone to prison and probably would have lived out the rest of his days on suicide watch. He never would have met Chris and, most likely, never would have found God. Chris may be gone from his life now, but he had been there at the time that Mitchell needed him.

Mitchell recalled a sermon that Rev. Inman had preached once. He'd said that God placed people in the lives of others for different reasons. Some weren't meant to stay forever. They were there for a specific purpose and to help fulfill a particular season. Mitchell had thought that he and Chris would be best friends forever, but now he was left to believe that their bond was a seasonal one. Chris's purpose was to give Mitchell a new start in life and to lead him to Christ. Even with the bitter way that their friendship had ended, Mitchell could find no reasons to be regretful.

Just as she had promised, Beverly was pulling up to the front door of the hotel at nine o'clock sharp; and once again, Mitchell was on time, for a change. It wasn't until he was inside of Beverly's car that Mitchell realized he would be arriving at a Christmas gathering with no gifts to give.

"Nobody cares about that," Beverly told him when he voiced his concerns. "In my house, Christmas isn't about gift giving. Christmas in Dr. Beverly Oliver's house is about thanksgiving. We thank God for family, friends, and food; and if you get a gift or two out of it, then that's just gravy. Besides," she added with a grin as she pointed to the digital photo card that she had placed in her ashtray, "I got mine."

Mitchell laughed and then thought about all that Beverly had just said. His mind went back twenty years. Isaac and Kate hadn't been religious people, but they hadn't been wasteful people either. There always had been more money spent on food than gifts. With his grandparents, Christmas had definitely been more about having a house full of guests than watching their grandson peel the wrappings from toys that he'd soon break or lose interest in.

As they reached the home that Beverly and Virtue shared, Mitchell saw no additional cars in the driveway or parked across the grass. The celebration here would be far less eventful than the ones that his grandparents had hosted. While he didn't want to appear anxious, once he was inside Mitchell's eyes immediately darted to every corner of the decorated living room. He'd not wanted to ask during the ride, but he hoped that Virtue would be joining them.

"Good morning."

Those two words formed the answer to his prayer. Mitchell turned around to see Virtue walking from the kitchen. Wearing a pair of jeans, a red top, boots, and her hair pulled back in a neat ponytail, she looked like the college girl that he had met in the canned foods aisle more than ten years ago.

"Good morning," he said as he watched her pass him and place a tray of assorted pastries and milk on the coffee table.

"This is for if you get hungry before the dinner gets ready," she said before turning away and heading back to the kitchen.

It concerned Mitchell that she never really looked at him, but he thanked her and then made himself comfortable on the sofa. While he enjoyed the Danish, Mitchell listened to the Christmas music that streamed from the speakers and watched the women work. Twice he offered to help, but Beverly refused.

"Is anyone else coming?" Mitchell asked when he saw the amount of food that was being placed on the table that seated six.

"Not unless you invited someone," Beverly said. "I should have invited Rev. Inman. I noticed he wasn't wearing a ring. Is he married?" She winked and flashed a smile at Mitchell, but disappeared back into the kitchen before he could answer.

Her words sparked an image in Mitchell's head. Beverly was a few years older than his pastor, but it just might work. He laughed to himself as he finished drinking a glass of milk. Standing from the sofa, Mitchell walked to a shelf that was cluttered with photo frames that housed pictures of people he didn't know. He assumed that they were relatives of Beverly's. One frame caught his eye, and he reached to carefully retrieved it so that he didn't disturb the others that stood nearby. With his thumb, he wiped away particles of dust that had accumulated on the glass.

"They look happy, don't they?" Virtue said, startling him.

Mitchell looked at her and then back at the photo of her parents. "Yeah," he nodded. "I'm really sorry about what happened."

"Me too," she replied.

Hearing the sadness in her voice, Mitchell wondered if he should change the subject, but there was more that he wanted to know. "What happened to Walter? Where is he now?"

"In the Mid-Michigan Correctional Facility," Virtue told him as she took the picture from his hand and admired it for a moment before placing it back on the shelf.

Walter Monroe had to be in his sixties now. Although he knew it happened all the time, Mitchell found it hard to picture a man his age locked behind prison bars.

"It will be seven more years before he's even eligible for parole," she said as she shook her head in sadness.

"Do you go by to see him?"

"He killed my mother, Mitchell," she said, avoiding a direct answer. "Every year I send him a Father's Day gift, but that's as much as I can do right now. I know he didn't mean to do it, but my mom is still dead. He's the reason I believe that any man who is capable of hitting me is capable of killing me."

Mitchell felt that the last statement was meant especially for him. "A man who doesn't know God is capable of doing anything evil, Virtue," he said. "But a man who knows Him is capable of doing anything good."

Virtue's eyes dropped to the floor, and then she sighed before turning her back to him. Stepping forward, Mitchell embraced her from behind and felt her body relax and melt in his arms.

"Just tell me how much time you need," he whispered in her ear. "I've waited seven years; I can wait longer."

Virtue freed herself from his hold and turned to face him. Cupping his face in her hands, she brought his face to hers and placed a light kiss on his lips. The unexpected touch from her lips gave his heart a jolt with a force that seemed to move it from its usual place.

"I don't need time to know what's in my heart, Mitchell," she said. "But I do want to take things slowly."

With the pounding that he could feel in the bottom of his stomach, Mitchell was certain that that was where his heart had relocated. In his mind, he pictured himself with a second chance to woo her again. A second chance for a first date. A second chance to propose—and a second chance to spend the rest of his life with her.

"I can do that," he said and then added, "But . . . but how slow are we talking about?"

Virtue laughed at his sudden concern. "How about we just start out as friends and take it from there?"

That was slower than Mitchell would have liked, but it was faster than any length of time he ever would have thought she'd give him. His response was a grateful nod, and then he added, "Okay, but sometimes friends kiss. Can we at least be kissing friends?"

This time, Virtue laughed out loud and then allowed him to give her a demonstration. "Okay," she said, looking into his eyes when he released her. "We can kiss every once in a while."

"Good thing he doesn't live right around the corner," Beverly said as she walked into the living room. "I'd have to quit my job just to keep an eye on you two."

"I'm sorry," Mitchell said, forcing himself to release Virtue.

"No need," Beverly said. "I'm happy too. From here on out, you don't ever have to think that you don't have family."

Mitchell found both her words and the long embrace that followed comforting. He was coming very near the point of tears when Beverly pulled away and announced that dinner was ready. They had settled down at the table and had just asked the blessing when the telephone rang. Excusing herself, Virtue vacated her seat and picked up the cordless phone that sat on a cradle beside the living room sofa. Mitchell had been enjoying light chatter with Beverly, but it didn't take long for both of them to realize that there was something special about this call.

Virtue pressed the mouthpiece of the phone into her stomach and walked slowly toward the table, coming to a stop beside Mitchell. "It's Christopher," she whispered.

Mitchell set his drink on the table and stared at the phone in her hand. He hadn't heard anything from his former partner and friend since the fight, and he'd never expected to hear from him again. Why was he calling now? After all, Chris was the one who pointed out to him that the operative word was *never*. For the life of him, Mitchell couldn't think of what he and Chris needed to talk about. He wasn't even sure that he *wanted* to speak with him. Memories of the painful punches and the hurtful words that were spoken to him replayed in Mitchell's mind. The more he thought of them, the angrier he became.

"How did he know you were here?" Beverly asked.

"He said his pastor told him that he might find Mitchell here," Virtue answered before turning back to Mitchell. "What do you want me to tell him?"

Standing from his chair and wiping his mouth with a napkin, Mitchell reached for the phone that was still pressed into Virtue's stomach. "I got it," he said.

When Virtue handed it to him, Mitchell walked to the living room and sat on the love seat before answering. "Hello?" Mitchell's tone was cold, mirroring the way he felt inside.

"Mitch, hey."

Chris's voice sounded different. It didn't sound angry and full of animosity as it had the last time Mitchell had seen him, but it also didn't have the relaxed tone of confidence that it carried on a regular basis. Mitchell didn't return the greeting, and after a short silence, Chris spoke again.

"Look, I'm going to get right to it. I called to apologize for what happened last Monday," he said. It wasn't what Mitchell expected to hear, but he refrained from immediately responding.

"I was wrong, and I'm sorry," Chris said. "I found out the truth, the story that you had been trying to tell me all along. I know I made a mistake by taking her word over yours, but I just couldn't believe that she'd do something like that."

"But you thought that *I* could?" Mitchell blurted, catching the attention of the women at the table.

"I know, man; I know," Chris said. "I messed up. I don't know what else to say. I'm sorry, dude. I'm sorry."

"That's all you got? You're sorry?"

"What else do you want me to say?"

By now, Virtue was sitting beside him for support, but Mitchell was almost too upset to realize that she was there.

"Man, I don't want you to say nothing!" he barked into the phone. "You said enough on Monday."

"I understand you being mad at me," Chris said. "I'd understand if you stayed mad forever. But I had to at least try and apologize and do what I could to make it right. I wanted to offer you your job back too, if you're still interested in working with me. I'm sorry for the name-calling and for hitting you, and . . ."

"Chris, you didn't just hit me; you hit me *two times*. You almost busted my ribs. I still have the bruises to . . ."

Mitchell's sentence drifted off when he felt Virtue place her hand on his knee; and for the first time, he heard the irony behind his own words. Turning to his left, his eyes met Virtue's, and he could read her every thought.

"I'm sorry, man," Chris was saying in his ear. "I can't believe I lost it like that. I mean, I want my friend back; but if I can't have him, I can't blame nobody but myself. All I'm asking is that you give it some thought."

In silence, Mitchell reached over and took Virtue's hand in his. As if she could hear both ends of the conversation, she gave his hand a tight squeeze and nodded.

"I'll tell you what," Mitchell said into the telephone. "Why don't we take it slow? Let's just start out as business partners and see where it goes from there."

With his voice full of relief, Chris replied, "I can do that. Thanks, man. This means a lot to me. Enjoy your Christmas. I'll see you in the office on Tuesday."

"I'm proud of you," Virtue whispered as she touched his cheek with her hand.

Mitchell reached for her and pulled her to his chest, wrapping his arms around her as tightly as he could. In his heart and mind, life couldn't get much better than this.

Readers' Discussion Guide

1 Fear is the word that best adequately describes Virtue's immediate reaction to seeing Mitchell for the first time in seven years. How realistic is it that she would still be afraid after so many years?

2 Were there clear, unmistakable signs that Chris should have discerned as inappropriate where Lisa's attraction to Mitchell was concerned or do you think she masked them well enough for her fiancé to be fooled?

3 Had Mitchell chosen to go directly to Chris and tell him of his encounter with Lisa, do you think it would have lessened Chris's anger toward him? Do you think Chris would have believed him?

4 Was Beverly too passive about the loss of her husband to another woman or was she right to release her un-faithful husband without a long-term fight?

5 Renee Bell tested Beverly's Christianity to no end. Was Beverly wrong when she finally reacted to Renee's taunting?

6 What do you think of Mitchell's family's reaction to Isaac's and Kate's deaths? Were they justified in blaming and excommunicating him?

7. Should Virtue have left Mitchell permanently after he struck her the first time, or was she right to give him a second chance, only to be hit again?

8 Both Virtue and Mitchell sought professional help for their respective issues. How important do you think that was for their total healing?

9 How did you feel about Virtue's choice not to visit her incarcerated father?

10 What was your reaction to Fynn's determination to hold on to the ritualistic beliefs of his father and grandfather?

11 Do you feel that Pastor Bradley's decision to remove Fynn from his position as youth pastor was too harsh? Why or why not?

12 Chris immediately chose to take sides with the woman he loved over his best friend. In your opinion, is that the stance that a man or woman of God should take when put in this situation? Why or why not?

13 For a moment, Mitchell lost sight of God during Lisa's last ploy to snag him and almost fell into temptation. What are your thoughts concerning his momentary weakness?

14 In your imagination, what do you think became of Mitchell's and Chris's partnership/friendship? Do you think it ever returned to its former state?

15 Did you like the story's ending? Why or why not?

16 Who was your favorite and least favorite character? Explain.

17 Was there any part of the story you would have changed? If so, which part?

18 It is estimated that a woman is battered every nine seconds. Why, do you think, that even in the twenty-first century, domestic violence is still such a taboo subject within the walls of many establishments (including churches)?

19 Domestic violence is categorized as any coercive behavior that is used by one person over another in an intimate relationship. It comes in many forms: physical (beatings), threats (verbal), sexual (rape), economic (forcibly taking away money), and psychological (mind games). Take a moment and discuss cases that you may be aware of.

20 The National Domestic Violence Hotline is 1-800-799-SAFE. Please pass it along to anyone you feel may be in need.

~ Acknowledgments ~

"In everything give thanks: for this is the will of God in Christ Jesus concerning you."
(1 Thessalonians 5:18)

Heavenly Father, my cup overflows with Your favor and Your grace and I don't have the time or the space to truly give thanks for everything You have provided. Thank You for my husband, **Jonathan**, who takes the meanings of pride and provision to a whole new level, and my babies, **Brittney** and **Crystal**, who have now grown into beautiful, gifted teenagers that You have already begun using for Your glory. Thank You for my parents, **Bishop H.H. & Mrs. Francine Norman** and my siblings, **Crystal (Albert), Harold (Gloria), Cynthia (Terry),** and **Kimberly** for giving me the kind of love and support that could never be bartered, bought, or borrowed. Thank You for the encouraging members of the **Holmes** and **Bellamy** families and for the love of my lifelong godparents, **Aunt Joyce** and **Uncle Irvin**. Though I only birthed two children, I thank You, Lord, for the growing list of young lives You've added to my existence in the form of godchildren: **Mildred, Jon-Jon, Courtney, LaMonte,** and **Cayla.** Thank You for my "bestest cousin" and associate publicist, **Terrance**. It's not possible to list all the invaluable support he provides; but Lord, You know. Thank you for **Heather, Gloria,** and

Deborah, who have been my closest girlfriends since childhood and with whom You still allow me to share a strong personal and spiritual bond. Thank You for the emotional flowing gracefulness of **Brenda Nelson** (TGCC), who inspired the profession of this book's heroine. Thank You for the birth and expansion of **KNB Publications, LLC,** and the literary family You've given me through the **Writer's Hut.** Thank You for all of the **book clubs** (too many to name) that have surrounded me with impassioned support and especially for **Circle of Friends XI**, for welcoming me into their reading family with open arms. Thank You for **Lisa** (Papered Wonders, Inc.) and **Dama** (God's Butterflies Ministries), the sisters You placed in my life especially for those times when I need a prayer partner and spiritual support system, and for **Jamill & Shunda** (Booking Matters, Inc), who've promoted me from the start of my career. Thank You for **Victoria, Jacquelin, Tia, Vanessa, Toschia, Deborha, Tanya, Eric, Hank, Travis, Jihad, Keith, Carl,** and **Maurice**, the fellow authors who take the time to encourage me the most. Thank You for my dynamic publicist and agent, **Rhonda** and **Carlton**, respectively, without whom this journey would be much tougher; and for every **reader** who has embraced the books that You have given me to pen. Thank You, Lord, for the years of divine support You've supplied me through **Revival Church Ministries** (where my father is founder and overseer) and most recently, my spiritual home away from home, **Total Grace Christian Center** and its leaders, **Bishop Johnathan & Pastor Toni Alvarado** as I fellowship with them regularly. Finally, thank You for the phenomenal vocals of **Brian, Fantasia,** and **John** that helped me avoid writer's block during the course of crafting this story; and the anointed vocals of **Fred, BeBe,** and **Smokie**, that kept me inspired and reminded of why I do what I do. It is in Your name, Lord, that I give thanks for all of these and other blessings. Amen.